Tranquil Moments Publishing,
A Division of The Nicole Bradley Experience
Orlando, Florida

1st Edition: 2008

2nd Edition: 2024

ISBN: 979-8-9873078-3-0 (PAPERBACK)
Library of Congress Control Number: 2024922027

Editing: Jahzara
Cover Design: Amy Queau - QDesign
www.qcoverdesign.com

Also By Jahzara

CONTRADICTIONS

MY LOVE WON'T LAST FOREVER: MATRIMONY

NEVER WOULD HAVE MADE IT: A TESTIMONY
OF WHAT GOD HAS DONE IN MY LIFE

THE DIVA'S DATING ASSESSMENT
GUIDE: Girl, Please!

MY LOVE WON'T LAST FOREVER:
CHAOTIC BLISS

MY LOVE WON'T LAST FOREVER: HIS WIFE

LOVE OF MY LIFE

Acknowledgements

To anyone who has ever been through
something … God is able.

*"With men this is impossible; but with God
all things are possible." Matthew 19:26*

Foreword

Authors from all over the world have produced enlightening, amazing, entertaining, and inspiring stories of human nature. Love Don't Live Here Anymore is such a book. It offers superlative content and is elegantly presented. I anticipate a screenplay, and so should you. Earlier this year, I had the pleasure of being asked to write the foreword for the book you hold now. I looked forward to it for two reasons. First, the author, Jahzara, holds a reputation for innovation and great writing. This, I first became aware of after reading her earlier works. And secondly, she is tremendously dedicated to entertaining her readers to the end. I can lay testament to her raw power of mastery, skill, and command of the written word. This work is heavily based on reality. Ironically, there are parts in the story where it actually suspends reality.

Be prepared to laugh, and cry. What's clear is that the author has an extraordinary bond with her characters. Each of the chapters had me guessing what twist or turn would they encounter, or create next. Any one of the characters could be in your life today. I admire the fact that Jahzara doesn't opt to exploit any individual, situation, or gender with her book. Nor does she underplay their contribution and importance; that's too easy. She simply tells it like it is. This book was written for you to enjoy. It doesn't lack integrity. As you read, you'll become mesmerized by this page-turner. My advice? Don't start reading this book unless you can do so without interruption. It is just that kind of an exceptional read; accept nothing less.

— Fran Briggs
http://beapaidwriter.com

One

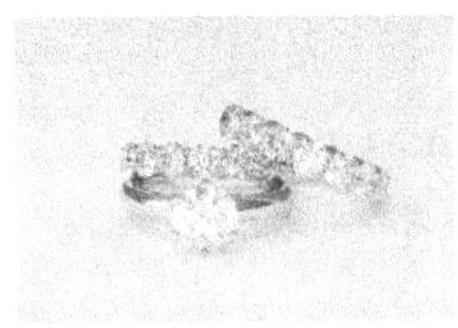

Six Months Ago

April 1995

"Biggie, give me one more," Nyree Shaw sang totally off key as she swerved her foreign vehicle into the parking lot of the church. "Damn," she mumbled as she turned down the music, and shoved the remains of her fish dinner from *Gowdy's II Restaurant* down her throat. She wished she would cook fish as well as *Gowdy's*. Perhaps it was a blessing that she couldn't – if she could cook she would probably be as big as a house. After licking *Gowdy's* signature sauce off her fingers, she commented, "Lord, you really must be looking out for me because I almost just hit Pastor Anderson's Lincoln. I don't know how I *didn't*. I need to turn this loud rap music down. Lord, forgive me for cursing on the church grounds. " Nyree shook her head in disgust as she pressed the down arrow for volume on her remote control.

If there was one thing that she could say about Pastor Anderson, it was that he kept a sharp car. When his wife was alive, she drove a nice vehicle as well. Part of her felt guilty for playing secular music so loudly in front of the church. What had she been thinking about? The fact of the matter was that she had not been thinking. She was too excited and stressed to think rationally. Two days from now she was going to be doing something that she said that she would never ever ever do- get married.

A part of Nyree felt a rush of satisfaction blasting that song; it was like she finally did something bold. People were always calling her "Miss Goody-Goody," and honestly, it got old. No, it was stale. One of these days, she was going to stop playing it safe, take some risks, and today felt like as good a day as any to start. Maybe, cranking rap music in a church parking lot might've been *a bit* over the top, but hey, you've got to start somewhere, right?

She used to think she was being risky with Malachi Chandler, but these days she was convinced she had him locked down. It wasn't always that way, though. She'd had serious doubts about him. Especially that day in August, lying on the beach in Jacksonville, when he casually dropped, "I think I killed somebody."

Wait, what? Nyree's mind screeched to a halt. "What do you mean, you *think* you killed someone?" she pressed, her stomach doing flips. In her mind, you either did or you didn't. Simple.

Malachi just shrugged, like it wasn't that serious. "I was reppin' my set. Somebody disrespected me, so I went to my boy's car, grabbed a gat, and handled it." His voice was so matter-of-fact it sent chills down her spine.

Nyree had heard enough stories about gang life to know it was messy, but this? This felt too real, too close. Suddenly, the man she thought she had figured out became a puzzle she wasn't sure she wanted to solve anymore.

"When are we going to come together and unite for a common cause?" Nyree questioned.

"Here you go with the Black history lectures, again. I don't need to hear it today. I know it by heart. You want me to recite it for you? You know what your problem is, Nyree? You're stuck up and think you're better than everyone else!" Malachi was yelling now.

It was as if he knew he could easily redirect the attention of other people on the beach to take notice of him and Nyree.

"Well, I guess I am stuck up if I think it's wrong to take a human life over some colors, stars, and numbers!" Nyree shouted back, not caring who was looking at them. Malachi huffed in frustration. He knew he wasn't getting through to her.

"Nyree, you just don't get it. You've always had both of your parents around. You don't know what it's like to come home and your moms is not there because she is working two jobs, and the only recollection you have of your dad was at your third birthday party. You don't know what it's like to be at Dunes Bowling Alley and wonder if the guy a couple of lanes down is your dad," he sighed as he recalled the times he had gone there as a kid. The first thing he would do when he ran through the door was to play one of the arcade games. Then he would go to the counter and see what lanes were available before obtaining his rental shoes. He continued his statement, "...Or the skating rink as a kid and see a guy who looks like he could be your father, but you don't know for sure because it has been years since you have last seen him. You have no idea what it is like to have to lie to the kids in your class about what your dad does for a living. How about even knowing small things about your dad? Like what's his favorite color, or favorite food. Do you know how envious I used to feel when kids would say, 'I hope my dad doesn't show up here wearing such and such,' because I would be embarrassed. Then there I was, wishing my dad would show up at school in a pair of drawers and flip-flops. Yeah, I might be embarrassed, but at least my dad's coming to the school to check on me. That would show that we had some type of relationship, some connection. You don't know how it feels to have your moms bring this cool guy around and to hope that she will marry him so you can have a dad. Then just when you start to get used to him… *Bam*! He's gone out of your life and then some new 'Joe' comes around to replace him. That's why I got in a gang, Nyree; for the family feeling and stability. Well, as much stability as you can have until one of your homies gets smoked or something. Don't judge me until you have walked a mile in my shoes. Everybody didn't have it as good as you did," Malachi told Nyree.

Nyree had no idea that Malachi's childhood had been that bad. But she for sure was not going to apologize for her childhood. The intensity in his eyes was something she had never seen before. Although he was looking in her direction he was not looking at her; and for that she was glad because she was uncertain of the expression on her face. She did not want to come across as uncaring and on the other hand she did not want to come across as an emotional basket case. Staring at the crashing waves and listening to the swoosh of the water, Nyree found herself silently thanking God that Malachi's childhood had not been her own.

There had been times when she felt her parents had been too hard on her and even unfair. Once she had gone into the bathroom and ran the water in the shower and yelled, "I hate y'all. I wish I had different parents!" Now she was thankful that she did not always get her wish? What if her wish had been granted and she had gotten Malachi's parents?

She almost wanted to tell him about her dad's tough beginnings, to show him she *got* it. But then she stopped herself. It would sound like one of those, "Oh, you think *your* life was hard? Let me tell you about mine" conversations, and she hated when people did that to her. It felt so dismissive, like they were competing for the worst sob story instead of just *listening.*

So, instead, she bit her tongue, keeping her thoughts to herself.

Two days before my wedding, I'm a hot mess. Now where did that zit even come from? Stress will cause all kinds of mess to come out. I don't need a big blackhead on my cheek. In less than forty-eight hours I will be saying two little words that have the potential to turn my world upside down.'

Most little girls dreamed of - marrying the man of her dreams. But at this moment, Nyree Shaw felt the weight of the world was on her shoulders. There were not enough hours in the day to complete all the tasks that needed to be done.

"Where is he? I told him to be here at five-thirty," Nyree asked herself, hoping that he would pull into the parking lot in his mother's Buick Regal. '*It is five-thirty*', Nyree found herself thinking. After rustling through mounds of paper in her Coach handbag, she finally found her cellular phone and attempted to reach Malachi Chandler at his mother's home. The phone rang six times before the voicemail picked up. *'I know this fool didn't forget about our appointment for marriage counseling with Pastor Anderson tonight?'*

"I can't go in here alone," Nyree shouted as she threw her cell phone at the window. "I'll look like a fool." This was going to be the first —and most likely the *only*—counseling session, given Malachi had just rolled back into town a week ago. With him stationed at the naval base in Mayport, Florida, their marriage counseling had been practically impossible to schedule. But here she was, about to face Pastor Anderson solo. Nyree checked her Movado timepiece—5:45. She slammed the car door harder than necessary, trying to mentally prepare herself for whatever was about to go down.

The walk from her car to the church door was barely ten feet, but it felt like a damn marathon. The hawk as she likes to refer to the wind was ruthless, smacking her, pushing her back, even whipping her hair into her face like it had a vendetta. *I'm not gonna cry,* she told herself. *I want to cry so bad, but I'm not doing it. I got this.* Despite the myriad of emotions raging inside her, she forced herself to hold her head high as she stepped through the church doors and headed upstairs to Pastor Anderson's study.

This is so embarrassing, she thought, fighting to tame her wild hair. *I probably look like a damn peacock right now.* She tried to fix her hair but didn't have a mirror, so she wasn't sure if she was fixing it or making it worse. She knocked on the door, then again. Nothing. Relief washed over her. *Maybe this saves me from total humiliation.* But just as she spun on her heel to leave, she heard that familiar voice.

"Come on in, Sister Shaw."

Damn. She was really hoping he wouldn't be here. But of course he was. Pastor Anderson was nearly 80, but he was one of the most reliable people she knew. If he said he'd do something, you could bet he'd show up every time. He'd even come to check on her at the hospital after a minor fender bender with a cop last year, despite her insistence she was fine. Baby delivered? Pastor's there. Death in the family? He's already by your side. Crisis of any kind? Pastor Anderson was front and center. Why she thought today would be any different was beyond her.

The counseling session barely lasted ten minutes. Malachi never showed. How unoriginal.

On the 30-minute drive home, Nyree's anger boiled over, and she cursed him under her breath the entire way. Every mile, every red light, every beat of silence—her resentment grew. *How did I get here?*

"Kyle, can you believe that douche bag stood me up for counseling? No one has ever stood me up. I can't believe he didn't show up for counseling," Nyree yelled into her cell phone as she drove home.

"Well, if you marry him then just know that he is going to be irresponsible. You might not want to hear this but he's not the one for you," Kyle warned her.

Nyree barely registered Kyle's voice in the background. *I'm not letting in any negative energy,* she told herself. The session with Pastor Anderson had left her with a question that gnawed at her: *Do you love him?* That simple question should've been easy to answer, especially with her wedding just two days away. But now, it was lingering, making her doubt. Malachi was smooth, knew all the right words, made her feel like royalty. But love? That was a whole different level. Sure, he was unlike any man she'd ever been with. Why was that word "love" tripping her up?

Malachi was all about the small, intimate gestures. He'd come over, run her a hot bubble bath, and then gently bathe her. His hands? Soft and deliberate, like he knew exactly how to touch her to make her melt. And the candles—he loved setting the mood. He'd buy the scented ones that you could massage into your skin from nicolebradleycandles.com. Malachi would light them all over her place, turning her apartment into a sensual oasis.

***

One Sweetest Day, when he was "low on funds" as he liked to say, he'd picked up steaks and potatoes from the grocery store and whipped up dinner for her. When Nyree told her friend Sasha Sinclair about it, expecting her to swoon over the romantic effort, Sasha wasn't impressed.

"Girl, you act like he really did something," Sasha had said, her tone dripping with sarcasm.

Nyree's eyebrow shot up. "Excuse me?"

"You're excused. Let me keep it real with

you," Sasha continued, relentless. "Aris and Antoine claim they're your friends, but they don't want to hurt your feelings. So they're staying quiet. But, girl, we all think Malachi is a straight-up bum. You're hyping up this man for using *your* pots, pans, and gas to cook *you* dinner? Like, okay, he bought the food, but that's bare minimum. No job, no money, no future plans. Do you hear me?"

Sasha's words hit like a slap. Nyree felt herself shrink, like a tiny speck on a page. Sasha had a special talent for raining on someone's parade, and her signature line, *Do you hear me?* always added that final sting to Nyree's already battered confidence. But here's the thing —Malachi *was* different.

When he spent the night, he'd wake up early, clean her place, and serve her breakfast in bed. Not just any breakfast either—he'd make her Mickey Mouse pancakes with Alaga syrup, her favorite. And when she was stressed, he'd massage her feet, his strong hands kneading away her tension. He gave the best pedicures and, to top it off, could perm her hair better than any stylist. Some might call it a little too soft, too feminine, but there was nothing soft about Malachi when it came to the things that mattered.

Those moments—the tender touches, the care he poured into making her feel special —were exactly why she wanted to be Mrs. Chandler. To be committed to him, flaws and all, until death do them part.

Still trying to recall if she had enough data to justify wanting to marry him. Her mind kept bringing memories to the forefront. What about the first time she had agreed to see him? That brought a smile to her face. She even laughed. They had met a year before he came to her apartment. Her sorority sister insisted she attend a fish fry. She remembered the day vividly. "I really don't want to go to the fish fry," Nyree had stated.

"Oh, Girl, come on. It'll be fun. I promise. You might meet somebody," Aris said in her most convincing voice.

Nyree knew where this conversation was going. If she knew Aris, she knew that Aris was up to something. "I'm not interested in meeting anyone. In case you have not been listening to me, I like being single, unattached."

Aris was not taking 'no' for an answer.

"Okay, Girl, whatever. I'll pick you up in about an hour." She hung up before Nyree could protest.

Aris had introduced Nyree to Malachi. The two had a couple of good laughs, but Nyree was not interested in him. He was not her type. She was not sure what it was about him that she did not like, but she knew that he was not the one for her. There was nothing about him that screamed, "He's the one," or better yet whispered that he could be the one. The gold around his neck, the oversized diamond stud in his right ear, the name-brand clothing, and his fresh, new Michael Jordan gym shoes made her do a double-take. He looked as if he had just stepped out of *Mocha Apparel* which was located at Eleventh Avenue and Broadway. Malachi looked like he was trying very hard to impress someone and with all her money she was not easily impressed. However, she had to give him credit for shopping at *Mocha Apparel*. "Simple goes a long way," she had heard someone say before. She was not sure if she would say that was her philosophy, but found it to be applicable in this instance, he had overdone it. He was doing too much. She couldn't quite put her finger on it, but something about his appearance was overdone. Maybe it was all of the jewelry.

Someone had given Malachi her telephone number; and if she were a betting woman, she would say, without a doubt, that it was Aris. Without fail every time she was home from school for a break he would call her without fail. Each time he called she would make an excuse about why she could not see him. When she moved into her townhome he managed to get her phone number from her mother. Ordinarily, that would not have been an easy feat. Nyree imagined her mother had given the telephone number to Malachi for spiteful reasons. Nyree figured that this was Margo Shaw's way of letting Nyree know that even though Nyree was grown Margo was still the mother and always got the last word, as they had been at each other's throats earlier in the day. Her father had commented that the reason that they did not get along with one another was because they were too much alike. Nyree had given her dad the evil eye when he said that she refused to believe that she was anything like her overbearing mother.

Reminiscing about the conversation that she and Malachi had that day, she had to chuckle.

"My car is sick. I want to see you, but it's

not running. None of my boys are home. I can catch the bus to your place," he suggested.

"Hold on a second," Nyree said while pressing the mute button on the telephone and holding onto the counter in her kitchen so that she would not fall over from laughter. After regaining her composure, she returned to the line and said in her most serious voice, "Brother, are you serious?"

He was serious and told her that he would do anything to be in her presence. If that meant catching the bus and walking half a block to see her, then that's what he would have to do. Nyree hadn't taken him seriously when he said it. Dudes are always trying to run game and be impressive. That's what she had chalked Malachi's spiel up to. When she heard the doorbell ring, she got up slowly as she clutched a piece of tissue, and walked to the front door.

"Hey," Nyree greeted Malachi with a folded tissue up to her nose, red- and -black bandana on her head and an Indiana University gray – and- red sweat suit. She tried to read his facial expression to see if he was turned off by what he saw. It was his great idea to come to her place and since she was both sick with a cold and bored, she had no intentions of trying to comb her hair or put on any make-up to try to impress him.

He smiled and said, "Hi," as he made his way to the living room area. He was dressed neatly. His clothes hung off him just right. She could tell that they had come from Mocha Apparel. She wondered if the store had ever considered him as being their poster boy. He exuded such confidence. He walked with all the confidence in the world and he smelled so good. Nyree was hating herself for paying so much attention to him. When she took his coat to hang it up, she noticed that he was thinner than she remembered. His goose- down Carolina jacket made him appear to be larger than he was. If only she could remove a layer of clothing and look thinner. She wished that was her problem. Her issue was that she liked to eat. Food provided her comfort. She celebrated milestones and accomplishments by going out to dinner. To tell the truth, when she was in any type of emotional crisis, happy or sad, she picked up a fork and put food in her mouth. Some people were addicted to drugs, nicotine, and other vices. She had an unhealthy obsession with food, and it was reflected in what she called her yo-yo weight. 'I *hope he ain't on that shit– that crack, or what if he has a disease, no I'm not going to even go there with it. He is awfully skinny and that's the truth. Grandma Lula could fatten him up. I'm tripping. It's not like he's going to be my man,'* she thought to herself. "Well, come on in and make yourself comfortable," she said with a sniff and a cough. "You have to excuse me; I have a little bit of a cold."

Malachi looked at her and asked, "Do you have some cold medicine?" Nyree shook her head to indicate that she did not have any. "Well, what about some chicken noodle soup, some lemon juice and some garlic?"

Nyree raised her eyebrow because she was not sure why he was asking about the contents of her cupboard. "I have soup, lemon juice and garlic," she responded.

"Good, if you show me to your bathroom I can wash my hands, and if you don't mind I'll make you some soup. You'll most definitely feel better."

"Are you serious?" Nyree questioned him because never in her entire life had a man other than her father and brother offered to take care of her when she was sick. This was a first, an unexpected first. A man other than her daddy taking care of her was something that she could get used to.

Malachi flashed a smile and said, "Yeah," while shrugging his shoulders to indicate that it was no big deal.

Nyree sat at the breakfast bar and watched Malachi go to work in the kitchen. He even served her. As she began to eat, he began questioning her about what type of cold medicine she used. He grabbed his coat and announced, "I'll be back in a minute." Nyree smiled at the sight of him leaving all bundled up to brace the cold December night air. She did not know what he was up to, but he was certainly making her question what it was that she did not like about him. He was a brave soul to go out in that weather.

Fifteen minutes later a very cold Malachi returned with a huge brown paper bag from Beach Pharmacy. It was filled with products that would ensure a speedy recovery.

"Doctor Malachi is in the house," his baritone voice announced, "I order you to lay here on the couch and let me take care of the rest."

"Okay," Nyree said, not sure if she should give this man free reign of her home, but how much damage could he do, she wondered. She was breaking one of her rules which was not to let a man have free reign of her house.

Nyree knew that when men are allowed to wander about the house, they begin to snoop and ask questions. They become too comfortable, in her opinion, and she didn't like that. When they started asking all those questions and snooping she was quick to remind them that she pays the bills at her residence and she does not have to answer any questions. The few men that she had allowed to visit her town home resented her bringing up the issue of paying bills. She surmised that they felt resentment because they could not afford to pay bills at her residence. If that was the case, then it only confirmed for her the reason why they had no business snooping around and asking questions such as "What is this?" "Where did you get this from?" "Who is this guy in the picture?"

Malachi poured her medicine on a spoon and ordered her to open her mouth. Then he opened up a jar of Vicks Vapor Rub and rubbed it on her chest, which caused her to feel some feelings that she had not felt in a long time. She watched his facial expression and from what she could tell, touching her chest had not caused his expression to change.

"Not trying to be funny or anything but I have to ask you a question," Nyree began and continued without his approval. "Are you gay?"

Malachi rubbed his eyes with his forearm and asked, *"What?"*

"Are you gay? I don't know how you can rub on my chest and not so much as crack a smile," Nyree teased him.

"I'm a gentleman. I don't take advantage of the sick but to answer your question I'm not gay. I like what I see," he said with a smile.

"Why don't you take a swallow of this? You'll feel better," Malachi told Nyree.

Nyree protested, "Are you serious? You want me to swallow some Vicks Vapor Rub?"

Malachi looked puzzled at her protest. "Yeah, my grandma, when she was alive, used to make us swallow it all the time. It will knock the cold out of you."

"Uh... I don't think you're supposed to eat it. I think you are supposed to apply it externally. That's why they call it vapor rub."

"Naw, you can swallow it. I'm telling you when I was a kid we used to swallow it all the time and nothing bad ever happened to us."

"I'm going to pass on it."

"All right, suit yourself. Do you have a blanket that I can put over you?"

"It's one in that closet over there." She pointed and watched him walk to the hall closet and retrieve a red, black, and green plaid blanket. He draped it over her body ever so gently and they talked for hours like two old friends. Nyree was amazed at how comfortable she felt talking to him. When her eyes became heavy, she told him that she was sleepy and offered to drive him home.

He told her that he could not allow her to drive as the medication had probably begun to take effect and he did not want her to get into an accident. "I'll call my brother and see if he will come and pick me up." When he told Nyree he was unable to contact his brother he grabbed his coat and stated that he would walk home.

"I can't let you walk home. It's a good thirty- minute drive from here to your house. You'll catch your death if you walk home in this cold December weather. I'm going to get in my bed and you can sleep on the couch."

"I'd rather sleep in the bed with you. I'll keep my hands to myself," Malachi said with a smile.

"Keep it up and your ass will be walking home," Nyree said and tossed him a blanket and pillow. *I can't believe I'm doing this.* She broke another rule which was allowing a man to spend the night on the first date, in this case the first encounter because this could hardly be called a date. Nyree tried to convince herself that it was not really a rule violation since he was sleeping in the guest room and there was no intimacy going on. As sleep overpowered her she told herself this would not become a habit.

*Damn, am I lying to myself? Because for real, for real this is how it starts. Dude spends the night once. Then the next thing you know when you look up he has a shirt in your closet, a pair of sneakers in the hallway closet, deodorant and a razor in the medicine cabinet, and pants and underwear in what was once deemed a spare drawer. When you're not paying attention, he's asking you when are **you** going to buy some more of his favorite snacks. Next he'll be scrolling through the caller ID as if he's paying your Ameritech phone bill; and if he has the* *access code to your voicemail, he will try to check the messages. Nope. No, this is a one-time thing,* Nyree promised herself. She liked flying solo and she did not need the drama that men brought with them when they entered your life. Her life was rather boring and drama-free and she had to admit that she rather liked it like that.

***

The drive from the church seemed like it took forever, even though she did sixty miles per hour the entire way home on the city streets of Gary. When she opened the door to her parents' house, she threw her purse, which fell on her mother's white sofa. If her mother had seen Nyree's purse land on her sofa, she would have had a fit. She would have asked Nyree, "What is your problem? Do you know how much it costs to have that white sofa cleaned?" Nyree would have snarled at her and told her mother to stop acting like a tightwad.

"It's Daddy's money. He has enough to get the sofa cleaned every day of the year, if he wants to," is what Nyree would have told her mother. Nyree hated when her mother asked her about money and if Nyree knew how much things cost. These conversations irritated Nyree.

Her mother was always talking about the value of a dollar, but her mother spent money like it was going out of style. Her mother had gotten so out of control with her spending that her father had to give her mother a monthly allowance. "The nerve of him! It's not like we don't have it," her mother had whined to Nyree about the allowance.

Her father responded that they were wealthy because he made good investments and did not squander money.

Nyree ran to the kitchen and snatched the cordless phone off the wall mount and placed it to her ear. The line was free. She hurriedly scrolled through the caller ID monitor to see if Malachi had attempted to call; he had not and this infuriated her even more. *'Sorry ass. It's over. It is definitely over. There will be no wedding on Friday evening. He can't make it to marriage counseling- this is bad. This is very bad. No telephone calls- no explanation- nothing. I've got to stop cussing. Well, it's not really bad unless you say it, right?'* When the telephone rang her thoughts were interrupted.

"Nyree? Hi, what's wrong?" Malachi asked casually.

"What's **wrong?** You did not show up for marriage counseling at five-thirty. It is **seven-thirty!** Where the hell have you been? You know what? Forget it; I don't even want to hear it. There's not going to be a WEDDING," Nyree yelled and then regretted having done so. If her mother heard this, she would probably lose her mind and tell Nyree that she did not have fifteen thousand dollars to throw away.

On the other hand, she imagined her mother saying, "Good. I never did like that no-good... Never mind that, we will just cancel the church and use the Dunes Pavilion to throw you an 'I'm- glad -I -didn't -marry -Malachi –party'."

"Baby, baby, calm down. Listen, I'm sorry. My mother had me out running errands with her and we lost track of time. I had no way to get in touch with you. You know you never keep your cell phone on. I'm on my way over there," Malachi made the bold justification and then, just as quickly, hung up the phone.

His head was throbbing. He wanted to take two Tylenol, chase them with a shot of his favorite drink Hennessy, pass the hell out and wake up to a trouble-free life. He was having a "Murphy's Law" type of day. If anything could go wrong, it definitely did. *Like was this the day that karma showed up?* He tried to remember what class in high school talked about probability. It didn't matter because he hadn't been paying attention.But... what was the probability of a man cheating on his fiancée with two different women? What were the odds of those two women who, by the way, don't know each other, calling him on the same day and informing him that they were pregnant with his child? Then to add fuel to the fire, his fiancée called the wedding off two days before the wedding because he did not make it to counseling. Life was definitely life-ing. It was beating the hell out of him. If he were keeping score it would be: Life:5, Malachi:-5. Yeah, life was showing out.

Two

Ninety Minutes Ago

Malachi and his cousin Frank sat on the couch while playing a video game in the game room of Frank's house. *He is slacking off. I wonder why he is not as competitive as usual,* Frank found himself thinking. "Hey, man, what's up with you? Are you excited about the wedding?"

Clearly deliberating in thought, Malachi shrugged his shoulders and responded, "Man, same ole same ole. I'm just ready for this thang to be over."

This certainly was not the answer that Frank was expecting to hear from a man who was about to embark on a lifelong commitment. He remembered how anxious and happy he was when he married Lynn. That had been three years ago and the joy was still there. He would smile just at the mentioning of her name. That enthusiasm was missing from Malachi and that worried him. "Dude, you look different- stressed- is everything all right? Tell me you're not having second thoughts."

Malachi let out a sigh and fixed his eyes on the portrait of Frank and Lynn on the wall. He envied his cousin, he had a beautiful wife, home and everything seemed to be going well for him. Frank used to be "Mr. Playa Playa" but when he met Lynn he settled down and turned his life around for the better. Frank was even going to church regularly. He said that he was saved and had found Jesus. Malachi often marveled at how Frank had changed his life. Frank had been in a gang in junior high school and most of high school. Frank was the person who had given Malachi his first joint. He even gave Malachi lessons on how to roll a joint and how to smoke it. Frank had taught Malachi how to steal from the local corner store without getting caught; and when they were short on money they would take the stolen merchandise and sell it to classmates at school or kids in the neighborhood. Malachi watched to see if he would catch Frank slipping back into his worldly ways. Secretly, Malachi hoped that he would be able to catch Frank doing something wrong so that he could shout to the world, "See, Frank is just like me. He ain't all of that. Trying to be holy and walking around doing the same stuff I'm doing," but he never caught Frank doing anything wrong. It bothered him that Frank went from being on the bottom rung of the ladder and was now on top with everyone giving him kudos, while Malachi received nothing. Although he waited and watched, Malachi could honestly say that he never caught Frank reverting to his old lifestyle. Malachi wondered if he would ever make a transformation like Frank did. In his heart he wanted to be the type of man that Frank was, but he was too engulfed in his flesh and found it difficult to let the fast life go.

By all accounts Malachi was what you would call a lucky man. He had snagged a rich, beautiful college graduate. Nyree, as the old people would say, "came from money" but she never made a big deal about it. Not once had she asked how Malachi intended to keep her living in the manner in which she was accustomed to living. Nyree worked hard at a job where she didn't have to work. She said she wanted to make it on her own and not use her family's name.

Malachi had chuckled at that statement. He was different from her. Once he remarked, "If my last name had been Shaw, I would be right there in the company boardroom running things." Nyree was different. Perhaps that is what had drawn him to her in the first place- she was different from any woman he had ever known. All of the women he knew were out there trying to get something for nothing and trying to see what man was going to take care of them financially. Sometimes he felt that Nyree was too good to be true and that he was not good enough for her.

"Man, I don't know. Did you ever cheat on Lynn- I mean, before you got married?" Floored by the question, Frank responded, "No. Lynn was - and is - my heart. The day I met her I knew she was the one and that I wanted to be with her for life. Never had a need or a want to cheat." *Who in their right mind would want to cheat on Nyree?* Frank thought. He was really hoping that this was a random question and that a confession was not going to follow. Malachi listened intently to Frank and shook his head in agreement, when his cell phone began to ring. Malachi's heart started beating rapidly when he looked at his phone. The number belonged to this chick named Terri that he had broken off with about a month ago. "Wait a minute. Let me take this call. Hello. Yeah. Um-humph. Whatever. I told you it ain't mine. Do *not* call me with this crap anymore. Yeah, I'm still getting married, why? Bye…"

After hanging up he turned to his cousin and said, "Frank, man, I got myself in an ill situation. I had been messing with this girl and she called me last week saying that she needed to talk to me. I told her no, we could not talk because that's how she likes to lure you into doing something. *You know what I mean?* I decided to be real with her. So, I tell her that I'm getting married to Nyree. She turns around and tells me that she is three months pregnant and it's mine. Bad thing about it is it could be, but my boy Stevenson got up with her a couple of times so it might not be mine, but right now I'm her target. She's in the Navy too but not on my ship. Anyways, she's threatening to have her ship's chief talk to my ship's chief and to have me take a blood test and consequently pay child support. I don't know if she's just pulling my leg or if this is something that can be really done. All I know is that I love Nyree and I can't lose her over no bullshit, over some chick that don't mean anything to me." Frank gently patted Malachi on the back and encouraged him to talk to Nyree about the situation.

"You can't start a marriage off based on a lie. Dude, it's six o'clock. What is she going to say about you not going to counseling?" Frank wanted to say more, but decided against it as he had been the one to cause a minor riff in the couple's relationship when they first started dating. Frank had accidentally slipped up and mentioned that he and Malachi had gone to a card party given by Shonta who was Malachi's ex-girlfriend one night. It just so happened that the night they went to the card party Malachi had feigned having the flu. Malachi told Nyree that he was not feeling well and was going to bed early that night. When Nyree heard that Malachi had lied about being sick, Frank wished that he had a magic wand and could make himself and Malachi disappear at that moment. Frank had never seen a woman lose it like Nyree lost it, for he had been cursed out by many women numerous times in his life. Even though Nyree had not been talking to him, she had instilled so much fear in Frank that he was afraid to move, let alone swallow.

After that episode, it was a week before Malachi returned any of Frank's phone calls. "Man, you talk too much," Malachi had whined when he finally started talking to Frank again.

"*My fault?* Man, how was I supposed to know that you had lied to Nyree? Next time you lie and don't want me to say anything, tell me in advance," Frank suggested.

Malachi drove to his mother's apartment in silence. *What have I gotten myself into? If only Nyree would have quit that stupid job and moved down to Jacksonville with me. This would not have happened. I'm a man. I have needs, right? Yeah, but now it's come back to bite me in the butt. In both booty cheeks. Like Malcolm X said, "The chickens have come home to roost.* Although not an avid reader, *The Autobiography of Malcolm X* had been one of his favorite books. He had even read it twice during his hiatus from school his sophomore year. Upon reading the book, he had promised himself that he was going to be a different person. He would seek knowledge, and be a responsible brother, which meant no more selling and using drugs. Also he was going to treat African-American women as queens and stop using them for sex and money. For a while he had changed, but what happened? He marveled at the responsible man he had once been and the miscreant he had become while seriously thinking about what Nyree would do to him if she ever found out.

***

Terri stared at the telephone in disbelief. *Who did Malachi Chandler think that he was?* How dare he play with her emotions? Lisa stared at Terri waiting for details. The suspense was killing her. Based on Terri's responses, Lisa could just imagine what Malachi had said was not good. When she realized that Terri was not going to be forthcoming with the info she queried, "Well?"

Through sobs Terri managed to say, "Well? Well, he doesn't want anything to do with me or the baby, and he's getting married to that girl from Gary! Remember the time we went to the one -hour photo shop in the mall and saw his photo on the wall with that girl. That's who he is marrying. I think her name is Nyree or Nila, something like that."

Lisa was shocked. She had not expected to hear this. "What is that chick doing with him?

She doesn't look like the type that would be with somebody like Malachi," Lisa said. Although Terri was her girl, Lisa had to keep it real and the truth was Nyree appeared to be too good for Malachi. And while she was telling the truth Terri could not compete with Nyree. If Lisa had to describe Terri in one word it would be: ghetto. Lisa hated that this term was often used to refer to African- Americans because that was not true. It actually means an area where groups of the same race or ethnicity live. This term was first used in reference to Jewish people. The term is also used to describe slum areas of a city. How it came to be associated with African- Americans, Lisa did not know, but she did know that Terri met the qualifications to be considered "ghetto". Most people are proud to be called intelligent, beautiful, and responsible. Terri, on the other hand, beams when somebody says, *'Girl, you know you ghetto.'* The way her face lit up when people said that one would think somebody had just said, "Girl, you know with your talents and ingenuity you are going places in life." Terri was the type of girl that would get a short haircut today and two weeks from now she would try to gel all her hair up into a ponytail more like a twig.

It would be a struggle to get the rubber band around the hair because loose strands would not stay. Her style of dress was hoochiemommaish. A pair of cut-off shorts that barely covered her behind, a halter shirt that showed too much flabby belly and white stack sandals are what she would wear and thought she was really looking good with a nasty, stank walk to accompany it. It would be a fight if you told her that she was not looking good. Terri lacked morals too. Once, Lisa had made the mistake of telling Terri that Johnny was a good kisser. The next time Terri saw him she walked up to him and said, "I heard you was a good kisser. Let me find out. Before Johnny could back up Terri laid one on him, tongue all down his throat. Annoyed by Lisa's comment about Nyree being too good for Malachi, she responded, "I don't care about her. I'm concerned about me and my baby..."

Lisa rolled her eyes at the comment that Terri was concerned about herself and the baby. Lisa thought to herself, *'Now she needs to quit. She knows that she is only concerned about herself. She ain't thinking about a baby, because if she was so concerned about her child then her child would be living with her and not her parents. Terri was thinking that this was going to be "a keep a man baby" and Malachi was like "Oh, no boo-boo." That is foul on his part, but it was foul on Terri's part to lay down with him knowing what kind of man he was. Sex does not change or keep a man. Men feel like they can get it anywhere, and that is something that is not going to change or keep them. It is too bad Terri had to find out the hard way. Maybe this would be the end of her going around talking about my Boo, Malachi.'*

"Well, if he gets married to her you're going to have to deal with *her*," warned Lisa.

That last statement resonated in Terri's head like the clanging of cymbals. *'Damn. I had not thought about that,* Terri thought. *I was so sure that I was taking him from her when we first met. I cannot lie. I am shocked to hear that they are getting married, because I thought that I had stolen him from her and that it was over between them. I remember seeing him sitting at the bar in Chuckey's. I spotted him from across the room. He was wearing a black silk shirt with black slacks. The black next to his ebony skin sent ripples through my body. Sexy was the first word that came to mind. When I sauntered over to him and introduced myself, he flashed those pearly whites and said it was nice to* make my acquaintance. I nearly died. God had heard my prayers. I did not blink an eye when he told me that he had a woman. Dismissing the statement, I said, "So. I can change that." He raised an eyebrow and chuckled. I took the chuckle to mean that he was up for the challenge. Perhaps, I misinterpreted his laughter. Maybe he laughed because he knew that I would never make him leave his woman. When he told me that he didn't date Navy chicks. That only intensified my quest for him. I have failed though. I just played my trump card- the baby- card and this time it was not a lie, it was for real. And what did he do? He threw out the Little Joker - the F-U card and then to add insult to injury he came back with the Big Joker- the "I'm marrying the love of my life" card. When he said that I could hear the lyrics of that old Kool Moe Dee song, "How You Like Me Now" I'm feeling like one of those broads off Maury's show. You know when they bring a guy on the show and say this is your baby and then the results come back and the results indicate it is not your baby. The girl only looks shocked for about three seconds before she says, "Oh, alright, well then, it's got to be Tommy's for sure." Do not get me wrong, I am not about to pin Malachi's baby off on somebody else. I'm just going *to see if I can salvage my relationship with Tommy. I wonder if Tommy still has feelings for me. Life is crazy. The man I adore hates me. Tommy adored me and I played him shady for a guy who could care less about me. I cannot believe I have been that stupid. How could I place myself in this predicament? I thought that I could win him over with sex. I'm mad at Malachi, but in a way I know that I can't be mad at him. He only did what I allowed him to do. Momma is going to be livid when she finds out about this. Since I am always traveling with the Navy, she and Daddy help me out with Tiya since I'm always traveling with the Navy. I cannot bring them another baby to take care of.'*

***

Ciara threw the phone that was nestled on its base at the wall which formed a hole. After throwing the phone, she was instantly sorry. Their sorry landlord would now have something new to complain about. He had been trying to evict them forever but never had the legal basis to evict the family. Pablo Martinez wanted the family off of his property so badly that he had gone so far as to plant marijuana on the property. One day after an inspection, Ciara's father watched Pablo walk out the door with his hand in his pocket. It was then that he observed Pablo force a dime bag of marijuana out of his pocket. When the plastic bag fell to the ground, her father yelled, "Hey man, you dropped your weed." Pablo nervously laughed, picked it up and placed it in his pocket. His facial expression screamed, *So much for trying to set them up with the marijuana. "Dang!"* Ciara yelled at the top of her lungs. To Alexandrina it sounded like the cries of an injured animal. She ran from the kitchen to find her child lying on the couch wincing in pain in the fetal position.

"Ciara! Ciara, *mi hija,* what's wrong?" her mother shouted. Alexandrina Sanchez could only imagine the worst. Had her child been shot? They lived in a rough neighborhood and drive-by shootings often occurred. Never had she seen her child in so much pain. When she reached out to touch her baby, the sobs grew louder and louder. Tears formed in her eyes. It hurt her not to be able to soothe her child and take this horrible pain away. There was no blood or broken glass, just the new hole in the wall. Although she was angry about the new eyesore, she was relieved to know that her daughter had not been shot. For Ciara the excruciating pain that she was experiencing now was similar to that of the pain she felt the day her mother left the family. Her father, Carlos, never said a word about her mother's absence to Ciara, but she had learned to eavesdrop at an early age in order to obtain vital information.

One evening while she was in the bathtub her father was in the basement talking on the phone about his wife. Through the vent in the bathroom, she heard every detail of what he thought was a private conversation. Apparently, Alexandrina had a nervous breakdown - whatever that was. She had run out of pills and left home to become a dancer. Ciara did not think anything was wrong with being a dancer, but the way her dad spat the word out you would have thought somebody had just served him fried feces dipped in chocolate.

"Mama, I'm pregnant. I told Malachi. He dumped me and by the way, he is getting married in two days. That whole story about him going home for his daughter's funeral was a lie. I don't think he even has any kids. There, I said it. I'm going to lie down."

Alexandrina had to hold her chest. She felt an anxiety attack coming on. "Ciara! Ciara!"

she yelled to her daughter as Ciara ran into her bedroom and slammed the door. Alexandrina thought about going to Ciara's room for further discussion, but she had learned long ago that when that door slammed to leave Ciara alone. She was furious and could only imagine how her daughter was feeling. As the eighteen-year-old girl lay on her bed with her head buried in her favorite pink plush bear, she replayed the phone conversation she had earlier with Malachi. She only called because after she and her mother dropped Malalchi off at the airport a week ago. He promised to call but had not. Ciara was trying to be the dutiful woman to be there in the time of his grief.

In a harsh tone, one that Ciara was not accustomed to hearing from Malachi, he answered his phone saying, "Yeah."

"Hey, baby, you don't know how to call nobody?" Ciara asked.

"Who dis?"

"Boy, you crazy, this Ciara."

"Oh," he said. The manner in which he spoke the word suggested that he would rather speak to a nagging bill collector than to speak to Ciara.

"Oh? What's up with that?" She was very curious about his put-off tone. It wasn't "oh" the last night he was in town and they were making out in her dad's car at the beach, she thought.

"Look, I'm really busy. What do you want?"

"I was just calling to see how you were. I mean with the funeral and all…"

"Look, I ain't been straight with you, but I'm 'bout to be straight with you now. I didn't come up here for a funeral…"

"No? Then what for? I got some good news."

"What is it? Did you get accepted to that college you were talking about?"

"Oh, I don't know yet. No, what I was going to say was you know how you always saying you want me to have your baby and how I should stop taking the pill…"

"Yeah and …"

"Well, I stopped taking it about four months ago. I went to Planned Parenthood today and found out that I'm eight weeks' pregnant."

"You're going to have to get an abortion. I came up here for a wedding. I'm getting married to my girl, Nyree."

"*Married?* When did this come about? You

said that she was your *ex* and it was over between you all…"

"Look, I just said that so that I could hit it and you could stop sweating me about her. Why do you think I hadn't been calling you lately or been around until the night that I left? The only reason I called you then was because I needed a ride to the airport." There, he had said it, and it was like a huge burden that had been lifted from him. He hated to be so blunt about the situation, but he had learned a long time ago that you have to get to the point with some women or else they will not hear the message. If he had tried to sugarcoat the situation with Ciara she might have thought that when he returned to Jacksonville there would be a chance for them to rekindle what had been.

"That's messed up. What are you going to do about this baby?"

"Look, Girl, I'll give you the money for an abortion, but other than that, I don't have anything for you."

"So what you are saying is: you could kill your child without a second thought."

"Don't try to put a guilt trip on me. It's not like you have never had an abortion before.

What, this will be number three, right? You should be familiar with the routine."

"How could you throw that up in my face? I told you that because I didn't want there to be any secrets between us, but I see there have been lots of secrets…"

"I don't have time for this; bye, rat." After hanging up, he felt remorseful for the way he had spoken to her. He knew that one day he would be lying on the ground reflecting on life as Cane in *Menace II Society* had done as he lay dying on the sidewalk. *Oh well, it won't be today*, he thought.

Ciara did not know how she felt about the child growing inside her womb. She had adored Malachi once upon a time. Her mother and father had given him money, let him come over to wash clothes, use their phone to make calls home, and even let him spend the night before he departed home for the alleged funeral.

Three

Nyree and Malachi settled onto the plush leather sofa in her parents' high-end, home movie theater. Just two months had passed since Nyree left her townhome in Lake Villa and moved back in with her parents. She had insisted on paying for half of the wedding out of her own pocket, so her father, Edwin Shaw, insisted she move back home to save. Nyree's stubborn independence puzzled him; she'd always rejected his financial help, choosing to pay her own rent in Lake Villa on a modest salary—even though he owned the townhomes and had told her she didn't need to worry about rent.

Unlike his daughter, his son, Kyle on the other hand reminded him of the prodigal son. Kyle wanted everything that he could get right now. "Why don't you all give me what you're going to leave me in the will now?" Kyle once asked his parents. When he saw they were offended, he laughed and said that he was just joking even though he had been serious.

Edwin had not been laughing the day he disowned his son for stealing half a million dollars from his property development company. At first, Edwin blamed his accountant, Thomas Reese. Reese had been with the company for years, and Edwin trusted him without question. But an internal investigation by the Dilworth Detective Agency revealed the painful truth: Kyle had betrayed him. Edwin could hardly believe it; he felt a sting that was deeper than anger—it was the agony of knowing his son had not only stolen from him but had done so without a trace of regret.

"Kyle, why?" Edwin had asked him, his voice thick with hurt and disbelief. "Why would you do something like this?"

But Kyle had just shrugged, his gaze cold and indifferent, as if he hadn't just shattered his father's trust and torn their family apart.

Kyle looked his father square in the eye and with a feeling of satisfaction he stated, "Because I could." They had been standing so close that each one could feel the other's breath on his face.

Edwin inched closer to his son, a man

who seemed quite different from the person he had reared, and said, "Because you could? Well, because I can, I disown you this day. Today I only have one child. You don't exist and will be written out of my will. Don't call. Don't set foot in my house."

***

Nyree and Malachi sat in silence, the movie flickering on the screen before them. But Nyree wasn't focused on the plot; her mind was miles away. She shifted a little, creating a bit of space between them before turning to meet his gaze. Malachi's eyes were deep, the color of black coffee swirled with a hint of cream, and his intense stare drew her in, making her feel like he could see right through her. Those eyes always had a way of making her want to believe every word he said. They'd just decided to give their wedding plans another shot, but Nyree's heart was still wrestling with doubts.

"So..." she said, keeping her tone casual but direct. "Is there anything you need to tell me?"

Malachi didn't hesitate. "No." His response was quick, too quick, and Nyree felt a pang of uncertainty.

She had to press him, no matter how uncomfortable it might get. Her friends had warned her time and again, whispered suspicions and doubts, and she needed answers. This was her chance. She took a steadying breath. "I mean… with you being gone so long. You in Jacksonville, me here in Gary…" She trailed off, letting the unasked question hang in the air, heavy with everything she was afraid to know.

She was doing it again—chickening out. One of her pet peeves, something she was guilty of, biting her tongue in the name of keeping the peace. The truth was she tried to avoid confrontation. But not this time. This time, the question was burning in her mind, and if she didn't ask it, she'd never forgive herself.

She didn't give it another thought. Nyree blurted out, "Have you been intimate with anyone else?"

This could have easily been a scene from her favorite soap opera, *Lies and Deception* when Malachi cupped his hands to her face and spoke barely above a whisper, "No. No!" He looked sincere, hurt, and taken aback all at the same time.

'Silly me. How could I have ever doubted him for a minute? Well, it's not hard considering all the times I have been lied to in the past and led to believe one thing only to find out later that the thing I believed was a lie.

Malachi hasn't given me reasons to doubt his word, no, that's not true. Sounds good to say, but there have been moments. Like the time when he wanted to rent a car to visit his aunt in Fort Lauderdale. I rented the car on my credit card, and he and his buddies drove down there. Unbeknownst to me he did not have any auto insurance. His license was suspended in the State of Indiana, and he got into an accident which the police deemed his fault. Guess who was responsible for the damages? Me. Malachi assured me that he was making bi-weekly payments to the rental car agency. After a month of missed payments, the agency contacted me requesting their money. When I asked Malachi about it, he told me that it was taken care of. I called the agency yelling at the representative that my fiancé said that he had taken care of it, so they needed to keep more accurate records. Boy, was I embarrassed when Malachi finally admitted that he had missed the payments because of... well, I don't remember what excuse he provided, but I know he *lied and made me look like a fool. However, he eventually paid off the debt, and that is really the only time, in addition to the time he lied about going to a party at Shonta's house, that he had given me a reason not to trust him.'*

Four

Six Months Later

The six months that Malachi had been away on a Naval Mediterranean tour of duty, felt like a lifetime to Nyree. There had been insane three hundred-dollar phone bills for long distance calls, lots of letter-writing, and way too many lonely nights in their bed. As they drove from Midway Airport they sat in silence. The silence was eerie. She and Malachi always had something to talk about in the past. They could practically talk about anything. Nyree had even confided in Malachi about here worst period days.

"Chi, I'm telling you I got cramps bad this month. My flow is heavier than Niagara Falls. I 'bout need to have a diaper on to catch this mess," Nyree had once confided in her husband.

"You just make sure you have that same flow when you get off the rag. I want you to wet me up real good," Malachi had responded.

"Boy, you nasty," Nyree had responded.

Nyree smiled to herself as she drove and remembered asking Malachi, "What's the wildest thing that you have ever done?"

Rubbing his goatee, he chuckled. "I hope you don't think differently of me after I tell you this. Honestly, the wildest thing I have ever done was once when my mother went out of town with one of her boyfriends… Monte' and I invited these females over and we took turns having sex with them. Man, that was wild." Malachi smiled as he reminisced.

"Okay, that's enough. Looks like you're still enjoying the moment," Nyree told him as she slapped him on the arm hoping to bring him back into reality.

Nyree and Malachi had even discussed their fecal matter and why sometimes it was brown and other times it was green. *If you can talk about shit,* you *can talk about anything* or so Nyree thought. Now it seemed as if neither of them had anything to say.

It was so quiet in the car that it was loud. As Nyree instinctively reached for the radio, tuning it to WGVE, to fill the emptiness with something other than her swirling thoughts. She wanted to say something, anything, but each time she opened her mouth, nothing came out. She felt a pang of nervousness, her mouth dry and words stubbornly hiding in the back of her mind.

Suddenly, the familiar voice of her friend Kia came over the radio. "This next one's for Nyree and her boo, Malachi, who just came back from overseas. Y'all enjoy Jodeci's 'Love You For Life.'" Nyree looked over at Malachi, catching his small smile at the shout-out. For a moment, a spark of the old warmth flickered between them, but just as quickly, it faded, and they both turned back to the road.

She had imagined this moment so many times: her running into his arms at the airport, planting a kiss on him that would take his breath away, his laughter in her ear as they held each other tight. But reality hadn't delivered that fairy-tale reunion. Instead, they were here, coasting down a stretch of highway with too much unspoken and too much distance between them.

Malachi cracked a smile after hearing the shout-out on the radio, yet they rode in silence. Having been apart so long, Nyree had imagined that when she saw him it would be non-stop conversation, but that was not the case. This was not how she imagined her husband's homecoming. The excitement that she anticipated that she would feel had been replaced with exhaustion. She often daydreamed about running up to him in the airport and laying a big fat juicy kiss on his lips and wrapping her arms around him so tightly that he would be left gasping for air. Well, that scene had remained a daydream and did not play out like that in reality.

His plane had been an hour late as there was inclement weather in Atlanta where Malachi had a brief layover. Then when he finally did walk off the airplane he looked like a thug. His pants were sagging halfway down his behind revealing striped boxer underwear. As he walked he pulled at his pants that continued to droop down while he tried avoiding a stumble which seemed inevitable. If that was not bad enough he had grown his hair out into a neatly trimmed Afro, but the style was not working for him. He looked a 'hot-mess,' however, by the way he was walking, one could tell that he thought that he was looking good.

Nyree thought that it was a shame that one of his boys had not pulled him to the side and told him that he should probably not greet his wife looking like that. There used to be a time when all Malachi would have to do was to walk in a room and Nyree's underwear would be practically saturated due to her excitement. She wondered how she would be able to produce that same excitement now. The thought of making love to him made her stomach turn. How would she politely broach the subject about his appearance? *How can I say to my husband who's been away for six months that he can expect to **not** be getting any sex until he cuts his hair and pulls his pants up?*

As Nyree drove she began thinking that she did not have much to say to Malachi. He had called several times during his voyage requesting that she send money via the currency exchange. During the fourth month of his voyage suddenly his checks were not being directly deposited in their joint checking account per his request. When Nyree questioned him about this, he pretended not to be concerned.

"So what you are telling me is that you're

working every day but not being paid? You're very calm about that. Friday has one time to come around and I don't have a paycheck and all hell is going to break out. Somebody would have to cut me a check right then and there. I don't want to hear we got to call so and so, or we don't have it now, but wait till Monday. I wouldn't care if they had to perform a magic trick and pull my money out of their asses so long as I got my money. I ain't never heard of any mess like this," Nyree vented.

"I don't know what the problem is. My chief said that maybe it's something going on in the states and they are looking into it. Why you tripping? You know your daddy will give his girl anything she wants."

"This is not about my daddy. This is about a grown man who can't take care of himself, who keeps calling me for money and telling me that he is not being paid. Besides, I would never ask my daddy for money and give it to your ass. I know they drug test you so you're not smoking crack, but what you said was some real crackish type shit. I make my own money or have you forgotten?"

Yesterday had been no different in so far

as requests for money. She received a call from Malachi in which he stated that she needed to wire him seven hundred dollars for rent and the security deposit. Nyree was a frequent customer at the currency exchange. The cashiers were on a first-name basis with her. Her favorite cashier Debbie had not been working. Instead Lynnette was. Nyree detested having to make transactions with Lynnette for a number of reasons. The first one was because she was rude. Never did she greet you with a "hello" or a smile. Her standard greeting was "What do you need?" Lynnette had a way of making you feel like you were bothering her when in reality you were just asking her to do her job. If she were on the telephone, you may as well leave and go somewhere else to handle your business because she was not going to hang up until she was good and ready. Of course, she knew that you were standing there waiting for service, but she did not care. If she were eating, you had better pray that she does not damage your document with the food residue on her fingers. Most times she was good about licking the residue off before she started handling paper transactions. To Nyree's surprise Lynnette was very pleasant and expedient on this visit.

Nyree had chosen to remain at home with her parents while Malachi traveled the world. Her parents insisted that she stay with them so they could make sure that she stayed out of trouble. The real reason they wanted her to come back home was so that they could hold onto their baby as long as they could. They knew when Malachi returned, their baby would be gone and they were unsure what to expect in regards to the future. Nyree and Malachi stayed with Nyree's parents before leaving Gary to go to their new home in Florida. Nyree wanted to visit with friends and family as neither was sure when they would be able to return for visits.

Two nights before they were to leave for Florida, Nyree received a telephone call from a *Fleet MasterCard* representative.

"Good evening, Ms. Shaw this is Carlton calling on behalf of your *Fleet MasterCard* account. Now, Ms. Shaw, I am calling because there has been quite a bit of activity on your card today. Ms. Shaw have you used your card today at the pawn shop or *Mocha Apparel*?"

"No, I have not. As a matter of fact, I haven't even left the house today. How much activity was it?"

"Twelve-hundred dollars. Is there another authorized user on the account?"

"Yes, my husband, Malachi."

"Well, do you think he could have made all those charges?"

"He's not here right now, so I can not say. I will check with him when he gets in and if it was not him then I will most definitely be giving you a call back."

"Well, Ms. Shaw, you have a nice evening. If you have any concerns later that I can assist you with do not hesitate to call me at one eight hundred..." Nyree had stopped listening a long time ago. Her mind had been blown when she heard him mention twelve-hundred dollars. She had worked hard these past six months to become debt free and in one day, Malachi had spent twelve hundred dollars. *'Where is he anyway? He left here at ten o'clock this morning and now it's eight o'clock in the evening. What's up with that?'* Nyree picked up the phone and dialed Mrs. Chandler's telephone number. When her mother-in-law answered, they exchange pleasantries. Over the past six months, Nyree had developed an extreme dislike for the woman.

Nyree had found many discrepancies in what Keysha said and Nyree was annoyed with the calls begging for money for so-called expenses that Malachi had incurred while living with her.

"Oh Dear, he's not here. He left here a couple of hours ago and said he was going to his cousin's house. Girl, I thought you all would still be doing the honeymoon thing. I know when I was first married my husband couldn't get enough of me. I guess you young people are different," Mrs. Chandler said rubbing in the fact that Nyree didn't know Malachi's where-abouts.

"I don't believe in smothering anyone. If you talk to him, tell him to call me. Bye," Nyree said without giving her mother-in-law an opportunity to say another word. Nyree was furious. *How dare he treat me like this?* She was becoming annoyed with Malachi. This was supposed to be technically their honeymoon period where they were still happy, no problems, and lovey-dovey, as he left on the Mediterranean tour of duty two weeks after they were married.

It was twelve AM when Nyree was awakened by the sound of Malachi undressing. He hurried and got into bed. She smelled liquor on his breath. *'Was that Hennessy VSOP? Where had he been'?* She wanted to know, but she did not want to be perceived as the nagging, jealous wife.

Nyree wrestled with Ms. B, her inner voice. Ms. B was the part of her personality that was blunt and got questions answered. Ms. B had taken over. Nyree switched on the light and her voice took a harsh tone, one that she did not use much. He had some nerve coming into her parents' home this late. No respect whatsoever.

"Where in the world have you been?" Her question and tone seemed to startle Malachi, who feigned tiredness as he rubbed his red eyes.

"I was over my mom's. Then we went by Fat Man's house and I got some sounds for the car..."

Nyree raised her eyebrow at that statement. He said "the car" as if it belonged to the both of them. It was her car; her daddy had bought her that car for her graduation present from Indiana University. She did not mind sharing what she had, but she did mind being taken for granted. Her car was a luxury model. It was not the type of car that you wanted people to hear coming around the block. It drew enough attention as it was, she did not need her trunk rattling from the bass in the trunk. Funny, that he thought he had done her a favor by "putting some sounds" in her car with her money. Wasn't she capable of going to an auto shop to have a sound system installed in her car with her own money?

"Did you use my credit card?"

"Uh…Yeah, I told you that I was going to use it earlier. *'Member?"* he told her as if she were a child slow to comprehend.

If he gets smart with me one more time, I'll slap the taste out of his mouth. His use of the card was not bothering her as much as his cockiness and 'I could care less' demeanor.

"No, I don't **re-mem-ber**. How much did you charge?" Nyree questioned. Malachi lay there in the bed, propped up on his elbows, with his right leg crossed over his left leg. Nyree stood at the foot of the bed as if she were a mother demanding answers from her young child. Malachi rolled his eyes as he answered, "A couple of hundred dollars, why?"

'That's not a sufficient answer. Press him on it. Your definition of a couple of hundred dollars may be different from his.' When Malachi realized that he was going to have to provide a numerical answer for Nyree he responded in a low, almost

hoarse, voice, "Five hundred."

'I'll be darned, he just lied. "Yep," Ms. B chimed in, "aren't you glad you asked him? Uh-huh. Ain't no telling what else he has lied about.'

"Five- hundred?   Uh-no.   Try twelve hundred. A credit card representative called me." The way she was grilling him she felt like an attorney. Humph, maybe she had missed her calling in life. Nyree always had a knack for getting to the bottom of a situation and arguing her case. Now it was no different. Malachi looked like a little kid caught with his hand in the cookie jar.

"I didn't know it was that much. Why are you trippin'? I'll take care of it, *damn!*"

"I'm trippin' because your ass just lied. I'm *trippin'* because if it wasn't for my good credit and allowing you to be on my credit card you would not have a credit card. If you'll lie about this, there is no telling what else you will lie about. Next thing I know, you will be telling me you got kids." She laughed at her joke for what seemed like a minute.

Nyree stopped when she realized that she was laughing alone. For a moment she felt that awkward feeling that she experienced when she told corny jokes that no one in the room could understand, so she had to explain them so that they could get it. She brought her laughter to an abrupt stop and zeroed in on Malachi's face. She couldn't recall the last time she had seen him look so serious.

No memories came to mind. Not even the night he proposed to her. Ah, that night. They had spent it at the *Embassy Suites* in Schaumburg, Illinois. He had bought a bottle of Moet. She was impressed because she did not think that his meager salary would allow him to afford such a luxury. They were watching a movie rental. The name of the movie escaped her at the moment, for it did not matter. It was not significant to the story anyway. The bubbly overflowed in the champagne glasses that he had purchased that evening from the mall. After a few sips from her glass, she was finished.

"No, you can't be finished. Go ahead and finish it off," he had insisted.

With a curious look she responded, "Maybe later. I'm okay for now."

Snuggling close to her and whispering in her ear, he said, "It would be good for you to do it now. It'll enhance the moment." His suspicious behavior really had the wheels in her head turning. *'I hope this isn't poisonous. Never has a man insisted on me drinking all of my drink. And what is this "enhance the moment" stuff? I don't need anything to "enhance the moment." I'm that good. I make him holler every single time we have sex.'* Reluctantly she drank from the glass finishing off its content only to find that there was a foreign object in her mouth. "Malachi, what the…" she began as she removed the one-carat diamond ring that she had fixated her eyes on months ago at Albert's Diamond Jewelers from her mouth. She figured her eyes must have been the size of saucers. Then, as if he had rehearsed this scene, he was on his knees, saying, "Nyree Ilese Shaw, will you marry me?" while sliding the ring on her finger. Fanning and waving her hands around like a fish out of water was all she could do. She nodded her head up and down. Malachi calculated that five minutes must have elapsed before he heard the single answer to the question he had posed. He was pleased with her positive response and said, "For a minute there you had a brother scared." They both laughed and it was a good night and good morning that followed.

Bringing herself out of her memories and back to the present moment, she was certain that Malachi had never worn a serious expression as the one that was present on his face now. It was so extreme that it sent a hot sensation through her body. Not the hot sensation that a lover sends, but the sensation that you experience when you dip your foot into a tub of water that contains hot, scalding water. Suddenly she was feeling like a child being scolded for having said something wrong.

She was reliving the moment when she was eight years old standing near the offering table in church where Eric Monroe had said something that offended her. Her hair had been styled in two ponytails. She wore a purple blouse with a purple skirt and was swaying her hips and patting herself on the behind while saying, "Kiss my grits!" Her mother seemed to have come from out of nowhere (like she usually did when Nyree was up to no- good) and clamped down on Nyree's right forearm while instructing her through gritted teeth to apologize and refrain from that language, as ladies do not speak in that manner. Nyree remembered her face feeling hot as she imagined her caramel skin was rosy. She apologized not knowing exactly what she was apologizing for. Flo on *Mel's Diner* always said it and no one ever made her apologize. It would be years later, when Nyree would learn that phrase meant "kiss my butt."

Nyree said for effect, "Next you'll be telling me you have a baby." She was really on a roll now. This lecture would teach him about lying to her. Who did he think he was?

"I do," Malachi said bluntly without expression.

Ms. B interjected, *"Oh no, he didn't just say that. Girl, he did not just say that. Somebody had better pinch me before I snap on this son-of-a –ooh. You must have heard him wrong."*

Nyree was pretty sure that she had heard him correctly. However, this is not the type of thing that you want to hear your husband tell you after six months of marriage, with all those months being spent apart. The notion of moving to a strange place had her under stress so it was quite possible that she could be hearing things. After all, Ms. B was talking a mile a minute in her head so she asked him to repeat what he said.

Malachi rolled his eyes as he repeated himself: yes, he had a child. The way he looked at her, like *what's the big deal?* almost made her blood boil. Five years together—minus a messy two-month breakup—and this was the first she was hearing of it. Nyree could barely process what he was saying. When they first met, she'd asked him straight-up: Do you have kids? Ever been to jail? Got a girlfriend? He'd answered "No" to each one without hesitation.

She swallowed hard, keeping her voice steady. "So… how old is this child?"

"He's a baby," Malachi replied, shrugging like it was nothing.

Baby? Nyree's mind raced, hoping he meant the kid was five, six—anything but what her gut was telling her. She pressed him, her voice sharp. "A baby? How old, Malachi?"

In a voice so low she almost didn't hear it, he answered, "One month."

The words hit her like a punch to the gut. She felt the air leave her lungs, her knees buckling as she collapsed onto the hard wooden floor. Tears blurred her vision, spilling down her face as she gasped for breath. The pain was crushing, like her heart had been yanked out of her chest. She clutched her stomach, feeling like she'd been sucker-punched, left breathless and broken. She'd never imagined betrayal could feel like this—like the life had been knocked clean out of her. Trying to pull herself to a standing position was difficult. Her lower body was numb. She was paralyzed with disbelief. If death came to her right now, it would not be soon enough. Pain and agony were no strangers to her, but at least in the past she had seen those twins coming. This experience was totally different. His hands were full of strength as they pulled her five- foot- two- inch, one hundred and five-pound body to its feet and laid her in the bed. With her hair brushed in a ponytail she appeared to be eighteen instead of twenty-six years old. The tears flowed like a constant stream. It was difficult to see his face through the tears, but what she could see was a man who appeared older than twenty-six. Had he aged right before her eyes? Now he seemed more relaxed- more relieved. Her body was too weak to pull from his embrace as he tried to comfort and console by rocking her. Her voice had been muted; it was an ineffable moment as she did not have the ability to speak. Lucky for him, for if she could be speaking, he would be every curse word she could think of.

***

Her mind kept flashing back to the evening of April 7, 1995, as she stood exchanging vows with this man at the candle- lit altar adorned with white roses. She recalled the beads of sweat on his brow as they stood before God, friends, and family taking their marriage vows. At that time she had the audacity to think that she had caused him to perspire. She heard the wedding march being played as she sat in the dressing room waiting for the cue, but did not budge. The phrase "cold feet" came to life and she began to cry. Amazingly enough, she had not ruined her makeup which was a good thing. Her makeup artists had been Diane, Jannis, and Gretchen of the Dilworth family and she was sure that they were in another part of the church making sure that the wedding was running smoothly. The ladies were also the wedding coordinators. They were top-notch. They handled many important events and did not come cheaply. How would she have gotten word to them that she needed her makeup touched up? Luckily for her she did not have to. A knock at the door brought her out of the dressing room. It was her dad. "Are you coming out? This is the second time the pianist has played the song." Nyree was sure that if her dad had not come to the door that she would not have left the room.

"I'll be out in a minute, Dad," Nyree said as she watched him close the door. She looked in the mirror and dabbed her eyes. *'I still look good. I look good even when I cry. I'm a bad motor scooter, watch your mouth.'* Then she blew a kiss to herself in the mirror and walked out of the dressing room. Nyree met her dad at the door to the sanctuary. He was there waiting patiently.

The usher at the door joked, "For a minute there, I thought you weren't coming up."

Nyree said seriously, "Me too."

Nyree smiled as she walked down the aisle. *'Please don't let me trip over my dress. That would be too embarrassing. I could see it now. The cover of the* Midwest Vein *would read Nyree Shaw stumbles as she says, "I do." Why is Malachi sweating? I must have that effect on men. I had him waiting so long he probably thought that I wasn't coming. That would have been funny if I stood him up like he stood me up the other night. I wish I had a handkerchief in this bra. I would pull it out and wipe his brow. I hope he doesn't make our pictures look bad.'* For the life of her, she could not figure out why he was perspiring so profusely. Now she knew why he was sweating like an NBA basketball player who had played all four quarters while resting on the bench for only five minutes.

Who was this man with his arms around her? Everything she thought she knew about him, about them, -was a lie. Hadn't she asked him if he had been untrue to her? And what did he do? He lied. *'What else had he lied about? How many other women had there been? I should have known better. How long have I been a fool? What about the other day when I found a condom in his Tommy Hilfiger jeans (the ones I bought him for Christmas last year), and he said that his friend asked him to hold on to it? Who in the world asks someone to hold a condom for them? You ask people to hold your drink, maybe your purse, or even your coat—but a condom? That's like me telling my girl at the club, "Hey Aris, can you hang onto this tampon for me? I'll probably need it later, just not sure when." Like, who does that? Some things are way too personal to hand off like a set of keys.*

Nyree, girl, how dumb can you be? she thought, her frustration simmering. It was almost laughable if it weren't so ridiculous, but deep down, she knew there was nothing funny about it.

Nyree began pounding on the bed and saying, "Oh God, help me. Help me, Lord. Why me Lord? Why?" This moment was surreal. She was there hearing and seeing everything, but she could not believe it. Like a rare occasion when it is bright and sunny outside. The breeze is ever so warm and gentle to the skin. All is well in the world and for once everything seems like it is going to be alright. The mood is peaceful and somber and you wish you could bottle it up and save it for a later date. And then out of nowhere on this perfect day without warning, it begins raining. It becomes dark in an instant. The thunder roars and the lightning crackles and the branches from the trees begin to sway violently. Some break and hit the ground. Damage occurs to the property of others and all you can do is hope that it misses you and your property. But no such luck. It was raining on Nyree and when it rained it poured. This was one of the darkest storms of her life and there was no umbrella in sight.

This ordeal was a learning experience for her and the more she reflected on past events the more she was learning. Lesson 1a: *Didn't Mommy tell me not to marry a man that I was not evenly yoked with? We lack the same spiritual and moral beliefs. Malachi cannot even provide me with the life that I am accustomed to living. Money is not everything but hey, I gotta keep it real, it sure does help having some. Have I always known that we were not equals and just pushed that fact to the side? I think that I was hoping that one day we would be playing on equal playing field. Lesson 1b: You should have known something was wrong when this man said he wanted to rent a hall and get married. His rationale was he would not feel comfortable in a church.*

She mumbled to herself, "And this too shall pass." She could not help wondering when it all would pass. All she could do now was to call on God and pray that He delivered her from this situation. There had been times she had called on Him in the past but not often. Many unfulfilled promises about changing her behavior and ways would follow her calls. She knew that she should pray more, go to church more, and work on her relationship with God, but she always had an excuse. Always promising to get around to it, but never fulfilling the promise.

Five

December 1995

The transition to Navy life hadn't been easy for Nyree. Sure, Florida's weather was gorgeous, and she loved cruising down highways lined with palm trees, but Jacksonville had lost its charm the moment she learned who else called it home. She hadn't known that Malachi's "other family"—the baby and his mother—lived in the same city until they were already halfway down I-65, leaving Gary behind. If it had been some random fling overseas, she might have found a way to accept it. But to be in the same city, forced to coexist with this reality in her own backyard? It was like a wound that couldn't heal.

Malachi had dropped the bomb on her somewhere near Evansville, Indiana, just as they crossed into Kentucky. Her mind raced with images of pulling over and leaving him stranded right there, her foot pressing the gas as he stared in shock at her taillights. Every mile they passed through Indiana had her envisioning it more vividly—watching him grow smaller in the rearview mirror as she sped away. And as they passed the rural stretch of Martinsville, she almost laughed out loud, imagining the irony. She'd heard too many stories of that place back in her college days at IU Bloomington—rumors of Klan sightings, unsettling tales that kept her from stopping for gas there.

In a way, she thought, maybe Martinsville wasn't the best place to leave him stranded, but the idea still brought a grin to her face.

Would anyone come to Malachi's aid in that town? Had he opened his mouth while they were in Evansville, Indiana, she would have probably kicked him out of the car right then and there. Nyree had learned from a research topic paper that she had written on racism in Indiana that Evansville, Indiana, was the place where the Klan originated. Why was she having so many twisted thoughts? Would the Klan getting Malachi really make her feel better? She had always taken her enemies head on. There was never a time that she could recall when she had allowed one enemy to handle another enemy.

Managing a local bookstore in Jacksonville was rewarding for her. Edwin and Margo did not understand why she was not pursuing jobs in corporate America, but they left her alone. Whenever they spoke with her they heard the sadness in Nyree's voice but Margo always dismissed it as Nyree being homesick. Edwin knew his baby girl and sensed that it was something more than homesickness that caused her to sound so dismal. "If that son-of-a… ooh, you almost made me curse and you know I ain't cursed in, well never mind all that. If that person is mistreating you in any way, I will kill him. You don't have that to worry about." Always trying to reassure her dad that everything was fine, she would smile and force cheer in her voice and say, "Oh, no, Daddy. I'm just tired and trying to adjust to a new place, new people, the weather, you know how it is." He would often agree with her, but he had always known her to be able to adapt to any situation.

On her off days she stayed in bed all day only leaving to shower, change clothes, and drink water. Her appetite had disappeared and she forced herself to drink water so that her skin would maintain its healthy look. She had scheduled herself off for three days in a row and had followed her day-off routine. Today she had decided to let some sunlight in the apartment and some fresh air. Malachi said that she had it looking like a mortuary. He would joke, "Who died?" She would mumble, "I did." It was difficult for her to deal with her situation. When Nyree loved she loved hard. She put one hundred twenty percent into her relationship with Malachi and even though she often felt short-changed she gained solace in knowing that she had gone above and beyond the call of duty.

Treat others as you would like to be treated was her motto. So she gave and gave and **gave** with the expectation that if she were ever in need Malachi would do the same. When others questioned her about Malachi's faithfulness to her in the past, she dismissed it as people "hating on her" and wishing that they had what she and Malachi had. In a million years she would have never thought that Malachi would put her through such turmoil. He was sexy in a peculiar way, but she did not think that another woman would give him the time of day. There were some brothers that were "all of that," but that term did not apply to Malachi, thus she never thought that she had anything to worry about.

In addition, he had led her to believe that he was so into her that he would never cheat on her. Nyree had not learned how to deal with her reality so she just slept for twenty hours a day when she did not have to work. At least when she was asleep she didn't have to think and she did not experience pain. As of late there were no dreams to recall either.

Ms. B told Nyree that Nyree would come back from the dead and that everyone who had ever crossed her in life would be sorry. Nyree wasn't certain about that or anything in life. The one thing that she had surmised was that everything wasn't always what it seemed. What happened to her fairytale life? Yes, there had been disappointments in life prior to this one that she was currently experiencing, but none of this magnitude and nothing that she could not overcome. In the past there had always been hope, light at the end of the tunnel. She could not see light or the end of the tunnel for that matter. She felt like she was sinking into a bottomless pit. Why did she continue to stay? *I want to make this work. I don't want to give up so early in the marriage, but I can't help ask the question that Keysha asked me five years ago: "What are you doing with Malachi?" Well, this is a fine time to be asking such a question. Didn't Keesh try to warn me in her own subtle way and I dismissed it? Had I listened to her then, I might not be going through this mess. Now I truly know what people mean when they say hindsight is twenty-twenty.* **Lesson#2** *learned: When a man's momma tries to tell you that her son is not worth your time you better grab your purse, get up off your behind and to quote the women in my family, "run like 40 going south" and be like Lot from the Bible and don't look back. My mother, my father, even co-workers tried to warn me about him. They thought he was after my money. I didn't listen to them and I probably should have. What I really can't get over, is that **his momma** tried to warn me about him. That speaks volumes over anything, but I couldn't hear at the time. I mean just think about when the woman who gives birth to a man tells you that that man ain't about nothing, she's probably telling the truth and you should listen. She doesn't have to give you that warning, because she was really losing out by doing so. How is she losing out? She has a grown man living in her house that she can easily get rid of by allowing you* *to think that you have a great catch. Thinking that you have a great catch you take him in and off her hands. So for her to tell you that you do not have the catch of the day is working to her disadvantage. She has nothing to gain by telling you that.'*

Six

"Nyree? It's mom and dad here. We're calling to wish you a Merry Christmas."

"Merry Christmas to you all too. Did you all get my gifts?" Nyree had asked as she had waited until the week before Christmas to send her gifts. She had not really been in the Christmas mood, but figured just because she was not in the mood that did not give her the right to disrupt her parents' Christmas.

Now Malachi was a different story. If he was looking for a present from her, he had better keep looking. There had been times that she thought of giving him an unexpected present. One day when she was baking homemade chocolate walnut brownies, which he really loved for her to make, she had thought of putting laxative in them. The idea had made her fall out laughing as she thought, *'It's mean, but so what? He's full of shit anyways, so no real harm would be done.'*

"Yes. Thank you," both of her parents said together in unison.

"So how are things going there? Can you talk?" her dad wanted to know. That's what she really loved about her dad. He did not do a lot of small talk; he just went for the gusto and got down to business. Her mother could go on and on for days without getting to the point.

Nyree let out a sigh and told her dad, "Yeah, I can talk. He supposedly went to the gas station to get some milk." She'd barely kept a straight face when he'd said it, knowing full well it was just an excuse to get out of the apartment. She'd bet anything he was either headed to Ciara's mother's place or somewhere on his phone, whispering sweet nothings to her. If he was really going to the gas station, he sure wasn't taking her car. She pictured him trudging down the street on Christmas Day, looking pathetic as he walked in the cold, and almost laughed. Still, a small voice nagged her—why hadn't she checked the window to see if someone picked him up?

Living like this was exhausting. She felt more like a CIA agent than a wife, analyzing every word he said, hunting for lies. It was like a twisted game, and right now, she was losing. She was determined to get one step ahead, to never let anything catch her by surprise again. But if someone had picked him up, they were long gone by now. She kicked the air in frustration, cursing herself for not looking out the window sooner.

Twisting the phone cord around her finger as she lounged on the sofa, Nyree decided to take a break from her constant "investigations." At least she was on the line with her parents, people who actually cared about her. They'd been pushing her to come home ever since she'd confessed to them over Thanksgiving about Malachi and his newborn son, Camron. Her mom, Margo, and dad, Edwin, had practically begged her to cut her losses. "Just come home," they'd said, but she wasn't ready to throw in the towel.

Her mom, a psychiatrist, had been especially concerned when Nyree mentioned her struggles with depression. Margo even suggested a visit to Jacksonville, saying she'd help "sort things out." But the last thing Nyree wanted was her mother analyzing her every move, poking and prodding at her emotions. She'd assured her mom she had it handled, determined that nothing would slip past her again. "The wife is always the last to know," she muttered to herself. Not in this case—not if she could help it.

Besides, when her mother came to visit, Nyree wanted to be sharp and alert, not a basket case. Margo had to respect her daughter's wishes, but the thought of her daughter suffering a nervous breakdown without any family to help her recover was unnerving. "Well, Dad, I can't lie to you all. It's not been so merry. You know when I called you and told you that I couldn't find my Platinum Visa? After Malachi watched me tear the apartment up, he reached in his pocket and pulled out the card and said, 'Is this card you looking for?'"

Edwin was sitting in his favorite chair in the family room and his leg was jerking. It was a sign of anxiety. He knew that whatever she was going to say he was not going to like it. "Yeah," he managed to say as pleasantly as he could. He had never liked Malachi, but he found him tolerable. Margo was just blunt and admitted a long time ago, "I can't stand the bastard. You see how he's always squinting. He never looks you in the eye. The bastard is hiding something. Nyree, you really should have him investigated. What do we know about his family and upbringing?"

When he stayed in the Shaw home, Margo avoided him as much as possible. There had been no sit-down family meals the brief time that Malachi was in the house. "I don't break bread with my enemies," she told Edwin one evening as she retreated to their bedroom and ate her meal there. "Oh, you're exaggerating, Margo," was Edwin's response.

Edwin considered Malachi a foe as well. Nyree continued, "Well, two days ago, I received my credit card statement and, lo and behold, there was two hundred dollars worth of charges to Toys Are Our Thing and charges to Victoria's Confessions..."

"Don't tell me he took your card and bought that bastar... baby stuff. *Victoria's Confessions?* If this snake has bought some whores lingerie on your credit card, you don't have to worry... I'll kill him with my bare hands," Margo yelled. The comment almost made Nyree laugh aloud. Her mother stood four- foot- eleven and probably did not weigh one hundred pounds. This was the same woman who would begin running a marathon when she saw a spider in the house. *How in the world was she going to kill somebody with her bare hands?* Nyree thought about what her grandmother often said about a woman protecting her children. According to her grandmother the weakest woman would step up to the plate to fight if she thought her children were in danger. This is the most dangerous type of woman, her grandmother had said. Her rationale was you think you know this woman, but in all actuality in a dangerous situation you don't know what she is capable of doing. *Could this be the case with my mother?* Nyree wondered. She hoped that she would never have to find out.

"Nyree, what did he say when you confronted him," Edwin asked.

"You don't even want to know. Malachi said that he didn't use my Visa. Malachi said

he used my MasterCard. So I canceled both of the cards and reported the fraud to the agencies. They had the nerve to tell me there was nothing that they could do about it, because he is a cardholder on the Visa. But you know I took the Visa that had his name on it from him.

MasterCard said that there was nothing that they could do. According to MasterCard this kind of thing happens all of the time. A spouse gets angry at the other one, and how did they know that I wasn't just making something up. The best thing that they could do was suggest that I call the police department if he forged my name on the receipt."

"Baby Girl, you don't have to put up with this. I know that you have to be tired of counting your money every day to make sure he does not steal it. Now you have to watch your credit cards…" Margo said.

"Mom, you just don't know how tired I am of having to hide my money in my underwear drawer and in the bottom of a sanitary napkin box. Yesterday, I almost hyperventilated. I had hidden my wallet in the bottom of my laundry basket before I got in the shower. I couldn't remember where I hid it, so I swore up and down he had stolen my wallet. Then I finally remembered what I did with it."

Edwin's heart went out to his baby girl. This was no way for anyone to have to live. "I know you want to do things your way, honey, but whenever you decide that you have had enough, home is here for you. You can come here whenever you get ready to, no questions asked. We will keep this in the family and this time the

Midwest Vein will not get hold of the story."

Nyree remembered the article in the *Midwest Vein* regarding her getting married to Malachi. She had once viewed the newspaper as a respectable source of news and thought that the article would be a delight to read; instead, it was more like yellow journalism. The article was embarrassing. The headline read, "Rags to Riches." The reporter drudged up all the dirt on Malachi that she could. It was reported that he had not graduated from high school; he had been arrested twice, once for possession of marijuana, and once for shoplifting. Both charges had been dismissed. The ultimate was when the reporter wrote Malachi Chandler had cashed in big time with marriage to real estate mogul's daughter Nyree.

Nyree wiped her tears away and thanked her mom and dad for listening. "So, when was the last time you guys talked to Kyle?" She knew that this was a sore spot for her dad, but it was Christmas, a time of cheer. "Nyree, don't get your dad started," her mom practically begged. Margo wanted her family to be happy as they had been once upon a time, but she did not want Edwin moping around all day complaining about "that thieving boy." It hurt Margo to have to choose between her husband and her son. Nyree apologized and encouraged them to talk to Kyle because life was too short to hold grudges and tomorrow is not promised to anyone. Her last statement weighed on Edwin's heart, so he promised to call his son and wish him a happy holiday.

When Edwin hung up the phone, Margo promised Nyree that she would have Edwin invite Kyle over for dinner. Margo anticipated resistance on Edwin's part. Nyree told her mother that sometimes in life doing the right thing could be uncomfortable. Margo could not help but wonder if that was how Nyree viewed her marital situation with Malachi.

Seven

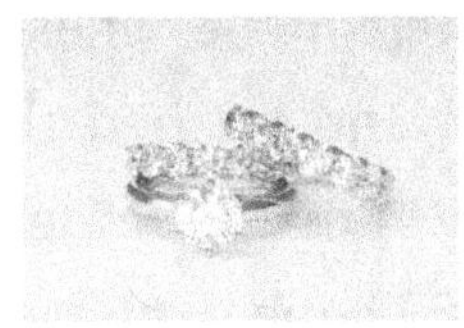

February 1996

The tension had been building between Nyree and Malachi for quite some time. She had set some ground rules about Malachi visiting his son. "Either I go with you to pick up your son or you won't be seeing your son," Nyree yelled.

"I'm not a little kid. I don't need you to go with me to get my *son*," Malachi yelled back.

"Well, I guess you won't be seeing the little bastard," Nyree yelled. She wished she could take the words back but it was too late. Her words had hurt Malachi and she was not sorry. *What about me? What about my hurt? It really burns me up to hear him say, "My son." Every time I hear those words it just reminds me that another woman has given my husband something that I, his wife, have been unable to give him. I feel like he is rubbing it in my face.*

Her feelings on having children were mixed. When she was at the mall and saw women with their little ones she became a little misty eyed and wished that it were she. When she heard tales of women's bodies being stretched out of shape and never being right since giving birth, she knew that giving birth was not for her. Once, while sitting in the hair salon, a woman told a story about how her daughter had told her that her stomach was fat and looked like she had a baby in it. The woman said that her daughter had asked why she had those ugly stretch marks on her stomach. At five years old, this mere child was telling her mother in a matter of words that her mother did not conform to society's beauty standards. The woman said that she told her five-year-old daughter that she was the cause of her fat belly and stretch marks. Nyree could not help but wonder how she would feel if her body lost its appeal due to her giving birth to an ungrateful child. While the child's comments sounded cruel and insensitive, the little girl probably had no idea how it tore her mother up inside; but Nyree felt the wo man's pain. What could you do? Send the child back?

The tension escalated even more when she went to the doctor in January because she would not stop menstruating. Her cycle usually went from five to seven days. She had heard of women having three-day cycles and only wished that she could be that lucky. When her cycle went to day eight, she thought that it was a little odd, but thought nothing of it. When it approached day ten she became a little alarmed but figured that maybe the stress she had been under had caused a continuation. On day eleven she could have turned a cartwheel when it appeared that her cycle was gone. Two days later she awakened to find that her little visitor was back. Her 'little visitor' remained with her for another two weeks. At that point she had become fed up and went to the gynecologist to discuss the problem. Dr. Madison had told her that it was probably nothing to get alarmed about as these things happen to women sometimes. A ten-day prescription of Provera seemed to solve the problem. When she shared with Malachi what was going on with her body, all he could express was how the situation was going to affect him sexually. When the problem occurred again in February, Nyree paid Dr. Madison another visit.

She told the doctor about the recurring situation.

"Okay, Doctor, are you going to give me another prescription for Provera? It really seemed to work the last time."

"No, Nyree. I think what we may need to do is what is called a D&C. It's a pretty

straight-forward procedure that can be done on an outpatient basis."

"I don't know. I mean I was hoping that you would just give me another script, and that would be that. You know?" Nyree had said hoping that she had caused the doctor to reconsider the recommendation for surgery.

"I think that the Provera is only a quick fix, but the D&C would solve the problem."

"Can I let you know?"

"Sure. It is something that you probably want to think over and discuss with your husband or family. If you decide to have the procedure, I can do it Friday."

"This Friday?"

"Yes."

"That's sooner than I thought. I mean it's Tuesday already."

"You want to get this matter resolved quickly, don't you? I can imagine that it is not much fun to be menstruating for such long periods of time."

Nyree snickered because the doctor was correct. Due to her cycle's inconsistencies, she did not know when she was really off her cycle, so she constantly carried sanitary napkins with her even though she preferred tampons.

"Well, you know what, Malachi? If taking me to the hospital is going to be a problem, I'll find somebody else to take me," Nyree had told her husband the day before her surgery.

"No, it's not a problem. The problem is that you don't want me to drive your car any other time, but now that you need something, it's okay for a brother to drive your car."

"Look, Malachi, either you're going to do it or not. I'm not going to kiss your ass for you to do something for me. I'll call somebody..."

"I'll take you," Malachi said unenthusiastically.

***

Nyree had a strange feeling as she turned the key in the door. Malachi was not home. *Where is he?* She had taken the car today, so he had no means of transportation. *Is that "Pleasures" I smell? Why do I smell my* Estee Lauder Pleasures? *I did not wear that today. I'm wearing Issey Miyake. Another woman has been in my home and has had the nerve to put on my perfume. NO, stop being silly!*

She surveyed the apartment and everything seemed to be in place. Nyree walked into the kitchen and opened the refrigerator to survey its contents. Out of the corner of her eye, she noticed that the lid to the trashcan was placed at an angle, as if someone had removed it and was unsure how to align it with the can. She peeped in the bag and noticed that there was a diaper in the trash bag. Then she heard the doorknob turn and Malachi entered. "Malachi, who has been over here?"

Malachi raised his eyebrows and glared to his left and then spotted the lid on the trash can. Nyree was a perfectionist when it came to things being put in their proper place. Why hadn't he taken the trash out before he left? Why had Ciara sprayed Nyree's perfume and too much of it at that? He was beginning to wonder about Ciara. What woman would want to be in another woman's personal hygiene items?

"What? What are you talking about? Nobody has been over here, Nyree," he said, hoping that he sounded convincing. He looked at her, trying to read her look, but it was puzzling. She looked like something out of *The Exorcist*. Not being a praying man, Malachi silently prayed that Nyree did not go into one of her rages even though he knew that she would be justified to have, as his mother would say, "a stone cold fit" on him.

Nyree's adrenaline was pumping and her thoughts were becoming irrational. Nyree was hearing voices. It was not Ms. B this time. *I must be losing my damn mind. What kind of disorder is this? My mother would know for sure. This cannot be real. It is real and there is nothing I can do about it. I feel so out of control.* A man was shouting, "Kill that bastard." A lady was saying softly, "It will be okay, dear." Then the man and the lady were arguing and Nyree's head was pounding. She wanted the chaos to stop, but she could not make it stop. The voices were controlling her. It was weird; she could hear the voices and her own thoughts about the situation all at the same time.

"Get out, Malachi!" Nyree screamed. She was trying to push him out of the kitchen and move him to the door.

"Get your hands off of me. Are you crazy?"

Malachi asked.

Nyree bobbed her head up and down to indicate that his statement about her mental state was correct. Then she let out a laugh that made him shiver as she walked over to the trash can, pulled out the soiled diaper, and threw it at him.

When the soggy, smelly diaper hit Malachi in the chest, she spied the cheap, red lipstick on the collar of his white shirt. Malachi watched the soggy diaper hit the floor. *Busted,* he thought. He just shrugged his shoulders to indicate that he had been caught and had no excuse for the diaper being in the apartment. What could he do? He could not lie because the evidence spoke for itself. *Why did I bring them over here?* Malachi wondered.

There was a running tally of all the dumb things that he had done that he kept in his head, but this by far had to top the list. Ciara kept asking him, "What would your wife say if she knew I had been in your apartment? I bet she doesn't know that you and I christened the apartment before she came down here."

Malachi had played the "I'm running this over here" act and told Ciara, "I wear the pants in this house. Don't worry about my wife. I'll handle her." Now Malachi was not so sure about that statement. In fact he was so terrified of Nyree that he felt like he might wet his pants. A more accurate statement would have been that he was the one wearing the panties because he was feeling like a pansy right about now.

The hostile male voice in Nyree's head was yelling again, "Kill him. He doesn't deserve to live. How long are you going to put up with his crap?"

The female voice instructed him to stop yelling. The hostile man lowered his voice and instructed Nyree to walk over to the third drawer above the dishwasher and take out the carving knife. Nyree did as she was instructed. She walked over to Malachi and placed the blade at his Adam's apple. "Now, you lying sack of shit, tell me who has been over here," she demanded. Fear was beginning to loom over Malachi. He could count the times that he had heard Nyree curse on both of his hands. She did not curse in casual conversation as he did. When she cursed, it was an indication that she was furious. He chose his words carefully.

As Malachi began to answer, the hostile

man began yelling to Nyree that his instructions were not being followed. "Shut up, okay," Nyree yelled to the male voice.

Malachi gave her a strange look. If she was reading the look correctly, he was thinking,'*This chick is crazy. One minute she is grilling me and the next minute she is telling me to shut up. Think. Think fast. I'm not going to be able to lie myself out of this one. It's best that I leave now.*'

"Malachi, get out," Nyree said, her voice low but steady as she waved the knife with a warning flash. That was all he needed. His long legs darted out of the apartment like his life depended on it—because this time, he knew it probably did.

He found himself pounding on Kenya and Dre's apartment door, heart racing as he waited. Memories of two weeks ago flooded his mind: that night he'd rolled into the apartment at two in the morning after hitting the local club scene in Jacksonville. The chain lock had kept him out, and he'd spent half an hour pleading through the door before Nyree finally let him in. The moment he stepped inside, he'd shoved past her, knocking her back. She'd hit the ground with a gasp of pain, but the liquor he had consumed earlier caused him to ignore it, heading straight to bed without a second glance.

Sure, she was mad about him staying out, but in his mind, she should've been grateful he came home at two instead of closing down the club at four. He could've gone to the after-party, hit up IHOP at dawn, but he'd "done her a favor" by coming home early. *Why's she gotta trip like this?* he'd thought to himself, irritated. *Even when I'm not doing anything, she acts like I am.*

Nyree, though, was far from "tripping." She'd sat up, watching late-night infomercials in a fury, listening to his snores fill the apartment. When the clock hit three, she'd slipped into the kitchen, her fingers curling around the cold handle of the butcher knife. She slid it under her nightshirt, tucking it securely against her hip with the waistband of her bikini briefs. She flicked off the TV, in the living room. Silence was the only silence to be heard, then tiptoed toward the bedroom, ready to finally make him understand just how done she was.

"Malachi. Malachi," she whispered. There was no response, he was out cold. She could smell the liquor seeping from his pores. He was sweating too. She nudged him hard in the ribs, still no response. *What if he died in his sleep?* A smile came to her face as she imagined shaking a lifeless, cold corpse. Carefully she placed the knife under her pillow and proceeded to mount him. *Ooh, I hope this does not arouse him and then he wakes up thinking that he is going to get some of this brown sugar.*

There was no response and she was glad. Minutes elapsed as she sat still in this position. Gently she stroked his "smooth-as-a-baby's-bottom" face and his neck with her fingertips. A tingly sensation went through her body. Then she grabbed the knife and placed the steel tip at his Adam's apple. This brought her sheer exhilaration. There was a moistness building up inside her as she stroked his Adam's apple with the tip of the knife. Oh, how sweet it was going to be when she went in for the final blow. The coolness of the blade at his Adam's apple woke him.

He grabbed the cool object with the palm of his hand not realizing it was a knife and cut the inside of his hand. The pain caused him to jerk and throw Nyree out of the saddle. "You crazy bitch!" he yelled as he ran to the sink to rinse his wound.

Normally Nyree would have been offended by the word, but she cackled like a witch on a Halloween and said coolly, "Yeah, I'll be that bitch," as she picked up the bloody knife and jumped on Malachi's back, wrapping her legs around his waist tightly, securing a choke hold on him with her right arm. With the knife resting on his neck, she said, "If you ever touch me again in your miserable, pathetic life, I'll cut you from ear to ear! Consider yourself warned." Then she jumped off before he could respond. From that night on she could have sworn that he slept with one eye open.

After the second knife incident, he started living on the base again.

Eight

March 1996

It was the morning after Nyree's birthday —a Saturday that she'd spent mostly alone. Malachi had ship duty and wasn't around, but honestly, even if he'd been there, she wasn't in the mood to celebrate. What was there to celebrate anyway? Another year, but with what to look forward to? More of the same exhaustion, frustration, and loneliness? She'd tried to lift her spirits by heading out to Jim's Spot with a few of her coworkers that night. The DJ gave her a birthday shoutout, and the drinks kept coming her way without her ever having to open her purse. But even as she drank herself into a fog, none of it numbed the worries lurking beneath the surface. Alcohol wasn't her escape —it only took her deeper into that dark place she was trying to avoid. By the end of the night, she felt drained, dizzy, and more hopeless than ever. When she finally stumbled into her apartment, she kicked the door shut and started stripping off the night. First off were her heels—the cute, stacked ones that looked amazing but were basically a trap for her feet. She kicked them aside, wincing as she glanced down at her toes. She could've sworn she'd developed a corn from all that dancing. Dropping onto the couch, she massaged her aching feet, muttering, "Never again." Those shoes were made for looking good, not for hours on the dance floor.

Dragging herself to the bedroom, she fumbled with the zipper on her CK1 jean dress, reaching around her back and slowly peeling it off. The night had been a blur, but now, standing there in the quiet of her room, all the pain she'd tried to drink away came flooding back. The dress accentuated her curves and showed off all of her assets. Had she gained weight since she first put the dress on? Had it been this difficult getting on? Nyree had no desire to struggle with this dress.

Nyree let out a groan, struggling to shimmy out of her dress until it finally fell in a heap on the bathroom floor. Standing there in nothing but her black lace bra and panties, she eyed her reflection, feeling a spark of pride. Those home video work-out sessions hadn't been in vain—she looked good, and for a moment, she let herself feel it. She flashed a grin, then attempted a celebratory squat, only to wobble and end up flat on her behind, laughing in spite of herself. "Some birthday," she muttered, snickering as she took in her makeshift party of one.

Reaching for her jewelry box, she glanced at the photo on it: her and Tyson, her sorority brother, the one who got away. Her mind started to wander down that road of "what-ifs," but she stopped herself—no pity parties tonight. She popped open the box, her eyes landing on her stash: ten neatly rolled blunts and a half-smoked one with a blue lighter resting on top. With a deep breath, she grabbed the half-finished one, flicking the lighter in her other hand, watching the flame flare and fade, almost hypnotized by the warmth and glow. She tried to imitate a fire trick she'd seen a kid do back in middle school, feeling a rebellious thrill even as she laughed at herself.

Memories of the kid with the sweater

vest and tie came to mind—the way he became the school's mini-celebrity for five minutes with his flame trick before losing all his cool points once he gave away the secret. She flicked the lighter again, bringing her palm just close enough to feel the heat without getting burned. Was she seriously playing with fire now? She scoffed at herself—maybe she was turning into a pyromaniac on top of everything else.

After a while, the fire lost its charm, and she found herself sniffing the blunt, cringing at the stale odor but sparking it up anyway. She exhaled a thick cloud of smoke, watching it swirl and dissipate in front of her. When it was time to ash, she paused, chuckling—she'd set a rule against smoking indoors, yet here she was breaking her own boundaries without a second thought. It hit her as ironic: she'd set up all these self-imposed rules to get her life on track, yet here she was, high and tipsy, laughing at her own broken boundaries. She raised her hand, slurring, "Who needs rules?" She cracked up, even as drool spilled down her chin, which she wiped off and examined in her hazy state, cringing as she wiped it on her thigh.

Stumbling to her feet, she tried to make it

to the bed, her head pounding. She had expected to feel that old college high, that escape, but it just wasn't hitting. The only thing swirling in her mind was her real life, all the stress, and the pain that never seemed to go away. She muttered, "Where's the peace in this? Where's that release?"

Suddenly, a soft voice seemed to cut through the haze, clear and almost close enough to touch: *ry God.* She froze, the words echoing like someone else was in the room with her, as real as anything she'd ever heard. She shook her head, trying to shake it off, laughing at the absurdity. "Great, now I'm hallucinating."

She muttered to herself, "But for real... *try God?* That's deep."

When she woke up at ten o'clock the next morning, she assumed she must have passed out when her head hit the pillow. Nyree jumped up when she heard Malachi's key in the lock. She hurried to close the bedroom door when she heard the laughter of men, but it was too late because Jason was surveying her. Malachi quickly stepped in front of his half-naked wife. Nyree pushed Malachi hard in the small of his back and said very sheepishly, "Hey, Jason.

What's up?"

In a nervous, shaky voice, he said, "How are you, Ms. Chandler?"

"Ok, you know yesterday was my birthday?"

"Oh, yeah? Happy belated birthday. What did you do?"

"Nothing much. Went to *Jim's Spot* and got messed-up..."

Malachi cleared his throat and backed her up in the room and said, "I'll be right back, Jason," as the door shut in Jason's face.

Malachi was agitated. What was wrong with Nyree? He had never seen her like this. When they first met she had been so shy about revealing her body. She often covered up after sex. He never could understand why she did it because she had the perfect body. Every chance he got to look at her body he did. Under normal circumstances he would be gawking at her body now. But it was difficult to do because she just stood topless in the doorway of their bedroom for what seemed like eternity, talking to another man. That hurt Malachi more than the time she threw hot coffee in his face. If he did not know any better, he would have thought that she was throwing herself at Jason.

"Put some clothes on," he scolded her.

She was standing toe to toe with him even though he stood a whole foot over her.

In a calm voice she said, "Get out. I want you to pack your stuff and get out. I should have never let you convince me into letting you come back."

He laughed at her comment. She had to be joking. He had gotten off duty and all he wanted to do was to show Jason this computer software he had just downloaded on the computer and go to sleep.

"Nyree, go on with all that. I'm not in the mood."

Nyree wasn't backing down. "Malachi, who the hell is Chantelle Imani?"

The question hit him like a bucket of ice water; she could see the shock all over his face. But nothing he felt could top how blindsided *she'd* been when their next-door neighbor, Kenya Brooks—who also happened to work on the ship with Malachi—had asked about Malachi's daughter. "Son," Nyree had corrected. Camron was his only child, right?

Jason heard all of the chaos and he did not

want to be around if something went down. He yelled out, "Hey, Chandler, I'll get back with you later," and he shut the door as he tiptoed out of the apartment. He could have slammed the door and knocked it off the hinges and it probably would not have disturbed the couple. Nyree and Malachi continued to argue. Malachi protested that he paid rent and he was not leaving. Nyree stated that she did not care what he paid and he was leaving "this day."

Malachi's voice filled the room, angry and raw. "I won't leave here alive! I'll kill myself!"

Nyree felt that familiar irritation rising. *This again?* Every time he got himself into a corner, he'd pull this stunt. The first time, she'd let it shake her. The second time, he'd taken it up a notch, grabbing a razor and turning it into a tug-of-war that left her hands sliced up. Meanwhile, he came out without a scratch. *Not this time,* she thought, rolling her eyes. Today, she was done playing his games. This wasn't her circus, and she wasn't about to dance around for attention anymore.

Without missing a beat, she grabbed her phone and dialed his mom back in Indiana. If anyone could hear what a mess he was making, it was the one who brought him into the world. When Keesh picked up, Nyree didn't hold back. Her voice rose with each word, giving full volume to the frustration she'd bottled up for too long.

"If he doesn't leave now," she yelled, "he's not leaving under his own free will later!" *I'm selling wolf tickets,* she thought, amused at her own bluff, *but Keesh doesn't need to know that.*

Keesh took the bait, her voice rising in panic on the other end. "Uh… put him on the phone!"

Nyree felt a surge of energy, fueled by anger. "Malachi! Malachi!" She shouted loud enough for him to hear through the walls. She let the phone fall to her side, her patience all but gone. "Get your sorry ass on the phone. It's yo' mama. She wants to talk to you!" She lifted the phone back to her ear, hearing nothing but silence from the other end.

Growing tired of the standoff, she stomped out of the bedroom, phone still in hand. Then she heard it—a loud thud from the living room. Her first instinct was annoyance. "You better not be messing up my stuff!" she shouted, storming into the room.

But her breath hitched. There he was, sprawled on the floor, blood pooling from his wrist, the butcher knife lying abandoned a few feet away.

She barely blinked, turning back to the phone. In a flat, annoyed tone, she said, "Keesh, I gotta go. Malachi's on the floor in the living room, wrist slit and all."

There was a stunned silence on the other end. Then Keesh's shocked voice broke through. "What?"

Nyree took a deep breath, steadying herself. "Yeah, Keesh, you heard me. I don't have time for this shit—I really don't. I have to be at work in an hour, and he's over here playing games." She hung up hard, slamming the cordless phone onto the base loud enough that she secretly hoped Keesh could still hear the impact. Maybe that would make her realize how serious things had gotten.

Returning to the living room, she found Malachi still on the floor, keeping his "act" going. *Doesn't he know I'm the queen of drama here?* she thought, crossing her arms, unimpressed. *Fine. He wants to play? Let's play.*

With a cool, almost mocking calmness,

she spoke to herself. "Okay, Nyree, let's do this. I don't have time, but if he wants a show, he's about to get one." She knew he wasn't really hurt; she could see the subtle rise and fall of his chest. So she crouched down, leaning over him and, in the sweetest voice she could muster, cooed, "Alright, Malachi. Game's over. You win... for now."

But he didn't move. Not an inch. Frustration churned in her, her patience snapping thread by thread. She clenched her teeth, her breathing heavy as her nostrils flared. *Forget playing nice. He doesn't understand that— never has, never will.*

In a rage of anger, she raised her foot and stomped down on his chest. Hard. But even then, he didn't react, lying there like he was unfazed. *I know he's not dead,* she thought, feeling a small, dark hope flicker that maybe, just maybe, he was. She instantly felt a wave of guilt for even thinking it, her mind echoing old Sunday school verses: *"Love those who misuse you. Fret not evildoers. Vengeance is mine, saith the Lord."*

Well, Lord, she thought bitterly, *when exactly is that vengeance supposed to happen?*

Needing to clear her head, she stormed

out of the apartment, her heels clicking on the pavement as she sucked in deep breaths of fresh air. Then she spotted Kenya on her balcony across the way, and it hit her—she knew exactly what her next move had to be.

"Kenya. Kenya. Hey girl, I need you to come over to my apartment and help me." Nyree began to look around nervously, as if someone were watching. Then she beckoned for Kenya to hurry. Kenya seemed to be enjoying the fact that she was needed and hurried to her friend's side. Nyree grabbed her by the hand and began walking her up the stairs while telling her about Malachi having slit his wrist. Kenya ran into the apartment and tried to convince Malachi to get up. Again he was unresponsive. He was even unresponsive to Andre when he came over and tried to get his buddy to get up. *Damn, he's good, but I'm better.* Nyree began sniffing and said that she was going to call for assistance. When the medics and the police arrived at the Chandlers' apartment, Nyree briefly explained that there were marital problems and what led to Malachi's current condition on the floor. There were two medics on the scene. The female medic was thin and had the mannerisms of a man.

In a Southern drawl, she said, "Sir, get up. Do you hear me?" Then she snatched Malachi by the arm and inspected the cuts on his wrist. She flung his limp wrist toward Nyree and said, "These are superficial cuts. Not enough to do anything. You can get up, Sir. You can stop faking."

Nyree stood with her arms crossed, watching the scene unfold like a twisted movie she couldn't pause. *This can't be my life,* she thought, almost in disbelief. But it was. Every time she'd thought, *It can't get worse than this,* life seemed to hear her and up the ante.

The male medic cracked open a bottle of smelling salts, waving it under Malachi's nose. Slowly, he blinked, coming back to consciousness, dazed. The police jumped in, questioning him on what happened, and his story lined up with hers—no surprises there. Then, one of the officers, sensing Malachi's naval pride, asked, "So, you're in the Navy?"

With a smug grin, Malachi nodded, "Yeah."

The other officer, silent until now, stepped forward, handcuffs out, and announced they'd be taking Malachi to the psychiatric ward at the naval hospital. The grin dropped from Malachi's face as the reality hit him. He began pleading, desperation setting in fast.

"Wait, wait—I'm not crazy! Don't take me —"

Nyree, a smirk playing on her lips, stepped forward, her voice dripping with mock sweetness. "Oh, baby, maybe you do need a little help. I mean, you did just try to kill yourself."

His face twisted in anger, realizing she was flipping the script on him. Malachi's calm shattered as he tried to lunge toward her, but the officers yanked him back, holding him in place. He snarled, "Nyree, you know I'm not crazy!"

She didn't flinch, just gave him a slow, mocking wink. "Well, I don't know what I know anymore. But I do know you just tried to hit me in front of half a squad."

One officer, glancing at his watch, sighed. "Let's move it. I was supposed to be off ten minutes ago."

A rush of relief hit Nyree as she watched Malachi get shoved into the back of the squad car. She was already picturing the paperwork she'd file when the dust settled.

Nine

One restraining order—check. Two weeks ago? Yeah. She'd made sure of that. Nyree's heart felt like it was going to jump out of her chest. As usual she was running late. *'Let me get a piece of chewing gum before I go inside.'* Even though it was only three o'clock the parking lot at Olive Garden was packed. Nyree agreed to meet Malachi for a late lunch so that they could discuss their joke of a marriage. She did not know why she was even entertaining the idea of discussing their marriage. Why was she here? Was she a glutton for punishment? What could he possibly say that she had not already heard before? It would be the same song and dance.

Now, as she scanned the restaurant, she didn't see Malachi anywhere. A young host with a lean build, light complexion, and a gold tooth in the front—too noticeable to miss—approached her with a goofy grin. It seemed every guy in Jacksonville had a mouth full of gold; back in Gary, she'd only seen it twice, and it just wasn't something she found to be appealing.

"So, ma'am, is dere any tang I cun hep you wit?" he asked, his thick accent punctuating each word. She bit back her immediate thought—*Yeah, genius, a table would be nice*—and instead managed a tight smile.

"Yes, I'm Nyree Chandler, and—"

"You're meetin' yo' husband, Malachi Chandler, for lunch," he finished with a smug smile, clearly thrilled to be in on her plans.

"Yes," she answered, wanting to know how he knew that.

"Follow me. He described you to a tee."

"Oh yeah? What exactly did he say?"

"Well, he said that you were honey -brown, five- foot- two, sexy with shoulder- length hair and that you had a nice shape. And that you would probably be a haf-hour late. He didn't lie, but what he should have said wuz that you da bomb diggity."

Nyree could not resist smiling as they approached a corner booth in the restaurant where Malachi was nibbling on some bread. "Enjoy your lunch," Aaron, the host, said and winked at Nyree as she scooted into the booth across from Malachi.

After inspecting Malachi's outfit, she suddenly felt as if she had overdressed for the occasion. Nyree was wearing a navy- blue pants suit and Malachi was wearing his favorite sweatshirt, a pair of blue jeans and of course, a pair of Nikes. He claimed that he could only wear Nike gym shoes. Nyree spied the small gold hoop earrings in both ear lobes and she had to admit that they looked nice in contrast to his ebony complexion. Malachi had a fresh haircut and he was looking pretty good. She was feeling the same way that she felt the day she first met him- a little uneasy. Her sorority sister, Aris Smith had introduced them at the fish fry. Aris had told Nyree that Malachi was "cool people" and suggested that she give him a chance. Aris had laughed when Nyree asked her to be a bridesmaid.

"Dang, Girl, who would have known that my playing matchmaker at a fish fry would end up in marriage? I'm happy for you. I wonder if Sean and I will make it that far."

Nyree wanted to tell her probably not. There was something about Sean that did not seem right to Nyree. For the life of her, she could not understand how Aris and Kevin were going together one minute and the next thing you knew she was going with Sean, Kevin's best friend. That sounded downright whorish, but Aris was not that type of girl. All Nyree could assume was that Kevin must have royally messed up.

Malachi was aware that she was observing him, and he could tell that she was pleased with what she saw. He shot her that notorious "I know I messed up" look which was always followed by an excuse and a sly grin. Despite the fact that she knew this tactic, oh so well, she fell for it every time. She had promised herself that she would not fall for it this time.

Nyree was sitting on her hands anticipating the line that would follow the flashing of the pearly whites. If she had timed it right, in two seconds she would be hearing the "I'm sorry, Bae" line which had also been working lately. *But not today,* she promised herself. She was tired of hearing sorry. Lately that is all Malachi was- sorry. He looked down at his watch and commented, "What happened to two-thirty?"

"Something came up as I was walking out of the door." He did not need to know that she had changed her mind at the last minute and was not going to show up for the lunch date.

"You were all of ten minutes from here. I came from Mayport, maneuvered through traffic, and still managed to get here on time," replied Malachi.

*Yada Yada ya. I don't need a lecture about being on time. Hey, he ought to be glad that I didn't stand him up. He's trying to earn points with me by taking me to my favorite restaurant. It's working a little. He had better be paying too. If I get stuck with the bill like I did when we went to Gino's East in Chicago with his cousin and his cousin's girlfriend there will not be anything lovely in here. Gino's East has the best pizza in the world. No other pizza house can touch them, I just wasn't trying to pay for everyone's meal that evening. I don't mind paying from time to time, but when someone invites me to lunch, especially a man, especially the lying snake that calls himself my husband, he had better be paying, no **ifs, ands**, and **buts** about it.*

"So how did you get here?" she asked as Malachi did not have any transportation of his own. Malachi's base was in Mayport which is twenty minutes away from Jacksonville. She was glad that he was living on the ship and that she didn't have to pick him up and drop him off on the base, or even worse, have to wait for him to pick her up from work.

Nyree was also tired of getting up at five-thirty in the morning so that he could be at work at six o'clock, especially when she did not have to report to work until ten o'clock. Besides, her car was not a taxi. At least not in America it wasn't, maybe it was in Germany where it was manufactured, but that wasn't her concern because she lived in America.

"I'm driving Stevenson's car. You know my boy Stevenson, the one with the white Prelude. He's been by the apartment before."

After taking their orders, their waitress, Leslie, promised to return with their salads since Nyree whined that she was starving.

"Why are you staring at me? You wanted to talk -well *talk*," Nyree told Malachi.

"Nyree, I'm sorry. I just wanted to say that I love you and I know things have not been good lately, but I want to make them right."

Here we go. I knew it would be just a matter of time before he brought out that tired line. I'm surprised it has taken this long to surface. Tapping her finger and letting out a deep breath, she questioned, "How are you going to make things right. What are you going to do?"

"I don't know what I am going to do. Just know that I am going to make it right."

Leslie appeared with the salads and left quietly. She could feel the tension between Malachi and Nyree.

Malachi shoved about two tablespoons of lettuce into his mouth with bleu cheese dressing oozing out of the sides. Nyree rolled her eyes at the sight and thought it was actually pretty funny as he claimed that he did not eat salad. How many times had she heard, "I don't eat that" only to find him eating it as if it were his last meal? Nyree had learned that even though Malachi claimed that he "didn't eat this and that he didn't eat that," Malachi would eat just about anything that you placed in front of him. She remembered telling Aris that Malachi would probably eat hot garbage if you made it look good. Nyree was tired of the lies and simply stated, "Malachi, I'm tired of you claiming to be serious and then giving me empty promises. I'm tired of Ciara and the baby. Every time I turn around she is calling, talking about what she needs, what she wants.

"And then on top of that, I have to deal with you and these drugs. Now tell me this, how is it that you are selling drugs out of the place where you rest? You're crazy, you done bumped yo' head," she yelled. Malachi had not been expecting to hear that monologue.

When he invited her to lunch, it had been his plan to pay for lunch and be at home this evening. This was not going well. If one more person on the ship asked him when he was going home to his fine wife, he was probably going to lose it. For months he had been walking around lying to everybody. "Yeah, my wife knows about ole girl and the baby. She ain't tripping, what can she do? This happened before we got married, but it's all good now."

Malachi knew he had to say something, anything, to get himself back home. He was done sleeping on that ship, cramped up with all those "hard legs," his not-so-affectionate term for the other guys. He'd considered crashing with Ciara and her sister for a bit, but that thought disappeared fast when he heard she had some dude from another ship staying over.

"Look, about Ciara—I'm sorry. I know I messed up, and I've been apologizing for that for five months straight. Camron's my son, and I have to take care of my kids."

Nyree's eyebrow shot up. "Kids? Last I checked, Camron was the *only* child you had. And let's get one thing straight: apologizing? That's the least you should be doing. You ought to be kissing my behind every single day for this mess. We've been married eleven months, and you *knew* this chick was pregnant before we even said 'I do.'"

She folded her arms, her stare cutting right through him.

He was looking stupid and dumbfounded. It was the same look he had on his face when Nyree was cleaning the apartment one day and found a female's telephone number in the pocket of his favorite jeans. When she said to him, "Malachi, what is this?" he looked dumbfounded and said, "I dunno what is it?"

Malachi was rambling on about something and Nyree was munching on her salad thinking about her trainer that she had seen the other day when she was taking a tour of the gym near the beach. Lust was a sin and she was fully aware of it, but she could not help it that man was

F-I-N-E. What was she supposed to do when her body was aching for love but would not allow her to indulge in such pleasures with her husband? The trust was gone and she would not let her mind think about love. If love was gone in the marriage how would she be able to remain married to him?

She thought about divorce several times, but she would not allow it to surface. She had something to prove to herself. If she could get past this, then she would be a better person, wouldn't she? The thought of the trainer's chiseled body surfaced again as she considered membership at the Beach Body Gym. She was ashamed to be having lustful thoughts about that man, but she couldn't help herself. She had not been intimate with her husband since they had moved to Florida.

Without trust, how could she give away her secret treasure? Additionally, all the what-if questions came to her mind when she thought of being intimate with him. What if he told her this? What if he held her like this? What if he did this and that with her? What if he had something and gave it to me? The answer to that last question was quite simple. If he were ever to pass a disease onto her it would be lights out for him. Her daydreams of the sexy man that she had seen the other day were interrupted when she heard Malachi say, "… so you see that's why I need to come home."

Waving her hands frantically, she replied, "Whoa. *Whoa*! Come home? Who said anything about you coming home? You have got to be out of your mind. No. ***HELL No.***"

Heads turned and looked in their direction. She hadn't meant to be that loud, but Malachi had gone too far this time.

He reached out and touched her hand. "Boo, just hear me out. You're not hearing me. We need to sit down and talk."

Nyree threw her linen napkin down on the table and said, "Thanks for lunch, Malachi. I'll be talking to you." As far as she was concerned she had done all the talking that she was going to do. The hands that she had once liked to touch her, hold her, caress her, now suddenly gripped her forearms and forced her down in the booth. His grip was so tight that she thought her arms might fall off into his hands.

"Nyree, stop running away from this, from

me. I love you and I want to make this right again like it used to be." Then a tear dropped from his eye. *Is this for real? He did not just pull the phony teardrop routine, did he?* Nyree thought. *Hell, I can make myself cry on demand if I want to, all I have to do is think about my godfather Joe's funeral and I'll start crying too.*

"Boo- hoo. Cry a river if you want to, but coming home is not an option," Nyree told him.

He sat there quietly and gritted his teeth. *What is going on here?* he questioned himself. There had been a time when he could have had anything he wanted from his wife; now it seemed as though that was becoming a thing of the past. Nyree supposed that they both must have been reminiscing about the last time they were together at the apartment.

Dining for lunch at Olive Garden meant both Nyree and Malachi were in violation of the order, but neither one of them had any intentions of reporting it. Nyree stood, situated her purse on her shoulder and with three fingers of her right hand pushed Malachi in the forehead while boldly stating, "I'm through with you! I'm not going through any more drama."

She then ran out of the restaurant, jumped

into her "Beamer" and drove until she ended up at the beach. She loved the Atlantic Ocean almost as much as she loved Lake Michigan. There was no place like home.

It was so peaceful at Jax Beach in Jacksonville. There were children playing, and couples laughing and playing. No one even noticed her sitting there alone in her linen suit. The air was warm and crisp as it danced across her body. The sun seemed to be smiling on everyone including her. All in all, this was a great moment until she thought about her miserable life. Was there anywhere she could go to escape her misery? She had often wondered why so much despair had come upon her. What happened to the carefree, careless days? The days when she had not one problem or care in the world where had they gone? "Why me? *Why me?*" She had been uttered by her so much in the past that she could not bring herself to even speak those pathetic words again. She contemplated, '*Could it get any worse than this?*' Nyree didn't dare speak that thought because lately every time she spoke those words, the unspeakable happened and it was worse than she could ever imagine. Then she heard the words of a pastor from home who said, "Fret not the evil doers." A voice whispered to her to read Psalms 37. Startled by the voice, she flinched and looked around to see who had spoken. There was no one standing in her vicinity. This was the second time this month that she had heard a voice that wasn't there. She wondered if it was God speaking to her. Nyree strayed off the right path so long ago, she wondered if God would talk to a sinner such as herself.

It seemed like every time she desired to do right, something would happen and she always ended up doing something wrong. It was a vicious, never-ending cycle that she wanted so desperately to change.

Ten

Nyree found herself driving down Beach Boulevard when she spotted the sign for Beach Body Gym. Quickly she veered into its parking lot. When she entered the building she was greeted by Colin Jordan. His green eyes drew her in and the muscles bulging out of his tank top mesmerized her. She was even more surprised that he was well-spoken. They sat in an office and discussed her goals for her body and then he said that he wanted to take her weight and measurements. "No, that's okay. I'll keep up with that information."

He snickered to himself. Women were so self-conscious about their bodies and measurements whereas a man would have stood there ready to have his measurements taken, despite a gut hanging over his belt. In fact, men loved to boast about their size whereas a woman who is a size twelve may speak her fantasies aloud by saying she is a size ten. "Well, now that you have completed the paperwork, when will you be starting?"

"Now is as good a time as any. Let me go to my car and get my bag," she said as she was leaving the office. After realizing that she did not know where the locker room was located she turned and asked for directions. He walked her out of the office, pointed her in the vicinity and informed her that she would need to bring her own lock for her locker and remove it when she left.

Later, Colin was standing with his clipboard as she walked on the treadmill. Nyree was wearing her emergency clothes that she kept in a gym bag in the trunk of her car. The tank top and jogging pants had seemed like a good choice three months ago when she had placed them in a bag in her trunk.

"Why do you have an overnight bag in the trunk?" Malachi had once questioned her.

She had rubbed his cheek and looked him dead in the eyes. "I never know when I might have to make a mad getaway."

Looking puzzled he said, "What's that supposed to mean?"

She had him thinking and she liked it, so she did not elaborate by telling him that everybody should have some emergency clothing in their vehicle just in case a situation were to arise and extra clothing was needed. Now that Colin was standing behind her she felt self - conscious about her gear. Had she picked up a couple of pounds? These pants did not use to fit this snugly. *'He's looking at my booty. I can feel it.'* She sucked in her stomach and tightened her buttocks to prevent it from moving up and down as she took her strides on the treadmill. Out of nowhere the lyrics to that old song, *Baby Got Back* came to mind. Boy, did she hate that song when it first came out. The guys in the neighborhood would sing the lyrics to the song out loud. When they got to the part when Sir Mix-A- Lot the rapper said, "Baby Got Back," they would pause and point at her buttocks to emphasize the point.

"So this is the routine that you will do every other day. The days that you don't lift, you can come in and just do the treadmill for thirty minutes, row for fifteen minutes, and do the elliptical machine for fifteen minutes, end with stretching. What do you think?" Colin asked.

"Sounds good; will you be here to help me out, if I need help?"

"I'm generally here until five most days. I take it kind of easy on Saturdays," Colin said with a smile. His smile was warm, and she was feeling at ease with him. She wanted to continue talking but how much could she say about the work-out routine. He was enjoying the conversation with her. Getting to know her on a more personal level had crossed his mind. Dating the clients was against his rules and with his recent break-up from Adrianne maybe he shouldn't embark on anything new. That tanned line around her left ring finger had caught his attention when she gripped the rails of the treadmill. This made her even more intriguing. She tilted her head to the side, smiled, and allowed her hands to hit her legs while saying," Well, I guess I'll go hit the shower. Thanks for working with me." Her graciousness was a welcome surprise to him. Most people don't say "thank you" these days. They seemed to think that they were entitled to everything. She, on the other hand, was genuinely appreciative. This quality was very attractive to him.

His ex, Adrianne, on the other hand, always expected him to do and do and do; and she never so much as said "thank you."

"You're very welcome, Ms. Chandler. When you finish up in the locker room, stop by the juice bar."

"Okay. By the way, call me Nyree," and she was off with a smile. Her face was so soft and warm when she smiled. When she didn't, she looked mean and evil. He imagined that she was not a force to be reckoned with. Even though she smiled, her eyes were sad. This woman had a story to tell and he wanted to hear it.

As she towel-dried from her shower and applied lotion, her thoughts ran wild about Colin. There was something about him that she liked. She was an unhappily married, nevertheless, a married woman; so there was no sense in entertaining the thought. Maybe she would bypass the juice bar and go home. She wondered if he was as attentive to all his clients as he had been to her. *'I wonder how much he makes. I'm not hooking up with another broke man, not to sound superficial or anything but what can a broke man do for me? Oh yeah, I know he can break my heart and steal from me just like Malachi did.'* Hurriedly she dressed and rushed from the locker room. Colin was nowhere in sight so she would be able to leave the facility without having to see him.

She made it all the way to the door, when Colin yelled to her from the office saying, "Nyree, I thought you were going to meet me at the juice bar."

She tugged on her bag and said, "Oh," pretending to have forgotten his invitation, but feeling that she had been busted trying to sneak out.

Colin heard the hesitation in her voice and said, "I mean, if you don't have another appointment, I'd like to treat you to a smoothie." *A treat*, she thought. When was the last time she had been treated to anything when there was not an ulterior motive behind it?

"Sure. I hope your boss does not mind. Or do you give all clients free smoothies?" Nyree wanted to know.

He denoted a tone of flirtation in her voice.

Funny, she thought he worked for the facility. It had never crossed her mind that he might own the place.

"No, I don't give everybody smoothies. Just you," he said as they walked over to the juice bar.

He was earning points with her. Something so simple and innocent could really make a person feel good. They both sat at the bar sipping on pineapple smoothies.

"I'm not keeping you from something, am I?" she asked as she noticed him glancing at his watch. It was a fancy watch that adorned his wrist. She found herself thinking and wondering what type of salary he earned from the gym that would allow him such a luxury. *He probably had to save up for a hot minute to get that*, she thought.

"No, I'm right where I want to be." Those words had sent a ripple through her body, much like the ripple that she used to experience when her husband would walk into a room.

"Colin, I must say this is the best smoothie I have ever had. What did you put in it?"

"It's a special recipe exclusively for the gym," he said, winking.

"Oh. I see," she said, admiring his loyalty to the gym. You just did not find too many loyal employees like him.

"You're not from here, are you?"

"Nope. I'm from Indiana," she said as she licked some of the strawberry residue from her top lip.

Why did she have to do that? Colin thought to himself as he willed his manhood to stay in place.

"Yeah, what part? I have an uncle that lives in Chicago."

"I'm from Gary; it's about thirty minutes from Chicago."

"I know Gary. I've been there a couple of times. I hope you don't mind me asking this, but I noticed your ring finger; and it looks like you used to wear a ring there…"

"Um… I'm separated from my husband, and I don't wear my ring anymore."

"I'm sorry to hear that. Maybe things will work out," he said while trying to mask his disappointment.

"I don't know. It seems like things are beyond the point of no return."

"All you can do is pray and leave it in God's hands." The way she lowered her head and shrugged her shoulders suggested to Colin that Nyree doubted that God could fix her situation. He wanted to say more but decided not to pry.

"Well, I got to go now. Thanks for the smoothie and the workout."

He didn't want her to leave, but what was he going to do? Scream to a woman whom he barely knew, "Stay. Don't leave." *See what curiosity has done? It ran her right out of the gym*, he thought to himself.

Eleven

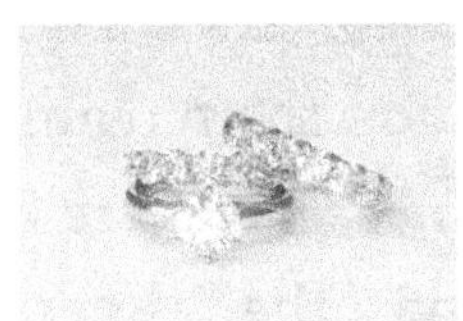

Malachi sat across the table from Dre while Stevenson and Mack sat across from each other. Malachi and Dre had just "set" Stevenson and Mack in the last hand of spades, so Stevenson and Mack did not make their bid.

"Oh! OH. So, you wanna go a blind now," Malachi taunted Mack "You weren't blind when you sat down."

"Yeah, that's right," Dre chimed in. "This y'all second blind this game. There ought to be a limit on how many times you can go blind during a game."

Mack was getting angry. The voices of his opponents were annoying. When Dre said the word "game," Mack could have sworn that some saliva had flown out of Dre's mouth and landed on Mack's hand.

"Say it, don't spray it," Mack said, sounding like a little elementary school girl. He hated to lose, and more than that, he hated being teased about his shortcomings. It was not his fault that Stevenson could not play the hand that he had been given. Stevenson always wanted to take the lead in bidding for their team and tended to overbid. Sometimes they were lucky enough to make the bid and other times they were not. Mack felt that he was playing pretty well for someone who had not played in years. Malachi was really getting on his nerves now.

"What's wrong Mack? You want to quit. You're not going to cry, are you?" Malachi had done it with that last comment. So what, that he tended to get emotional from time to time. That was no reason to bring it up in front of everyone in the lounge.

"Yeah, I'm crying, just like you were when they sent you to the Navy hospital for that suicide attempt."

Stevenson snickered and belted out, "Dayum, dawg! That was cold."

Mack was on a roll now "Not as cold as that steel his wife put to his neck. I don't blame her though. Fine as she is, she ain't gotta put up with his shit. Shoot, if she was my wife I wouldn't be creeping. I'd hit that every night."

Malachi's eyes were bloodshot-red, "Dude,

keep my wife out of this."

Mack threw his cards on the table. "I can't do that. You started this and I'm going to finish it. Why are you getting so mad about your wife? You weren't thinking about her when you were out there screwing everybody and making babies with everybody. I mean, if you were taking care of home…"

Malachi's fist crushed Mack dead in the nose. Holding his nose, Mack doubled over. After Malachi's size-twelve shoe made contact with Mack's genital area causing him to fall out on the floor, there was laughter in the room.

Kenya stood over Mack as if she were a referee in a boxing match, "**ONE, TWO, THREE, FOUR, FIVE, SIX, SEVEN, and EIGHT**. I dare say you got knocked the fuck out," she said, imitating Chris Tucker's character's voice from the movie *Friday*.

Malachi wiped his bloody fist on his pants and announced, "Game over."

Dre whispered in Malachi's ear, "Man, you better go back to the barracks. If the chief hears about you messing up again, yo' ass is grass. I think he's gonna send you to the brig. He's still pissed at you about that money that came up missing when we were out to sea."

Malachi was steaming. He was tired of hearing about that missing money.

Mack had gotten caught slipping, simple as that. You don't leave your money out on your bed and expect it to be there when you come back. Mack was from some backwoods town and that's how they did it back there. You could leave your front door unlocked and nobody would violate your property.

Malachi had told them that he was from "Gangsta Island," a nickname for Gary, Indiana. Malachi stated that he was from the "G," another nickname for Gary; it didn't go down like that. What was the big deal anyway? Mack cried to the chief, but three of Malachi's checks went to Mack for the money that Malachi had taken. Malachi had told Mack it wasn't any skin off Malachi's back because Malachi's wife had more money than Mack could ever dream of counting in a lifetime.

"Yeah, right. That's why you are on the ship stealing from a brother," replied Mack.

"A brother, a white dude, a Mexican, Puerto Rican, whomever. I don't discriminate. I catch you slipping and I'm taking your loot, simple as that," he had responded while pinching Mack's chubby cheeks. Malachi had no respect for the five-foot-six robust man. He often called him "Butterball."

Lying in his bed, Malachi thought about his indiscretions. Mack was right. Malachi was a dog, but Mack had no right putting Malachi's business out there. The lyrics to a song popped into Malachi's head, "Damn, it feels good to be a gangsta." He smiled while trying to remember who made that song. Somebody was coming down the hall and by the sound of their steps it didn't sound like they were going to be the bearers of good news.

A baritone voice spoke, "Chandler. Chandler, chief wants to see you at twenty-one hundred. We don't want to have to come back and get you, so make sure you're there at twenty-one hundred." *They would send old Uncle Tom, Macey and that "he-she," Richards. Boss man wannna see you. You betta be there or else we's gonna hafta come back for you. You hear me, boy?*

It bothered him that when some Black people were given a little authority they took it too far. Especially Macey. He was always acting like a "yes" man. Malachi could imagine Macey back in slavery running behind the master saying, "Yessir, boss. I'll get those Negroes in check. You wants me to beat them for you?" Malachi had respect for authority, but you wouldn't find him sucking up to any man. He had told Nyree that his mouth wasn't made for kissing up to anyone. Twenty-one hundred, maybe he would be there, maybe not. The Navy and all of its demands were starting to wear his nerves.

Malachi made it to Chief Turner's office with thirty seconds to spare. *What is he calling me in for now? I can tell ole boy ain't part of the hair club for men. That comb back is not working. He needs to get some of that stuff and see if he can grow some hair and stop combing it to the side.* Malachi did not know how old the chief was, but if he had to guess, he would say sixty something. Chief just looked old and wrinkled, despite the fact that he dyed his hair jet-black.

"Alright, Seaman Chandler, let's get down to business."

Malachi sat with his fingers intertwined trying to resist the urge to pop his knuckles.

"Let's," Malachi said curtly.

Chief Turner did not care for Malachi and

the fact that Malachi seemed to lack respect for ranking officers did not sit well with Chief Turner.

"Chandler, every time there is a situation on the ship, your name comes up. We have tried to work with you and be fair, but you continue to screw up. You should have been out of here after your hospitalization, but the doctors did not find you to be suicidal or with neurological damage. Then, your marital situation has become everyone's business. Are you in compliance with the restraining order?"

Malachi looked down at the floor. *Is this what this meeting was about? That was not any of his business*, Malachi found himself thinking.

"Yeah," Malachi lied.

Chief Turner knew a lie when he heard one, and if ever he had seen a liar he knew that Malachi Chandler was one. He was so cool and nonchalant; and, in Chief Turner's opinion, that is what made Malachi dangerous.

"Listen up, son; you are not to leave this ship for the next thirty days. You are only to leave to report to counseling sessions here on base with Dr. Cohen. Under no circumstances are you to leave this base. Understood?"

"What about my wife and my apartment?"

"I repeat, under no circumstances, are you to leave this base. You leave the ship only for counseling. **UNDERSTOOD**?"

"Understood," Malachi said half-heartedly as he walked out of the office. He hated the Navy. Signing up for the Navy was the worst decision he had ever made in his life, followed by sleeping with Ciara and Terri. He had only signed up for the Navy to impress Nyree, and even then he hoped that she would have begged him not to go. Initially, he would have given her the story about it being his duty to serve his country, but hoped he would have eventually been convinced by her not to go. To his dismay that conversation, the begging and pleading had never occurred and he went to the Navy. He never considered himself to be a quitter but suddenly going AWOL seemed inviting. He knew that it would earn him a dishonorable discharge, but when was the last time he had done something honorable?

Malachi ran to the phone. He had to call Nyree and tell her what was happening. After the fourth ring he realized that she was not home. Where could she be? He just knew that she would be home in bed. All she did since they moved to Florida was sleep. "You've reached Nyree Chandler. I'm unavailable. Please leave your message at the tone."

What happened to my name being in the message? It's like I don't even exist. "Nyree, this is Malachi. This racist chief says that I can't leave the ship for thirty days. I want you to come see me tomorrow. We need to talk. Love you. Bye."

Twelve

After hearing Malachi's message about being confined to the ship, Nyree slept like a baby. Despite the fact that there was a restraining order, Malachi would still drop by the apartment. She had complained to Malachi's chief but was not satisfied with the results of the meeting. The only thing that Chief Turner said was that it was a civilian issue and not a Navy one. He suggested that Nyree contact the police.

***

Nyree stopped dead in her tracks when she saw Malachi sprawled out on her imported Italian leather sofa, cradling her prized Hennessy Cognac Timeless. Her breath hitched —her heart racing in disbelief and irritation. His head was propped on one end, his feet dangling off the other, and that $4,000 bottle rested lazily on his chest. She clenched her fists. *He better just be hugging that bottle. If he's actually been drinking from it... oh, it's over.*

This wasn't just any bottle of liquor you cracked open on a rough day. This was the kind you showcased, saved for epic moments—if it ever got opened at all. She'd been raised to know the value of things, and as her mother always said, *if they don't know about it, keep them in the dark.* There was no way she was letting Malachi, of all people, claim even a taste of this treasure. Not him, with his discount Cognac and audacity, taking liberties with what wasn't his.

Nyree crossed the room in three strides, snatched the bottle from his grasp, and held it up to the light, inspecting the seal. Relief flooded her; he hadn't opened it. Cradling it like a newborn, she kissed the bottle's neck, then set it back in its rightful spot beside her other prized "trophies." There was the Hardy's Cognac Perfection, $5,800 a bottle, worth every penny with its mix of flavors dating back to the 1830s, as Kyle used to say. And then the crown jewel, her Courvoisier L'Esprit Decantes, a $6,000 masterpiece sourced from centuries-old vintages that had marked moments like Napoleon's coronation and the French Revolution. She'd pulled favors to get that one, her own personal history lined up on the shelf.

Malachi grunted, stirring, still blissfully unaware of the near wrath he'd just escaped. She had to laugh. He'd actually dared to think he belonged in this world of legacy, while all he'd ever contributed was a bottle of Meukow Vanilla Cognac which cost twenty-five dollars. Nyree had asked him if he really wanted to place that bottle in the liquor cabinet with her cognac. He shrugged his shoulders and grinned while saying, "Yeah. Why not? I picked up at *Chip and Nuts*. I figured if it's sold at *Chip and Nuts* it must be top-notch. "

Nyree did not have the heart to tell him that a twenty-five dollar bottle of cognac had no business sitting next to a six thousand-dollar bottle of cognac. As he saw her nose wrinkle up, he continued to press for an answer.

"Well, it's like putting a hamburger next to filet mignon," Nyree explained.

Malachi laughed. "Meukow is top-of- the-line stuff." Nyree let her forehead rest in her hands because he was giving her a headache and because he did not know "top of the line," it was useless arguing with him.

***

Nyree lit a candle from Nicole Bradley

Candle Co. She massaged the oil from the candle into her skin,. She hadn't felt that relaxed and soothed in a long time. It was going to be a great day and she did not want to spend it at work. There were a few items that she had to take care of before she slipped into relaxation mode. She called in and informed Crystal that she would not be in. Crystal was surprised to hear that her boss would not be in.

Nyree stared at the phone before hanging it up. *I know this heifer didn't just try to get smart with me. I cannot stand her. She comes in dressed in stretch pants with the stirrups and big tee shirts. It just isn't professional for management staff. Her attitude is poor. Enough of thinking about her; it's time to think about me.*

Nyree called Colin and left a message stating that she wanted him to pick her up tonight for Bible study at his church.

Nyree snuggled in her favorite chair and began meditating. It had been a long time since she had reflected on her life. The unanswerable question hung in the air: Why had she married Malachi? It was one question she did not want to address, but it could not be avoided. She decided that she would attack it right now for good.

'Truthfully, I don't know why I married him. When I first met him, I swore up and down he was not my type and he was not and still isn't. I was taken in by him. I had so many failed relationships in the past and I think that I just didn't want to have another failed one. I gave and gave and he taught me some things about life that I did not know. We had fun together and he made me feel like I was number one. For once in a relationship, I did not feel like I had to prove myself to someone. I did not feel like I had to be perfect. I was not in competition with anyone. Actually, I had the upper hand and I liked it. I liked being in control as opposed to being controlled. Now that I think about it, I was being controlled and did not know it. The fact that he has lied to me so much was his subtle way of controlling me. Two days before the wedding I had my doubts and I should have followed them. After the Midwest Vein wrote that horrible article, I did not want to give anyone anything to talk about and calling the wedding off would have been something else for that rag to make a dollar off me and my family. It sounds crazy but that's where my head was then.

I have also come to realize that I have issues with myself. I look for love to come from others, and I don't love myself like I should. My self-worth is equated with how others feel about me. I surround myself with the finest things in life, but I neglect me.

When something stops making me happy, I go out and buy something to replace that void. I have to start filling the void myself and that means dealing with some issues that are painful, but I only hurt myself by masking the void and piling things on top without dealing with it.

I have never been real religious. I don't even know what it means to be religious. I look at people's behavior and it gives me an idea about what religious means. I believe in God, but although it sounds bad to say I haven't really trusted God. I have to be honest with myself and this is the truth. I did ask God to give me a sign about marrying Malachi, but then I put a stipulation on it. I said if Malachi does so and so then I will know that this is a sign from God that I should marry him. The problem with that is the thing I was waiting for Malachi to do was something that he always did, so it was something that I expected. I think that deep down I knew that this was not whom God had chosen. I just took the first man that came along because later down the line I didn't want to have regrets or spend my life thinking, "What if I had married Malachi?" Now, I cannot help but think what my life would be *like if I had not taken that stroll down the aisle with this joker. I need to call Grandma Lula. She will have something inspiring to say, and I could use a kind word now.'*

Thirteen

"Hello, Grandma Lula."

"Ree, is that you?" Lula was the only one who got away with calling Nyree "Ree." Malachi had tried it once and she told him that no one called her that but Grandma Lula.

"Yes, it's me. Who else would it be?"

"Child, don't be getting flip at the mouth with me. You not too old for me to take a switch to your tail. Since I haven't heard from you in a month of Sundays, I didn't know who it was."

"Oh, Granny, it hasn't been that long." Nyree chuckled at the thought of her grandmother spanking her. Although when she was growing up, she had experienced what one might classify as some classic whippings; and there had been nothing humorous about those spankings. The most vivid spanking that came to mind was when she had been in the fourth grade and put Lula's Chihuahua, "Snuggles" in the dryer and turned the dryer on. Lula had been furious with Nyree's behavior. "Why would you do a thing like that?" her grandmother had questioned. Nyree had shrugged her shoulders unaware of the seriousness of the act.

"Grandma, I was only doing a science experiment. I wanted to see the effects of a blow-dryer and clothes dryer on a dog," Nyree had said with great enthusiasm. Kyle had taken delight in going outside to pick the switch from the tree that would be used for the spanking. It was generally him on the receiving end of the switch, so it felt good for him to be the observer for once.

After a long pause, Lula continued her conversation with her granddaughter.

"Yes, it has. I figured you went down there to Florida and became a superstar and forgot about ole Lula. You used to call me all the time and talk, now you… how is it the young people say, 'a big baller?' and don't have time for Granny."

"No. It's not like that at all. Malachi is a stone-cold trip. He got two girls pregnant before we got married and both of the kids have been born since we've been married. I only found out about one right before we moved down here, and I found out about the other one since I've been here. He's only claiming the little boy, which is the one I found out about before we moved. He said that he had a blood test for the little girl, and she's not his child. Malachi refuses to have a blood test for the little boy because he says deep down in his heart he knows that Camron, that's the little boy's name, is his baby…"

"Well, how are you doing with all of this?"

"I'm doing better now. I was really a basket case at first. I met a guy and I'm going to Bible study with him tonight."

"Ree, I don't think you need to be taking up with some guy because you are angry with your husband."

"Oh no, it's not like that."

"Umph-humph."

"What's that supposed to mean?"

"It means I haven't gotten to be this age by not seeing and hearing a lot of things. You're hurt and vulnerable; and while going to Bible study sounds innocent, I'm concerned with the fact that you are going with a guy."

"Granny, he knows that I am married and he's not like that."

Lula, in all her years on this earth, had not come across a man that was 'not like that.'

Now a man might say he was 'not like that,' but when tempted there was no telling what a person would succumb to. The fact that her granddaughter was spending time with the man was a problem. It was like dangling a piece of chocolate in front of a person who is on a diet. If the chocolate is dangled in front of that person enough, eventually he or she is going to snatch that chocolate and take a bite. After the first bite there is no turning back and the person will devour the whole piece of chocolate because cheating is cheating. There is no such thing as a little bit of cheating or erasing cheating.

"I'm not trying to tell you what to do; I'm just telling you that you don't want to put yourself in a compromising position."

Lula was trying to tell Nyree what could happen but Nyree was like her father. Once they made up their minds about something it was difficult for them to see the other side of the situation. Nyree was tired of the lecture so she changed the subject. "So, Granny, how are things with you?"

"Fine. I can't complain," was Lula's standard answer to the question whenever someone inquired about her well-being, as she felt the question was a rhetorical one and no one really wanted to hear about her ailments. Her blood pressure was a little high, but that was because she found it difficult to eliminate salt from her diet as the doctor had instructed her to do. No sense in telling Nyree that. She received enough lectures from Edwin so she wasn't up for dealing with one from Nyree. Besides, if Nyree found out Nyree would be calling every day insisting that Lula go to this doctor and this class. To Lula it wasn't that serious.

"Granny, I gotta get ready to go now. Do me a favor and sing some of that song, 'I Won't Complain.'" Lula beamed at the request. Lula couldn't remember the last time Nyree had asked her to sing a song let alone that one. When Nyree was twelve, she had asked Lula to sing that song. Lula thought that it was a strange request for a young girl; nevertheless, she honored the request. When she finished singing it, Nyree had told her that the song gave her strength. Lula honored her granddaughter's request today and sang the song with heart and soul. Nyree thanked her and then hung up but not before promising to send her a special package. Lula told her, as she always did, that it wouldn't be necessary. Nyree dismissed the statement and told her to be looking for a package from her in the mail. If she didn't receive it in the next few days, she suggested she inquire at the post office.

Fourteen

April 1996

Malachi lay in his bed on the ship feeling depressed and sorry for himself. Being on restriction had been a grueling experience for him. He was surprised that he had made it through this past two weeks. As it was his first-year anniversary and he was confined to the ship, today had been extremely hard for him. He called Nyree earlier to wish her a happy anniversary but there was no answer so he was forced to leave a cheesy message. One good thing had come out of today and that was his therapist had come to visit him. He had to admit that he felt special as it was Easter Sunday and she had taken time to come see him. He appreciated that because he knew that she could have been home or at church with family. Initially, the thought of seeing a shrink made him feel angry and inadequate. He had never felt comfortable sharing his deepest innermost thoughts and feeling with anyone. Nyree was the only person he had been able to open up to, and even then he still guarded himself and was careful about what he revealed.

It was different with Dr. Cohen. She listened intently and did not criticize. Her questions were thought-provoking and made Malachi look at things from a different perspective. "Hey, Chandler, you got a call," somebody yelled to him.

Malachi bolted out of bed. Nyree had not forgotten their anniversary and had called. He was happy and skipped all the way to the telephone. "Hello," Malachi said, hoping that it was Nyree on the other end of the line.

"Chandler?" the female voice questioned. It was a familiar voice, yet he could not place it. He did not care to hear what she had to say as it was not Nyree on the other end.

"Who is this?" Malachi's tone was blunt and did not conceal the disappointment.

"This is Kenya. I thought you might want to know that your wife has company."

"So?" Malachi said as he was very aware that Kenya was an instigator. Because she was the one who had told Nyree about Chantelle, he did not have much to say to her these days. Malachi had no intentions of Nyree ever finding out about his affair with Terri as he was not the father of Chantelle. Kenya and her big mouth had ruined that plan and added more fuel to the fire.

She was also the one who had spread all of Malachi's business on the U.S.S. John Hancock about Malachi trying to kill himself with a dull kitchen knife.

"**So!** It's Colin Jordan, the owner of Beach Body Gym..." Kenya paused and waited for an answer only to hear a dial tone.

Malachi paced back and forth while contemplating his next move. His hands were tied in regards to what he could do. If he left the ship, he would be in hot water. If he went home, he might kill that dude with his bare hands and for sure would be in hot water. It was a no-win situation.

How could Nyree do this to him on their one-year anniversary? Any other day of the year would have been bad, but today of all days. That just put the icing on the cake. Malachi convinced Dre to sneak him off the ship and to take Malachi by his apartment. Stevenson agreed to lie in Malachi's bed and pretend to be sleeping just in case anyone came by to check. Stevenson did not like this idea and Dre was even more uncomfortable with it, but each man empathized with what Malachi must've been feeling at that moment. On the drive to the apartment complex, Malachi was quiet. Dre broke the silence by asking, "Man, how do you know that ole boy is at your crib?"

"I got a phone call."

"From who?"' Dre wondered who in their right mind would call Malachi knowing that he was on restriction and drop such a bombshell.

"Kenya."

Dre shook his head in disbelief. "Man, I told her to stay out of yalls business. All she does lately is gossip and keep up mess; I'm starting to regret my relationship with her. It might be a false alarm."

"I doubt it."

As soon as the car rolled up to Malachi's building, he flung the door open before it fully stopped and dashed out, barely hearing Dre shout after him. He stormed up the twelve stairs two at a time, his pulse racing, and Dre hustled to keep up, knowing his job was to make sure

Malachi returned to the ship, no matter what.

At the door, Malachi fumbled for his keys. He tried one—nothing. Tried another—still nothing. "She changed the locks," he muttered, his frustration building as he pounded on the door.

Suddenly, the door swung open, revealing a man in a crisp, beige silk shirt and dark slacks. Behind him, there she was—Nyree, sitting on the couch in a sheer, periwinkle sundress, looking serene with a Bible resting in her lap. The sight of her, angelic and calm, made the rage bubble up inside him. Malachi barely registered the man's annoyed look as he brushed past him, shoving his way into the apartment.

"Uh, the word is *excuse me*," the man said, stepping aside but watching closely, prepared for whatever came next. This was Colin—a former semi-pro boxer, well aware of what his fists could do. The last time he let his fists loose was in a Jacksonville nightclub, when a guy got too bold with his girl. That night, Colin's temper had nearly landed him in jail after he almost killed the man.

But now, as Malachi stood fuming in the doorway, Colin held himself back, hoping he wouldn't have to teach Malachi the hard way.

It angered Colin when someone tested his manhood, and that is what had just happened in the apartment.

"Nyree, who is this cat answering the door? What is he doing here?" Malachi asked.

Nyree jumped up and ordered Malachi out of the apartment. The fact that she did not offer an excuse or explanation added to Malachi's anger.

"What's going on here, Nyree? No, never mind that. Dude, what are you doing here with my wife on our anniversary?"

Colin looked shocked as the word "anniversary" resonated in his ear. He knew that Nyree was married but sometimes forgot. Hearing that word "anniversary" brought it back to memory. Nyree had not mentioned that it was her anniversary. Colin had nothing to feel guilty about as they attended evening service and dinner at the church and then returned to the apartment to read some more scripture.

"Man, I'm not looking for any trouble. You and your wife need to talk. Nyree, I'm going to go. I'll talk to you later."

Nyree did not want Colin to leave. She told

him that he did not have to go, and again she ordered Malachi to leave. Dre interjected and told Malachi that they should be going. He reminded Malachi of the situation and told him that this situation looked innocent as there were two Bibles opened.

"I'm sorry about that," Nyree told Colin when Malachi and Dre left the apartment. Beginning to calm down, Colin was pacing the kitchen floor. He had anticipated having to fight and he did not like it. His adrenaline was pumping and he was in desperate need of releasing that energy. Colin was swinging at the air as if he was fighting someone. Nyree started to look at him as if he were crazy. It reminded her of the time when she was in college at IU. This boy from her hometown was standing out in front of Briscoe dormitory doing karate kicks during the time that students were going to dinner in the cafeteria.

"Why didn't you tell me it was your anniversary?" Colin asked in a tone that suggested that his feelings were hurt.

"It didn't seem important. It is not like Malachi and I have some kind of great marriage. I don't know why he is acting all sentimental. It's just another day to me. Look, I don't want to talk about that. We were having such a good time…"

"I should be going."

"Why? Because of Malachi?" Nyree did not want him to go. Colin did not like the underlying question that suggested he had been run off.

"No, not because of Malachi. Well, yes, because of him. Look, I can't lie to you. I like our conversations and spending time with you, going to Bible study and working out, but…"

Any time someone said, 'but,' Nyree found that it negated the first part of what they had just said. Why didn't he come out and say it? He didn't want to be bothered with her anymore. It would be hard for her to hear, but it was better than trying to sugarcoat it.

"But, what?" Her tone was harsh and she did not try to hide it.

"But, I'm feeling something for you more than friendship. You are on my mind all the time. I daydream about what it would be like to be your man, to take care of you, to love you like you need to be loved. I'm fantasizing about a married woman and it's not right," he said and walked out of the apartment without looking back.

Fifteen

Malachi quietly tip-toed into the barracks and tapped Stevenson on the shoulder.

"I'm back. Good looking out, man. I appreciate it. I can't afford to get in any more trouble."

"What happened?" Stevenson asked.

"Ole boy was over there. It looked like they were having Bible study. Man, I don't know. I'm so pissed."

"It's going to be alright," Stevenson said and gave Malachi a hug to reassure him that everything would work out for the best.

Lying in bed he closed his eyes tightly and asked himself when had his life gotten so messed up? It had been the day his mother informed him that his father was gone for good and would never be returning.

Keysha Chandler said it in a way that cut him at his very core. It was as if she had taken pleasure in telling him that his dad was gone for good. His mother had been the first woman to ever hurt him. She had broken his heart with the news. When he cried about his dad being gone, she laughed at him and said, "Boy, please, it ain't that serious. It's not like he was really a dad when he was here."

Malachi knew that his father spent a great deal of time away from home. He recalled waiting up all night long for Terrance Chandler to return home. Sometimes when Malachi woke up in the morning, he would find out that his dad still had not come home. But the times when his dad was home were great. His dad would let him eat chocolate chip cookies with ice cream and hot fudge for breakfast. Malachi loved when his dad would take out his bass guitar and smoke some of those white short fat cigarettes with a peculiar aroma.

He wished Nyree could understand why he needed to be a part of Camron's life. It did not matter to him if it was rumored that Camron might not be his son. He just wanted to correct a wrong that had been done to him. If Malachi could be a part of that child's life, maybe he could let go of the hatred he harbored toward his mother and father and become the man that he needed to be. Malachi felt that he might be able to make a difference. He often wondered how his life would have turned out if his father had been a part of his life. If his mother had been stricter and instilled in him the value of an education, he might have been a doctor, lawyer, or a business owner; however, he was a man in the Navy on the verge of being discharged. Malachi did not want to be kicked out the Navy, but without Nyree at his side, he could not see himself succeeding in the Navy. Without Nyree he was nothing and his life was nothing. *'Maybe this is my payback. This is payback for every woman that I have ever done wrong. I love that girl so much, and she's treatin' me like I'm nothin'.'*

Sixteen

Nyree walked into Trinity Baptist Church for the Sunday morning service, her heart heavy with a mix of curiosity and discomfort. It was Colin's church—his place—and she hadn't planned on being here, but here she was. Just a week ago, he stormed out of her apartment without so much as a goodbye. If she hadn't been married, she would've sworn the place had been left for dead. But married or not, she couldn't shake the feeling of abandonment.

She had every right to be here, didn't she?

The pews were packed, but by some miracle, she managed to snag a spot at the end. A few familiar faces from Bible study waved and smiled her way, and for the first time in days, Nyree didn't feel like an outsider. She wasn't stalking him—not today.

As she flipped through the bulletin, her gaze was drawn to the entrance. There he was—Colin. And beside him? A tall, curvaceous woman dressed in lavender, with a matching lavender hat that looked like it had been plucked from a magazine cover.

Of course, Nyree thought bitterly. *It didn't take him long to move on.*

The woman looked flawless, radiant, as if she belonged to another world—one where things were perfect. *Maybe this is his thing—meet women and bring them to church*, Nyree mused. Her eyes narrowed as she watched them settle into a pew together. The choir began singing one of Kirk Franklin's songs, but Nyree was lost in thought, trying not to stare at them.

The sermon ended, and Nyree, still caught in a haze of hurt and jealousy, moved toward the pulpit to shake Minister Hamilton's hand. His message on forgiveness had struck a chord with her, and she knew she needed to hear it. But as she turned to leave, she was stopped by the woman in lavender.

"Hi, Sister. It's nice to meet you. I'm Tina," the woman said, her voice warm and inviting.

Nyree's hand hesitated before she extended it. "I'm Nyree," she replied, forcing a polite smile.

The lady gave a strong squeeze to Nyree's

hand, encouraged her to come back, and then walked out the door. Nyree stopped and exchanged pleasantries with some of the other members she had met on the few occasions that she had attended Bible study. Some of the ushers had congregated in the parking lot and were discussing going out to dinner, so they invited Nyree to come with them.

Nyree thanked them for the offer but pleasantly declined. There was a steak defrosting in the refrigerator at that very moment and she had to get busy tidying up her place for her parents' visit on Tuesday. As Nyree sauntered off to her car, she noticed Colin whip past in his cherry-red Lexus with "hat lady" chatting away in the passenger's seat. A pang of jealousy hit Nyree. If the "hat lady" had been ugly, it would have been better, but she was not. Even up close "hat lady" was flawless. Her skin was even golden-brown like fried chicken. The only makeup she wore was soft-gold lipstick. Once upon a time, Nyree had been able to go without foundation, but that had been eons ago. Not that Nyree caked on foundation, but if she were to go without it, someone would swear up and down that she was ill. Some women had all the luck. The "hat lady's" teeth were nice and straight and looked like someone had painted them white. Nyree was a little self -conscious about her chipped right-front tooth. Though it was a slight imperfection that no one noticed, Nyree was quite aware of it. Her friend Aris had suggested to her that if she were that concerned, she should see a dentist. Nyree only went to the dentist for her regular cleanings twice a year and was always relieved to hear that she did not have any cavities. The horror stories of people going in for other procedures and leaving with swollen mouths, infections, and pulled teeth that had seemed perfectly fine were enough to make her accept living with a minor chipped tooth.

As Nyree drove through the gate of her apartment complex she debated calling Colin. If she called first it would seem like she were chasing him. If she didn't call him, then he and "hat lady" might become an item. *'If, if, if. For such a small word, it sure did have large connotations attached to it. The only logical thing I can do is to focus on me and getting myself together. I have to stop trying to engulf myself in relationships to avoid dealing with my problems. I got to get this place fixed up before my parents came.*

If Mother were to see all that dust on this table she would turn her nose up and have a fit. What will I tell them about Malachi? I'll worry about that when the time comes.'

Nyree sat across from her parents at the table at Olive Garden. She marveled at how well they looked.

"You guys have lost weight. I mean, not that you all were fat before. You all look good. Mom, is that a new ring you are wearing?"

Nyree knew full well that it was a new ring and that Margo was waiting for her to acknowledge it as she kept constantly flashing her hand. Her mother had small fingers and it looked like the ring was weighing her hand down. *'How many carats is that thing?'* Nyree wondered. That rock illuminated their dimly lit table. Margo beamed. Her perfectly straight teeth reminded Nyree of the slight imperfection in regards to her own teeth. This was twice in one week that she had been reminded of her own teeth. *I might just have to break down and go to a specialist and get my teeth fixed.* Margo said in a soft voice while she rubbed her fingers across the ring on her right middle finger, "Oh, this? Yes, this is a little something that your dad picked up for me last month. You like?"

'A **little** *something. Now that's an understatement if ever I've heard one.* **Like?** *Heckie yeah, I like it.'*

Nyree responded, "Like? No, I love it, Mother. What was the occasion?"

Margo laughed. "Nyree… Nyree." She sang, "Honey, there never has to be a special occasion for diamonds. You would know that if you had a decent husband. By the way, where is Malachi? We've been here for two days and have not seen him let alone heard mention of him."

Edwin nudged Margo in the ribs and scolded her through clenched teeth. How many times had he spoken to her about her thinking that a man defined a woman? Did she ever listen to him when he talked about how Lula raised him alone and it was from a woman that he derived his morals, values, and strength? It angered him to hear women, especially Black women, define themselves in terms of men.

Edwin often spoke with Margo about this, but she just did not comprehend. She complained about the status of Black men and often put down people who were not their economic equal. Edwin told her that there are not many people who live like they lived and that he was grateful for the fruits of his labor. He had not forgotten where he had come from and she should not either. "Easy come. Easy go," was his motto and was why he did not get caught up in material things.

True enough, he lived well and had nice things to show for his wealth, but it was not what defined him. He tried to tell his wife that instead of tearing down the Black man, because that is who she often berated, do something to uplift the race.

Nyree loved her mother but knew that it would only be a matter of time before Margo got on her nerves. They made it two days before Margo insulted her. Edwin saw the uneasiness in Nyree's face and said, "Nyree, this is a nice restaurant. I see why it's your favorite." Nyree was quite aware of what her father was doing and she appreciated it, but felt that she had to address the issue or the next two days of their stay was going to be awful.

"Malachi is on the ship. He's on restriction now but will be off next week. Mother, I want us to have a good visit; so if you promise to not bring up Malachi, I think that we will."

Edwin smiled at his daughter and then turned to his wife, "You promised that you would behave."

Margo pouted and pounded her hands on the table. "All right; all right! I will not say another word for the rest of the visit. You two are always ganging up on me. I should have stayed home." Nyree hated when her mother did that. Mother was wrong but made others feel guilty for hating her negative behavior.

Before she knew it, Nyree said, "Mother, I am so tired of this. Why does it always have to be about you? Do you ever stop to think and consider how your condescending ways make others feel? No one is trying to gang up on you or trying to make you feel bad. Just once think about how you make others feel. Do you think it makes me feel good to have a no-good husband that can't provide for me? Do you?"

Margo felt sorry for her behavior when she saw a tear trickle down Nyree's face and saw her rush off to the ladies room. Edwin shook his head in disappointment at Margo who sat there speechless.

"Don't just sit there. Go and tell her that you are sorry. Comfort her. Do something."

Margo let out a sigh and said to Edwin, "Did you hear how she just talked to me?"

Edwin was becoming annoyed and gently pushed her to the edge of the booth and said sternly, "Margo, I'm warning you." Margo grabbed her Prada clutch purse and marched off to the restroom. Edwin was starting to irritate Margo with his take-charge attitude. It was perfectly fine to have that demeanor in business, but she was not accustomed to his using it with her. Perhaps that is why they had gotten along so well for the past twenty- nine years. He let her do what she wanted to do.

Edwin and Margo smiled at each other and chuckled at Nyree's comment. Nyree marveled at the fact that after thirty years of marriage the two of them still appeared to be madly in love with one another. Although she and Malachi had achieved one year of marriage, she could not imagine thirty years with him. She knew the vows that they took read, "Until death do us part," and she was almost sure that if their marriage did not end in divorce, death would be how they parted and Malachi would not die of natural causes. Again she was having homicidal thoughts about Malachi. She tried to limit those thoughts to a few times per week and so far so good. This was an improvement as she often experienced those thoughts several times per day.

"I'll only discuss it with you if you decide to come home and work with me," Edwin said, puffing his chest out and giving Nyree a wink.

Returning the wink, she said, "You know I am not going to do that."

Edwin looked at Margo as if to say, "I tried," and turned to Nyree, "Well, I don't want to jinx myself, but I'm working on a new complex. This guy that I'm meeting with would be a good asset, for he would be able to extend his services to several of our locations in the Midwest."

Nyree raised her eyebrow and wondered if she had heard of this "guy."

"And does this *guy* have a name?" Nyree asked.

Edwin sensed that he had piqued her interest. *This may be the bait to lure her back home,* he thought. He knew that his daughter danced to her own beat. Nyree did not like anyone trying to upstage her with her father. Edwin rubbed his hand over his goatee and said, "Hey, I'm trying to have dinner here. I don't want to talk about business. What's the use…? I mean, it is not like you're going to join the team. *Right?*"

Nyree wiggled her nose at him. "Okay, keep your little business deal a secret. You'll end up telling me eventually."

Seventeen

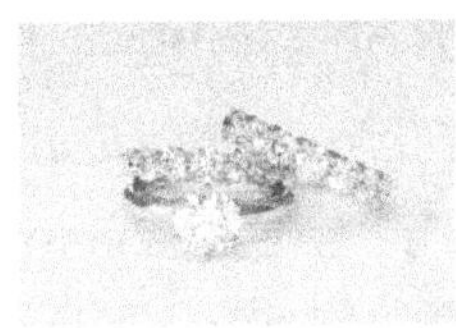

Nyree had seen her parents' plane off and decided to drop by the bookstore as she had not been to work since her parents' arrival. She had taken her mother to the bookstore and for once her mother Margo did not have a snide remark. She simply said, "I love the atmosphere here. I'm impressed. Maybe I'll talk to Edwin and see if we can get a store in Gary."

That comment had brought a smile to Nyree's face. It was one of the nicest things that her mother had ever said to her. While Nyree often tried to convince herself that she did not care what her mother thought, deep down she did care. It mattered very much to her what her mother thought. The only thing that was different now that she was an adult was that she did not break her back trying to seek her mother's approval.

***

"Crystal, how is everything going? The store looks great," Nyree told Crystal.

Crystal did a double-- take. *'A positive comment from Miss Perfection?'* Could it be possible that Nyree could say something nice to Crystal? The other employees gasped when they heard the comment as they were aware of the feud between Nyree and Crystal.

"Thanks. Everything has been going well. One problem was that the new Jahzara book had to be back-ordered. For some reason, there was a delay with the publisher," Crystal told Nyree.

"Really? I wonder if it's a publicity stunt *and* a highly anticipated book."

Crystal shrugged as she hadn't considered that. She was really waiting on this new book, *Contradictions.* Nyree had read an excerpt on the internet and was impressed.

"Well, I'm going to go back to the café and grab a cheese Danish and then, I'll be leaving for the day," Nyree told Crystal.

Nyree sat in the café area of the bookstore nibbling on her Danish. The two older gentlemen's conversation behind her had grabbed her attention. They were discussing politics. The one who looked like Grady from

Sanford and Son was saying that Republicans were the problem with the country. The other man agreed and said that only rich people were Republicans.

"Yeah, that's right. You ain't never heard of anybody Black being a Republican," the Grady look-a-like said.

His friend chimed in, "Yeah, unless he's rich."

Nyree shook her head in disagreement. She wanted to tell them that greed and corruption were the causes of the problems that the country was experiencing. Blacks supported the Republican Party since the time of President Abraham Lincoln. African-Americans did not really start supporting the Democratic Party in large numbers until the election of 1936. However, she decided to keep her two cents to herself because she did not think these men were ready for a history lecture. She really did not have time to go into depth. At that moment a hand grasped her shoulder. The touch was warm and familiar and as embarrassing as it was to say, it sent a warm tingly feeling throughout her body. He was standing behind her at an angle and she didn't want to turn around too quickly. She played it smoothly. Her eyes glanced down and noticed his brand--new white K-Swiss sneakers. He scored points for the shoes. Jeans were starched and creased and hung slightly off his frame. More points for appearance so far. The smell of Calvin Klein's Eternity for Men penetrated her nostrils. That was Malachi's signature scent and it drove her wild. When she turned to face the person with the warm touch, her eyes connected with Malachi's eyes. He flashed the million--dollar smile and said, "Hey," as if to say, "I'm back."

The smile was misleading. His eyes were bloodshot--red. Either he had not had any sleep in a while or he had been crying. *Don't rule out the possibility of his smoking marijuana or drinking,* she told herself.

"Hey. What are you doing here? I thought you were on restriction," Nyree replied.

"I am. I know that I am not supposed to be here or even talking to you, but I need to talk to you. I didn't know who else to go to. Please don't call the police. I can't go to jail. Can I talk to you outside? I don't want everybody all in ours..."

"Yeah, I'm on my way out of here," she said as they walked to the front of the store.

Something was bothering him and she would listen to him.

Forgiveness was something that she was trying to work on even as she harbored anger toward him. She knew that the anger that she was holding inside could not be healthy and that she had probably missed several blessings as a result of it.

When he opened the door for her to exit, he mumbled, "Frank had a heart attack last night and died. Lynn said that when she got off work, Frank was in bed saying that his chest was hurting. He thought that it was heartburn. She went to the store to get some antacids. While she was in the store she saw a girl that she knew from high school. Lynn began chatting and lost track of time. When she got home, Frank was still in the bed.

"She took a shower and slipped into bed with him. She touched Frank and he was still warm, but not breathing. He was lying on his side. There was a trickle of vomit on his pillow. She called the ambulance.

"He was rushed to the hospital. When he arrived at the hospital, Lynn heard one of the nurses refer to Frank as a DOA (Dead on Arrival).

Thirty years old. Whoever heard of a man going to work, coming home, having a heart attack and dying just like that? That's fucked up. Why did it have to be Frank?" Malachi told Nyree.

Nyree turned to face Malachi as they approached her car. She heard him but then she did not hear him. Frank was dead. That was hard to believe. Frank was a good person. Had he told her somebody else had died she would have had no problem believing it, but Frank; that was a shocker. She wondered why all the good people seemed to die and the drug dealers, thugs, rapists, and hard-core criminals seemed to go on living, some without a care in the world.

Then she was reminded of a sermon that Pastor Anderson had preached years ago about not being envious of evil doers because God deals with everyone. "God's time is not necessarily your time. Some of you need to be glad that God doesn't operate on your time," Pastor Anderson had remarked. She recalled nodding her head in agreement thinking that many people would be dead if God operated within her time frame.

Malachi held onto Nyree for dear life and literally cried on her shoulder. Through sobs, he said, "He's gone and I'm never going to see him again. The next time I see him he will be in a casket." Nyree embraced him as a mother would her child. Her moment of sorrow was interrupted when she heard the sound of screeching tires in the parking lot. When she looked up, she saw Colin speed by in his red Lexus. She lowered her head and shook her head in disbelief. If it weren't for bad luck, she would not have any luck at all. Nyree was getting used to it now as it seemed to be the story of her life. Nyree felt like yelling, *"Damn. Damn. Damn!"* like the family on the sitcom *Good Times* did when they found out that James had died.

Eighteen

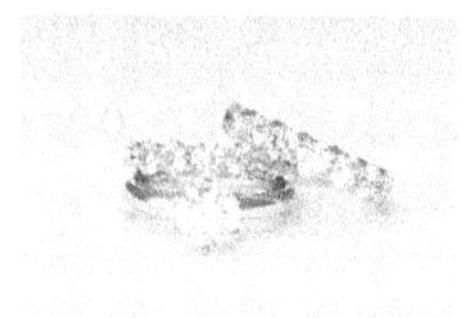

"Come with me," Malachi pleaded as he held Nyree in his arms. The voice over the intercom instructed passengers with boarding numbers sixteen through forty that they could now board the plane.

"I can't. Tell everyone that I'm praying for them," Nyree said as she watched him board the plane. She could have gone if she wanted to, but she did not want to send him mixed signals. It was probably too late for that as she had allowed him to stay over at the apartment last night and they had shared the same bed. To be quite honest they had done more than just share the same bed; it had been a night of heated passion. Guilt flooded Nyree as she drove over the St. John's Bridge and thought about last night. *Why should I feel guilty? I mean we are married, right? I have needs too and he is my husband.* "Oh, give it a rest, toots," Ms. B responded callously.

What? Nyree questioned her alter ego.

"What...," Ms. B responded in a whiny voice, "you let him back in the apartment and you fell weak to your flesh. Where do you think he is going to crash when he gets back to Duval County?"

Nyree had not given thought to that when she allowed him to stay last night.

"In his mind he thinks that everything is A-O-K," Ms. B said.

I don't know how that could be, Nyree said to herself.

"Yes, you do," Ms. B said. "You gave him some and a place to lay his head, so everything must be peachy-keen."

Nyree's anxiety rose. She had opened Pandora's Box and now it was probably too late to put a lid on it.

When she pulled the car into the lot of Beach Body Gym, something told her to check to see if her spare key and spare change were in the zipper part of her Dooney & Bourke purse. They weren't there. *Take a deep breath and calm down.* Frantically she dumped the contents of her purse onto the passenger's seat. There were items in her purse that she had forgotten about, but to her dismay no spare key or spare change.

"I can't believe this. He got me for my key and fifty dollars. I better check my wallet." Her heart pounded as she thought about the fact that her real cash and credit cards could be missing. After checking twice, everything appeared to be there. She was thankful. *What was I thinking?* She thought and spoke as she pounded her fists against her head. What was it going to take for her to get it? Was somebody going to have to literally come and knock her upside the head for her to realize that Malachi was a "nothing type man."

"Ugh. **UGH**," she groaned loudly. It hurt her to have to admit that she had married a lie. She had been charmed by Malachi's charismatic ways, but he was far from the portrayal. There were some people in life that you could vouch for and say, "He/she would never do something like that…" However, with Malachi there was no telling what he might do and Nyree hated that. She had prided herself in the past on being a good judge of character. Boy, had she missed the boat when it came to Malachi and that hurt.

Nyree noticed that there was a gold Lexus in the parking lot and wondered if Colin had traded his car in for another one. She was not in the mood for working out today; she wanted to talk to Colin. The last couple of times she had come to the gym to work out she had purposely planned her visit at times that she was sure that Colin would not be around. Nyree walked into the office hoping to see Colin sitting behind the desk.

Disappointment loomed as she saw the "hat lady" sitting behind the desk. Trying to regain her composure, she said, "Hi, is Colin around?"

Tina looked at Nyree and gave her that "I know I know you from somewhere look" and said, "No, he's out of town on business."

Not trying to mask her disappointment, Nyree said, "Oh," and began walking out of the office. Tina wondered what had the woman so down. "Is there something I can help you with?"

Nyree shook her head. "No."

Tina pried, "Well, do you want to leave a message for Colin?"

Nyree hated how the "hat lady" let Colin's name roll off her tongue.

"Um… would you tell him that Nyree came by?" Tina perked up in the chair.

"So, you're Nyree. I remember meeting you at church but I didn't put the two together."

Nyree was becoming annoyed. "What are you talking about?"

Tina smiled. "You're all my brother talks about. Nyree this. Nyree that. Girl, I don't know what you did to him, but honey, he has been in a funk…"

Brother? Nyree squinted at the "hat lady." "Colin is your brother?"

Tina said, "Yeah, that knuckle-head is my baby brother. I'll tell him that you came by."

"Thanks," Nyree said and left the building feeling relieved that the "hat lady," Tina, was not competition but Colin's sister. She had to laugh about being jealous of Colin's sister.

Nyree plopped down on the couch in the apartment and then swung her legs around and placed them on the couch while kicking her Manola Blahniks to the floor. *It has been some day,* she thought. Ms. B told her that it must have been a grueling day for her to kick a four--hundred dollar pair of shoes to the floor without a single thought. Nyree agreed that it was just that kind of day.

Guilt forced her to get off the couch and

to place her shoes on the shoe rack in the walk-in closet. As she put the pair in the empty space on the rack she heard Malachi's voice jokingly say, "Imelda Marcos." Then she caught a glimpse of something black peeking at her from under Malachi's shirt. Why couldn't he use the laundry basket like normal people? Curiosity got the best of her and she lifted the shirt to see the black leather planner that he always carried. His initials, "M.C.," were engraved in gold on the front of it. He kept that thing so close to himself that he practically guarded it with his life. She was surprised that he had left it behind. He was so protective of the planner that one might think that he had some classified government documents in it. What was in this planner? It wasn't like Malachi conducted business.

Nyree had to know, and if she did not look in it now she may never get the opportunity to inspect its contents again. When she opened it, she noticed that there was notebook paper that was blank. When she looked closer, she could tell that someone had used the paper as a cushion to write. The invisible writing belonged to a female named Felicia, and she had scribbled her telephone number. There were some business cards and one belonging to Yo-Yo whose title was dancer/entertainer. For Nyree, that meant stripper. Why would he need a stripper's card? What man would pay to see a naked woman? Oh, one who can't get a woman, Nyree thought. There was a crumpled piece of paper with the name "Shay" scribbled on it and a two-one-nine area code. How many times had she seen that number on the phone bill? Too many. Since it occurred so frequently and it was a Gary phone number, she assumed that it was one of his cousin's phone numbers. But he did not have a cousin named Shay. She was sure that if this person was his cousin, she would have met this person before and that was not the case.

Another compartment contained two cherry--flavored condoms. She was feeling ill. If she stopped searching now she might be able to ward off that anxiety attack that was slowly creeping up on her. In the back was a large slot that contained an envelope. A letter, Nyree suspected. Should she read his mail? Why not? He did not respect her privacy, did he? No, and it was evident every time he went into her purse he stole money, keys, and credit cards. How did that saying go? "What's good for the goose is good for the gander." She yanked the envelope out of the slot. The bubbly writing on the envelope belonged to Terri Webber. She checked the postmark date. It was April 12, 1996. The letter was dated April 7, 1996. It started:

Dear Malachi,

It's been one year that you've been married to old girl. I can't believe you married her knowing that I was carrying your baby and how much I loved you. Even though I'm married too, I still long for you. I was glad to see you when your ship came down here. If Tommy ever found out about our little rendezvous on his dead grandma's couch he would probably kill me. (*Oh, ya'll just was real trifling to be "doing it" on the man's deceased grandmother's couch,* Nyree thought as she continued to read the letter.) **At least you got to see your daughter. Kenya tells me that your girl doesn't want you to go see your son. What kind of mess is that? Speaking of mess, how you gonna get another bitch pregnant while you and me was dealing? I was really pissed that you didn't even try to make it and be there with me for the birth. Tommy knows that Chantelle is yours and he doesn't even care.**

What a sucker, hunh? Well, he's going to adopt her. Well, I gotta go. I still love you and if you're ever down this way again, call me. You know the number.

P.S. Don't write back at this address. Send it to my mom's house and she will get it to me.

Love Always,

Terri

Nyree was flabbergasted by the letter. The cheating had not ceased. Her whole life with Malachi was one big lie after another. What was wrong with him and Terri? Don't people take the institution of marriage seriously? Don't vows mean something? Why do people get married if they are going to cheat? Why did Malachi cheat on her and then get married? She had thought that since the cheating had occurred prior to their nuptials that she could deal with it especially if it were not going on during the marriage. Who was she fooling? Cheating, especially when you are the one being cheated on, hurts no matter when it occurs. For some reason she had expected that their separation would have brought forth improvement in Malachi, but it didn't. Nyree had thought that she was hurting him as she was depriving him of the "good-loving," but apparently he was used to getting "loving" from everywhere. Not having hers was not hurting him. She felt silly now because she really thought that she was teaching him a lesson. How did her grandma say it, "Once a dog always a dog"? Or was it "Can't teach an old dog new tricks." She was unsure which of those dog statements applied to Malachi, or if both did. The only thing that she did deduct from the statements was that Malachi was a dog. Maybe he and Terri were made for each other. This Terri sounded like a real character. No, a real whore. Tommy, from how she described him in the letter, seemed like the perfect man, but Terri did not want him. She wanted a man who was taken and she could care less. Nyree pondered about why she couldn't meet the perfect man. Was something wrong with her? How was it that she kept attracting "Mr. Wrong" and not only attracting him, but falling for him? When she spoke with her mother again, she would consider that maybe there was a personality flaw within her that caused her to keep falling for this type of man.

The phone startled Nyree. She took several deep breaths in order to regain her composure.

"Hello."

"Uh, hello, is Malachi there," a female asked.

"Who is this?" Nyree snapped.

"Ciara, his baby momma. Don't play, put him on the phone."

'His baby momma. Does she know how ignorant she sounds? Does she realize that is all she will ever be is a baby's momma? I mean she is saying that as if it is an accomplishment,' Nyree thought to herself. She had to admit that it did hurt that this woman had the one thing that she did not-- a child by her husband. But maybe it was good that she did not have a child by him. What type of life would her child have? Finances were not a problem, but what about a loving caring home? Could she or Malachi provide a child with such a thing? Finally, she told Ciara, "He's not here."

"Look, I ain't got time to be playing games with you today. He called from there this morning when I paged him, so I know he's there," Ciara said with venom. She had heard that Malachi was on restriction, so why was he calling her from the apartment. 'He probably just told his boy to tell me that so I wouldn't get suspicious about him not calling or coming by. I'm getting tired *of putting up with his mess. Why can't he just be honest? One minute he's telling me that he does not want to be with his wife and then the next thing you know he is calling me from their place. I mean what's the sense in that,'* Ciara thought to herself. Her dreams of living happily ever after with Malachi were fading right before her face.

"Correction was here," Nyree said not believing that Malachi had the audacity to call this woman on her telephone. How dare he call this girl from her phone? Who did he think he was? He can't have his cake and eat it too, Nyree whined to herself. She wondered when he had called Ciara. Ms.B told her that he had probably called Ciara at the same time that he was stealing from her purse. It didn't take Malachi long to do his dirt. He was the type of person that needed to be watched at all times because if you blinked you could become a victim.

"Put Malachi on the phone. Camron has a temp of one hundred and four."

"Why don't you take him to the hospital?" This was a no-brainer, Nyree thought, but then she had to remember to whom she was speaking. According to Malachi, Ciara was nineteen years old. Young and dumb is how he described her.

Nyree often wondered what Malachi could want with a young girl like Ciara. He was practically ten years older than her.

"I can't because I don't have any insurance and Malachi never put Camron on his insurance, so I need to get some money from him so I can take him to the doctor."

Nyree had no response to Ciara's last statement. All she could do was laugh. Her laugh infuriated Ciara.

"What you laughing at? You think it's funny that my baby's brain could be frying. I ought to come over there and kick your…"

A threat, how funny, Nyree thought to herself.

"Bring it, little girl, because I got something waiting for you. You people… I don't have time…"

"You *people?* I know you're not trying to be racist, because I'm Puerto Rican," Ciara stated.

'Puerto Rican?' Nyree thought. She had never seen this girl before and that bothered her. What if she was the girl behind the counter at the restaurant taking her order? Or what if she was the girl who bumped into Nyree at the mall feigning that it was an accident? Nyree felt like

she was at a disadvantage because she did not know what Ciara looked like, but Ciara had seen her picture. At least that is what Malachi told Nyree. Nyree still could not get over that this girl had just told her that she was Puerto Rican. Her racial background did not bother Nyree. However, for some reason, she presumed that Ciara was African-American. Her mind began to wander. Why do Black men find it necessary to go outside of their race? That was something she would ponder later after she got the answer as to why Malachi found it necessary to continually cheat on her. This day just gets better and better, Nyree thought.

"No, I'm not racist, Ignoramus. I mean you people in terms of you and Malachi got a baby and don't know what to do with it. What kind of mother would let her child not have medical coverage?"

"It's not my fault that I missed my aid appointment and they canceled my benefits."

'I hope she is not looking for sympathy from me. She has a baby with my husband, gets child support every month, and has the nerve to come up in here when I wasn't here. Humph, I ain't got nothing for her but a good butt kicking.'

"Well, whose fault is it?" Nyree asked not really caring to hear her pitiful excuses. The conversation was boring Nyree and she was barely listening until she heard Ciara say something about her mother not coming home in time to pick her up.

"Your mother? Malachi said your mother was dead," Nyree said in a frustrated tone.

"*Dead?* My mother isn't dead. I guess that's what he likes to say when he doesn't want to deal with a situation."

"What?"

"When he went home to marry you, he told me and my mother that his daughter died and he had to go home for the funeral. In fact he spent the night with me and in the morning my mother took him to the airport."

Nyree did not know if she believed the girl or not, but she for sure could not rely on anything that Malachi said to be the truth. The only way she would believe him was if she saw it in writing from a reliable source. Whenever she finished talking to Ciara, she would call her mother to inquire if she had heard anything about Frank's death. For all she knew Malachi could be lying about that. What about all the times he swore on his grandmother's grave to prove to her that he was telling the truth? What if he had a grandmother that was alive and well somewhere? That would be a trip, she thought.

"Well, I don't know what I am going to do about Camron." Ciara babbled.

"I don't know either." Nyree said nonchalantly.

"You are one uncaring, selfish, self-centered bi…"

"Ask me if I give a damn about the fact that you lay down, opened your legs and had a baby with my husband? What you do with your child is your business. I'm sorry to hear that the kid is sick, but it's not my problem. How you handle your child is between you and Malachi. I didn't lay down with you, so you'll never get a dime of my money," and with that she slammed the phone down in Ciara's face. She checked all of the dialed calls and sure enough the number that Ciara had just called from was one of the numbers that had been dialed from her cordless phone. She entered the block option on her phone to keep from receiving calls from Ciara.

A knock at the door sent Nyree running. Her heart raced as she thought that it might be Ciara. Nyree went back into the closet and retrieved her gold-plated gun, which she referred to as her peacemaker. Nyree had a license to carry it, and she was not afraid to use it. Peeping out of the hole in the door, she was satisfied to find that it was Dre minus Kenya. After placing the gun on the top shelf of the living room closet which was located near the front door, she looked in the mirror, smoothed her hair down, and opened the door.

"Where's Malachi? You know he's AWOL," Dre rambled on without so much as a "hello, how are you doing."

"AWOL?"

"Absent Without Leave," Dre told Nyree. Nyree knew the acronym; she just didn't understand how he arrived at that conclusion.

"Dre, he's not AWOL. He had death in the family and went home."

"He didn't get permission to leave. He was still on restriction."

"Oh," Nyree said unworriedly. Dre looked puzzled at Nyree's lack of concern.

"Do you know what could happen to him?" Dre asked.

Nyree rolled her eyes as she watched him

pace her living room. "Ask me if I care."

Dre focused on her to see if there was anything that indicated Nyree cared. He could not find anything that even remotely suggested that she might. "Man, that's cold. Well, I guess I will be getting back to the ship."

Nyree said in a monotone voice, "Take care," and slammed the door behind him. Nyree mimicked him, "That's cold." If he wanted to know about cold she could tell him what was cold, but that would cause her to start another pity party, and she was tired of feeling sorry for herself. 'Forget him and his little smart comments,' she thought.

Nineteen

Karen Easter, general manager for *My Sistah's Library,* had been pleading with Nyree for the past thirty minutes to stay on and manage the bookstore. Much to her dismay nothing was working. "Nyree, what can we do to get you to stay? I can probably talk to corporate to see about increasing your salary by five thousand dollars." Nyree smiled. It felt good to be wanted. It was funny to Nyree that the woman that she considered to be a mentor thought that Nyree was playing hardball.

"Karen, I really do appreciate the offer. It's not an issue of money. I really like this job, but my reasons for leaving are related to my personal life and at this time it is best that I return home and be with my family."

Karen gave Nyree a hug and wished her well as she left the office. It would be difficult to find a replacement for Nyree as Nyree had made significant progress in the short time she had been working at the bookstore. Customer complaints had been reduced by thirty percent and sales associate sales had increased by twenty percent. Karen liked Nyree. Nyree had a pleasant demeanor and was all about business.

There was something very sad about that young woman, yet pleasantly sweet, Karen found herself thinking. Karen could not help wondering if what her nephew Mack had told her about Malachi Chandler's indiscretions were true. Nyree had said that she was leaving because of personal reasons. If what Mack had said were true, Karen admired Nyree's strength. She noticed how Nyree always appeared to have everything together. Given the same situation and set of circumstances the forty--five—year—old Karen, Karen knew given the same situation and set of circumstances, she would fit the qualifications for "basket-case."

Nyree went home and fell into a deep sleep.

"Nyree, Nyree. Girl, wake up," Aris ordered.

"Aris? Why are you calling me at three o'clock in the morning? Somebody better be dead," Nyree said half-jokingly.

"Girl, your brother is crazy," Aris told

Nyree.

"And? Tell me something I don't know. I know you didn't wake me up to tell me that."

"Me and Sean went to the *Cave* tonight, last night, however you want to say it, and we saw Malachi there. Why didn't you come? Anyways, Kyle saw him talking to some girl and he went up to Malachi and said something. Based on what he said to Malachi, you could tell Malachi didn't like it and he tried to jump hard with Kyle. Malachi pushed Kyle and got up in his face and was like, 'What you gonna do?' Kyle told him to step outside. Malachi went outside and next thing you know, you hear blood-curdling howl… Malachi is bleeding and Kyle is nowhere to be found."

"When did this happen?"

"About twenty minutes ago."

"I'll call you back." Nyree rolled her eyes and tried to make sense of what she heard. '*Here we go with some more drama.*' She dialed Kyle's cell phone number. He picked up on the first ring.

"Kyle?"

"What's up, Baby Girl?" he said in his normal nonchalant tone.

"**What's up?** I need to be asking you what's

up. I heard about you at the club…"

"Stop hollering at me. I know you are not about to snap at me about Malachi when he was up in the club trying to holler at everything that walked by. I just let him know that he was not going to be disrespectful while I was in the club. Your boy tried to get hard and I brought him the business. I ain't never liked that punk."

"I'm not tripping on that. I don't want you to get in trouble. Get on the next plane and get down here. I got a situation and I'll tell you about it when you get here."

"What's up, Baby Girl?" Kyle asked his sister.

"No time for talk. Get down here before the police start looking for you."

"I'll be there, but I'm not worried. There's a code in the streets. Plus… never mind the less you know the better…"

"Get here. I love you. Bye," Nyree told her brother and then rolled over on her side and tried to get some sleep. Her mind flashed to funeral services for Malachi. She envisioned how she would look in her black dress that was custom designed by the famous designer Blueberry while sitting in the front pew of the church or maybe at his funeral. Maybe she would have the bastard cremated. Would she keep the ashes? Maybe she would disperse the ashes over the city dump. Would she cry? Life was funny, she thought. The saying, "Every dog has its day," was true.

"Hello,"Nyree said groggily as she held the phone.

"Bae. Bae." Malachi said in short exaggerated breaths, hoping to get some sympathy.

"What?" Nyree said in the nastiest tone that she could produce. *'So much for him being dead; but he does have shortness of breath; perhaps death is imminent. Is it wrong to wish this bastard was dead after all that he has put me through? Will I go to hell for thinking like this? Okay, I don't wish him ill; I just want him to stop bringing me so much heartache and despair.'*

"I've been stabbed."

"Yeah right, Malachi. You lie so much."

"I ain't lying *this* time. For real, somebody stabbed me in the stomach. I think it was Kyle."

"*Kyle?* My brother, Kyle? Why would he stab you?" Nyree was really pretending not to know anything about the situation. If she kept this up, she could be the next Erica Kane. Her favorite soap opera was *All My Children.* Erica Kane was the witch that you loved to hate. Erica Kane was so melodramatic and Nyree loved that about the character.

"I dunno. We were at the Cave and he was just hatin' on me," Malachi said. Nyree's nostrils flared up and she snorted like a pig. She hadn't meant to snort, but it was an uncontrollable gesture that occurred when she became angry. *Here we go again with the lies,* she thought to herself. It pissed her off that Malachi thought that she was naïve and gullible. Once upon a time she had been naïve and gullible but that Nyree did not live here anymore.

"Hating on **you**? Is you crazy? Why would he hate on your sorry ass? You ain't got shit to hate on. If it wasn't for me you wouldn't have a place to lay your head." Nyree generally did not speak in that manner, but she was at her wits' end and had to speak to Malachi in a manner that he could comprehend. It was time out for being nice. What has gotten her so far? Nothing. It only validated the saying that she heard all her life that nice guys, in this case, nice girls finish last. She was tired of coming in last and coming up short.

"Screw you, Malachi. I don't care if you bleed to death. Call one of your hoes and tell them. I mean that is if you really got stabbed. I applaud whoever stabbed you; it keeps your blood off my hands."

"Nyree, you don't mean that." Malachi hoped that she didn't mean that, but realized that she probably did. After all, she had attempted to stab him on more than one occasion. He had heard Tupac rap about a woman scorned, but now he was experiencing firsthand the effects of a woman scorned.

"How are you going to tell me what I mean? I mean it. Do the world a favor and die."

"That's cold, man."

"Oh, well."

"Look, I didn't call to argue. I'm down here at the emergency room at Methodist Hospital on Grant Street…"

"Oh, then it's a real possibility that you could die." Nyree laughed. That emergency room was constantly filled with people and the fact that you could have your guts hanging out would not give you preferential treatment or more expedient service. You waited your turn just like anyone else and you had better have proof of medical insurance when your turn came up or else you would be turned away.

"My momma wants to talk to you," Malachi said in the voice of a frail child. *She thinks she wants to talk to me. That woman does not want to talk to me.* Nyree felt as if she had taken a truth serum and when it came to telling the truth she was no--holds barred. If she were to talk to Keysha right now, there was no telling what might be said. In addition, Nyree did not have time for dramatics so she hung up the phone.

Twenty

Keysha and Monte sat restlessly in the waiting area of the emergency room as Malachi completed his conversation with Nyree. Malachi's facial expression revealed that all was not well at home. In addition, the bits and pieces that were heard from the conversation confirmed it. He begins rapping parts of a Tupac song, *'I ain't got time for witches. Gotta keep my mind on my mother loving riches.'* Then he turned to Keysha and said, "Momma when I die, don't mourn me. Bury me a 'G'."

"Well, what did she say?" Keysha asked, knowing full well the answer to her question and ignoring what he said about dying.

"She hopes that I die. That was the gist of the conversation," Malachi said in an annoyed tone. He hated when his mother asked him questions of which she knew the answer. It had been quite evident that she was listening to the whole conversation, so why did she have to ask what had been discussed? That irritated him to no end.

"I'm going to call that heifer and give her a piece of my mind. Let me see that cell phone. Never mind, I think I have mine in my purse. If you ever needed her, now is the time." Keysha fumed. Monte had been quiet to this point, but he had to interject.

"Don't call her. Why would you call her? She is entitled to her feelings. Look at all the drama Malachi has put her through. You are only hearing one side of the story. You don't know her pain and agony. Give her a chance to come around…"

If Malachi had had the strength, he would have punched Monte in his smug face. "Whose side are you on, man? You're supposed to be on my side," Malachi whined.

Monte darted back, "When you're right, I'm on your side; and when you're wrong, I have to tell you about yourself. This time you're wrong. You brought this upon yourself. You shouldn't have been in the club in that chick's face. You need to grow up and be a man. If you are going to be married you need to act like it."

"Ain't this about a *bitch?* How are you

going to give me advice on being a man when you got this woman here and that woman there?" He hated cursing in front of his mother and he only uttered such words when he was truly angry. Why had he let Monte provoke him to that point? Why was it that everybody was on Nyree's side?

"The difference between me and you is that I'm not claiming to be married. And to set the record straight I'm only involved with one woman now. I'm too old for that trying—to—be—a--player mess. I'm not trying to end up with some kids by a woman that was a booty call. And I'm for sure not trying to end with a sexually transmitted disease. But you can't speak on either one of those as you have experienced both," Monte told his older brother.

"My son was not the result of a booty call." Malachi wanted to ask Monte if marriage was so sacred, why Nyree had that dude over to the apartment on Easter Sunday which also happened to be their first--year anniversary. He decided not to bring that issue up because that would probably only give Monte more ammunition to fire with. Besides, it made him feel like a fool. One way to strip a man's dignity is for his wife to have another man laid up in his home. And was he supposed to believe that lame story about them reading the Bible? That was a good one if ever he heard one, but he did not buy it. He had to admit that Nyree was good because they surely did have those Bibles out on the coffee table.

"Maybe he was. Maybe he wasn't. But how many abortions have you paid for? Huh? And how many visits have you made to the free clinic?" Malachi looked at his younger brother who was the spitting image of Keysha and all he felt for the man was rage. His brother had spoken the truth, and there was no rebuttal to the truth. Monte saw defeat written on Malachi's face. He had won that match. "Alright then, that's what I thought," Monte said, rubbing the fact that he was right in Malachi's face. Malachi groaned in pain, hoping to gain some sympathy from Monte. Monte turned his back to Malachi and picked up the latest issue of the <u>Vibe magazine</u> and began reading it.

Keysha had had enough of sitting and waiting so she walked to the restroom and telephoned Nyree. She didn't care what Monte said. She was going to give Nyree a piece of her mind. When the phone rang again, Nyree just looked at the caller ID and let the answering machine pick up the call. She heard Keysha scolding her about not caring about Malachi and something about Nyree needing to be mature and how her husband needed her. That was the funniest thing Nyree had heard this year. *'My husband needs me. Huh, did he need me when he was screwing everybody in the world? Let one of them hoes take care of him and come to his rescue. I'm through and I mean that from the bottom of my heart.'* Nyree was the type of person who tried to be understanding and compassionate to others. She cut people slack when others were quick to throw in the towel. However, when she made up her mind that she was through with a person and wrote them off, there was no going back. She didn't hold many grudges in life, but when she had a vendetta against someone, it could get real unpleasant.

"Chandler. Chandler," the nurse called for Malachi to come back to triage.

Keysha grabbed her purse and followed behind Malachi. "It's about time," she snapped as she brushed past the nurse and then she turned when she noticed that Monte was not behind her.

"Are you coming? Come on," she said to

Monte.

Monte rolled his eyes and said, "I'll wait here."

Keysha yelled, "Suit yourself." Keysha didn't understand what Monte's problem was. His brother could have been killed and instead of being concerned he was acting like a snot-nosed brat. Why was the world against her baby Malachi? Sure Malachi was no angel and he had done his share of wrong, but he didn't deserve this hand that life was dealing him. Maybe it was her fault. If she had been a better mother, not worked so much, not had so many around her children, they would have turned out better. At least Monte was doing well for himself. He had moved out, was working steady and able to support himself. Keysha had thought that Nyree was going to be their meal ticket. She honestly thought that Nyree was going to share the wealth and allow the family to prosper. Boy, had Keysha been wrong. Nyree made it clear that Malachi was the man of the house and would be doing all of the supporting, not vice versa. Keysha's feelings had really been hurt when Malachi called Nyree on three-way one time asking for money for Keysha's cable and light and gas bill. Unbeknownst to Nyree, Keysha was on the phone.

Nyree's response to Malachi's request was, "Doesn't your mother work everyday?"

Malachi had responded, "Yeah."

Nyree said very smugly, "Alright then. I'm not Captain--Save—a--Hoe."

Malachi had become extremely angry asking Nyree who she was calling a whore. Nyree apologized stating that she was only quoting the words from a song and did not mean it literally, but she had no intent to bail out grown women and she stuck by that statement.

Once they settled into area number seven the nurse took Malachi's vitals and asked what happened. A few minutes later a police officer came to take a report of the incident. "And do you know who did this to you, sir?" Malachi shook his head to indicate that his answer was "no."

Keysha was quick to say, "Malachi, tell him the truth. Who are you trying to protect?"

"Ma, I don't know for sure who did it. It happened so quickly. All I know is that I had beef with ole boy. We went outside, exchanged more words. The next thing you know I had been stabbed, but he wasn't the only person up in my face..."

"Look, you know like I know that it was Kyle Shaw. Tell the officer. I'm tired of these Shaws thinking that because they have money that they can get away with murder. You see Nyree don't give two..."

"Ma, stop. Do you think pressing charges against her brother is going to help my marriage?"

Officer Simon Lillie had heard more than he would like to have heard. This was some real--life drama. He had heard about "Mr. Nyree Shaw" but now he had the opportunity to meet him up close and personal. Everyone wondered what made this guy so special that he got to marry Nyree Shaw. As far as Simon could see there was nothing extraordinary about him. He just looked like the average; wanna-be thug that he saw on a daily basis. If he had to re-create the scene, Simon would bet any money that Malachi was talking trash and somebody called his bluff. Simon couldn't wait to get back to the station to complete this report. Simon couldn't help hoping that Malachi would not want to press charges against Kyle Shaw. Although Simon had only lived in Gary for five years, he had learned in that short time that the Shaw family was a family that you didn't want to mess with. Not that he was afraid of anyone; he didn't like making unnecessary enemies. He really didn't want to pursue something if Malachi was not sure.

"So, do you know who stabbed you?" Officer Lillie inquired of Malachi.

"Yeah, Kyle Shaw."

"Alright; I think I have everything that I need. We'll be in contact with you," Simon Lillie said as he exited the room. This was going to be an interesting investigation.

Twenty-One

"Thanks. Have a good day," she called to the two young gentlemen from the Salvation Army as they carted the last of the furniture out of the apartment. Kyle wondered aloud why she had given away everything in the apartment.

"Too many memories that I didn't want to take with me," Nyree said as her eyes made contact with her brother's deep brown eyes. She turned her head quickly because she did not want him to see her pain. It was too late because he knew her as well as she knew herself and saw through the facade.

He hugged tightly. Kyle wanted to say something to soothe her pain, but he did not know what to say. He had never experienced what she was going through, and it would be cliché to say, "I know how you feel," because he didn't. He fantasized about finding the right woman, settling down, and having a family. The right woman had not come along yet. There had been many impostors, but they always gave themselves away. Nyree rested her head on his chest and sobbed like a baby. It was an awkward position for him to be in. He decided to let her get it all out. She had told him bits and pieces about Malachi and his infidelity and he understood why she was upset. Kyle had no regrets about stabbing Malachi; he only wished that he had known then what he knew now.

"Baby Girl, you got everything that you want out of here?"

"Yeah, I guess." She hated the way he had said "here." He said the word as if the apartment was a dump, some hell-hole, the armpit of the South.

"Well, let's go. I'm taking you home," Kyle said with authority. Nyree watched him walk down the stairs to her car. *Why didn't he have a woman in his life?* she wondered. Kyle was tall, with a peanut—butter complexion. His crooked grin and dimples made the most ornery person soften up. Under his hard-core exterior he was a teddy bear. His bark was worse than his bite, but you didn't want to put him in a position where he was forced to bite because when forced to bite, it was a vicious, almost lethal bite.

Nyree gave the place that she had temporarily called home one last look. She was not going to miss it. Jacksonville had been a nice place to visit, but it never felt like home. Perhaps if the situation had been different she might have liked Jacksonville. There was that word again, *if.* She remembered Grandma Lula's favorite saying: 'If '**if**' was a fifth, then we'd all be drunk.' There was no time to dwell on what could have been. Nyree had given her all to her marriage and it did not work. It was a bitter pill to swallow, but it was the truth and now Nyree had to move on. Nyree slammed the door shut and hopped into the passenger's seat of her BMW. She was glad that Kyle had taken a one-way flight out and agreed to drive her home.

Nyree and Kyle talked for hours as they drove home. Finally in Kentucky they decided to stop and stay the night at a hotel. Kyle pulled the covers up over his lean body as Nyree lay stretched out on her bed watching television.

"Well, I think I'm going to call it a night now."

"You never could hang," Nyree teased jokingly.

"What? Who fell asleep at Rocky's

birthday party?"

Nyree chuckled. She had forgotten about that. "That party was so boring..."

"Stop. Whoever heard of anyone falling asleep at a party?" asked Kyle.

"Okay. You got me. Hey, I've been meaning to ask you what happened with you and Dad and the money and all..."

"Tell you the truth; I don't know why I did it. I think it was revenge for how he treated me as a kid," Kyle told his sister.

"What do you mean?" Nyree asked her brother.

"I don't expect you to know how I feel, being that you were his favorite."

"I know you're not talking about being a favorite, when you were Mom's favorite. Let her tell it, Kyle could do no wrong," Nyree said with a hint of jealousy.

"And let Dad tell it, Nyree could do no wrong. You don't know how humiliating it is to have your dad think that you are a total failure."

"It's not like Mom dotes on me. She is always looking down her nose at me as if I am some reject."

"That's not true. Mom looks at everyone

like that," Kyle said, imitating the notorious look of their mother. The two of them howled with laughter.

Then in his best Margo voice, Kyle said, "Dear, you don't know what it is like to be labeled as a behavioral problem and put into special classes."

Nyree sighed. "Are you still bitter about that?"

Kyle was becoming angry because she did not comprehend what he was saying to her. "Hell, yeah, I'm bitter. I did not have a problem. My problem was that I questioned authority and did not conform to the rules, and the teachers didn't know how to deal with that so they shoved me off in some basement classroom so that they would not have to deal with me.

"It happens to too many African-American males and Dad never once stood up for me. That's what I am most bitter about. My dad did not speak up for me and my mother did, but in the end she was outnumbered."

Nyree shook her head and thought about what Kyle had said. She had to admit that he had made some valid points. "I'm sorry, Kyle."

He shrugged her statement off. "Sorry for

what. You didn't do anything."

"No, I didn't, but I always thought that you had an anger problem."

He flashed his goofy grin. "Yeah. I can't lie. I do have an anger problem, but who doesn't. The difference between me and others is that other people choose to manage their anger and sometimes I choose to and sometimes I choose not to. I like being that guy that lives on the edge. I'm the type of brother who can show you better than I can tell you. I'm dangerous to a degree because some people you can read and see coming. **Me**, you don't see me coming until I'm up in your face and then it's too late… like your boy Malachi. He tried me and underestimated me because I am generally calm and easy going. Oops, his bag… Well, I'm going to get some shut-eye now. Sleep well."

Nyree rolled over and turned the light off on the nightstand beside her bed. As she drifted off to sleep she couldn't help but think that her brother was a little bit crazy. If he were crazy, she quite possibly could have some of the same craziness in her. People often underestimated her until she showed them what she was capable of. Hadn't Malachi underestimated her? She had not shown him anything yet. Her plan was just being put into motion. When she finished with him he was going to wish he had never met her. For her that was not a threat. That was a promise.

Twenty-Two

Malachi hadn't realized just how chaotic his family was until the day of Frank's funeral. From the moment he walked in, he could feel the tension hanging heavy in the air. Aunt Francine, Frank's mother, seemed determined to ruin the day with her bitterness. She was livid, and she had decided that her target was Lynn, Frank's wife. Francine openly accused Lynn of being responsible for Frank's death, ranting that if she'd come straight home from the store with the antacid tablets, Frank might still be alive. She didn't stop there, even hinting that maybe Lynn hadn't been at the store at all, but out with another man. The autopsy had clearly shown Frank's arteries were blocked, something that had developed over years—not in one night. But that didn't stop Francine's blame game.

The morning's drama didn't end there. Lynn wanted the funeral procession to leave from her house, but Francine demanded it start from her place. Confusion spread among the family as everyone tried to figure out where to gather. In the end, they went with Lynn's plan, but Francine showed up thirty minutes late, claiming she had to "make an entrance," as if her son's funeral was her personal event.

As the cars lined up, yet another argument broke out. Malachi watched in disbelief as his cousin LaToya announced she was riding in the limo—*her* first time, and she wasn't going to miss out on this "chance." Little Man, who easily tipped the scales at two hundred fifty pounds, shot back with a comment about how she could've had a limo ride at prom if she'd ever been invited to anything classy. LaToya shot him a venomous look and snapped, "Look, Mr. College Man, just because you go to Purdue doesn't mean you're better than the rest of us!"

Trying to keep the peace, Lynn told LaToya to take her place in the family car and reminded everyone they were already late. Meanwhile, Francine turned to another cousin, Keysha, daring her to say anything "smart.".

Malachi couldn't believe the drama unfolding around him. At a funeral, of all places. *This family,* he thought, watching as everyone piled into the cars, tension simmering under every word. It was a side of them he'd always known was there—but never fully realized until now.

When the family finally arrived at the church, the church was filled to capacity. Instead of everyone lining up in an orderly fashion to enter there were people complaining about who should be standing in front of this person.

Malachi heard people murmuring things like, "Frank didn't even know him." "Who is that?" "He's not a cousin." The worst was when people started arguing about who should be sitting on the front pew. Malachi surmised that a funeral was like a wedding in many ways. People would show up just to see what they could see and what type of service, or in this case, performance it was going to be. Malachi knew people who went to funerals for the heck of it. He called them "funeral hoppers" because they did not necessarily have ties to the deceased. They attended the funeral for a form of entertainment. Malachi detested going to funerals and rarely ever went to the gravesite. Today would be one of those rarities.

The ushers stood at the door in their dark

suits holding the programs and waiting to usher the family in. The older thin, frail lady leaned over to Lynn and in what was supposed to be a whispered tone said, "The funeral was supposed to start at eleven o'clock. It's eleven forty-five. We thought that you all were not going to show up. Pastor was getting ready to start."

Lynn was tired of everybody and their smart comments. At this time she could no longer be polite or cordial, so she leaned over and told the old woman, "I doubt that you all were going to start this funeral without me."

The old lady, misunderstanding what Lynn was saying to her, grinned and nodded her head. "Oh, yes we were. Pastor said he had another engagement today."

Lynn rolled her eyes and simply said, "Oh well. You can show us in now." *The nerve of that old woman to say that to me*, Lynn thought. Lynn was not sure if the pastor had said all of that or not, but she thought that the lady should have had enough sense not to repeat it. If she were going to repeat, now was not the time.

As soon as they walked through the doors Francine began her performance.

"Oh, my baby. Frank. *Frank...* Not my

baby." On cue Francine began falling to the ground.

Lynn caught her elbow and said through clenched teeth, "Francine, get it together."

Lynn was mourning and grieving as well but found that Francine's performance was just that-- a performance. Lynn doubted that Francine was that broken up about Frank's death as they had not spoken in the past three months. Francine became upset when Frank would not cosign a loan for three thousand dollars that Francine wanted for a down payment on a 1995 Mercedes.

"You could deny your mother her dream car," Francine stated when she learned that she was not going to get the money from Frank.

Francine ignored Lynn's request and continued hollering about her son and how she wished God had taken her instead of him. Lynn whispered to Francine and told her that it was not nice to play with God. She had better be careful what she wished for because it might just happen. Francine drew in a breath and huffed at Lynn's remark. When they reached the front pew, Francine noticed that Lynn was sitting at an angle toward her. Lynn's back was facing

Francine. Lynn was well endowed with hips. Although Lynn had her right leg crossed over her left one, Lynn's right hip seemed to brush Francine away. Francine interpreted Lynn's body posture as if saying to her, "Kiss My Butt."

Malachi had to close his eyes tightly so that he would not cry while Autumn Summers sang *Going up Yonder*. '*Whoever knew that Autumn could sing like that,*' Malachi thought? As the young woman sang, Malachi began thinking about his life and wondered where people would say he went when he died.

He knew Nyree would say, "hell," without a second thought. Where would he go? His close brush with death the other night had him seriously considering his fate. He would like to think that he would go to heaven, but he knew that he had not really lived a life that would merit such a reward. In life he had been used to getting by and getting second chances. When Autumn finished singing that song, there was not a dry eye in the church.

The service was going along nicely. People were staying within their two-minute remark time and then Frank's twelve-year-old-son, Frank Junior, from a previous relationship stood up and commented that he loved his father but wished that his father had spent more time with him. Frank Junior stated that the child support checks were nice, but time spent with his dad would have been better. He had only had an opportunity to develop a relationship with his dad during the past two years. He acknowledged that his stepmother, Lynn, had been very instrumental in developing their relationship and to her he was grateful. Many of the people in the church batted their eyes as Frank Junior's comments, though true, were not in conjunction with all of the syrupy, sweet things that they had heard about Frank heretofore.

It took all the restraint that Lynn could muster to deal with the young man with an Afro. He was wearing black jeans, a pair of black suede Nike Cortez sneakers and a black tee shirt with Frank's picture on the front and the letter "R.I.P." above it. He walked up to the microphone and slurred some remarks regarding Frank.

"Good morning church. I'm Samuel," he paused and continued, "My man, Frank. *My man, Frank.* Now he was the realest nig…oops, can't say that in church, huh? He was the truest 'G' I knew. And even after he changed his life, he didn't turn his back on his friends--his boys. I mean, if you saw Frank in the streets, he would throw his fist up, nod his head, and ask you how things were with you. If he had it, you had it. That's just how Frank was. I remember the time we..."

His remarks seemed endless until Monte walked up to the microphone, patted Samuel on the back and gently escorted him to his seat. As Monte escorted Samuel, you could see people whispering and eyes following Samuel. People wondered out loud if Samuel was inebriated and questioned how he could enter church in that state.

Pastor Gray announced that was the conclusion of the remarks portion of the service and announced his sermon for the day. "You want to live your life in a manner that is pleasing to God. How many of you know where you would go right now if you were to leave this place now? My sermon for today, and I will be brief, won't bore you. My sermon is 'Will you be ready when death comes knocking?' See none of us know when our time is coming, but we must all account for the time spent here on earth. Are you spending your time wisely? Take a moment and reflect on that question. Are you spending your time wisely? I heard a young man remark to another fellow recently, 'How you living?' I am going to pose the same question to you all today, 'How are you living?' Is your lifestyle pleasing to God? Don't look at your neighbor. Close your eyes and reflect on yourself."

Malachi had not been to church since last year and here he was in church for a funeral. He felt the eyes of Pastor Gray locking on him. Every time Malachi turned to avoid eye contact, he looked back up and he and Pastor Gray were looking at each other. Did Pastor Gray know how he was living? Malachi pondered.

Even if Pastor Gray did not know, Malachi knew that he was living a dangerous and reckless life. Past and current events came to Malachi's mind, and he was feeling very uncomfortable at the present moment. He could track down the people that he wronged and say sorry, but that would not right the wrongs he had committed. What about the people who were dead that he had mistreated? Malachi felt as if Pastor Gray were preaching to him. He had never experienced a sermon like this. The sermon was thought provoking and meaningful.

His previous experiences with church had never been like this. There always seemed to be lots of singing that he was unfamiliar with, lots of talking about things that were unimportant to him, and the sermon never seemed to make sense to him. Malachi always had difficulty following the sermon, however, this was different. He appreciated that Pastor Gray supported what he was saying with scriptures from the Bible. He actually read the scriptures more than one time and this was important to Malachi, as he had difficulty locating them. Since they were being read multiple times, he could read along when he finally located the scriptures.

As Malachi and the other pallbearers carried the casket out of the church, he found himself nearly tripping over the pants legs of the suit that Monte had lent him. Nyree's words, "You ain't nothing but a bum," blasted in his head as he thought about how pathetic he was to have to borrow a suit from his younger brother. Even though he had been told that it was bad luck to buy an outfit for a funeral, he would have purchased one if he had the funds to do so. When his debit card was rejected at Man Alive in the Southlake Mall, he darted out of the store to the nearest ATM. When he requested a balance he learned that he had a negative balance.

The tension at the gravesite was thick. Lynn took her seat and watched as people elbowed one another in an effort to get a seat in front of the casket. Lynn sighed when the casket was finally lowered into the ground. She placed three white roses on top. Others placed flowers on the casket. Lynn felt the heels on her shoes sink into the moist ground. It felt as if her whole life were sinking. How could she go on without the love of her life? Although Frank had been dead a week, it had not seemed real to her before. Even seeing him in the casket at the wake last night did not seem real. It seemed surreal. She kept thinking that he was going to pop up out of the casket and apologize for the sick joke. Some of the guests had commented that Frank looked like himself. She guessed that they were just trying to be nice or did not know what to say. Nothing lying in that casket resembled how she remembered her husband. Amanda Payne had done a good job with the body, but looking like himself would have meant that he was alive and active. When the casket was lowered into the ground, it became real to Lynn that Frank was gone forever and his death became very real to her. She heard conversations about going back to the church for the repast. Lynn did not want to eat or talk to anyone. She just wanted to go home, get into the bed she had shared with Frank, pull the covers up tightly and tune the world out. It would look bad if she did not attend the dinner, but she did not care. She had lost her husband, her soul mate, and now it was time for her to grieve. Not once had she cried since Frank passed-- not because she was heartless, but because she was going through the motions. She felt like she was living someone else's life, but now it was real. She had felt the sting that death had left and it hurt. It hurt very badly.

After the burial, family and friends returned to the church for dinner. Keysha was in the stall of one of the bathrooms in the church when she overheard a conversation between two ladies who were at the sink. Peering out of the small space between the door and the doorjamb she noticed that one of the women was wearing a dress that was more suitable for going to a club, not church. The other woman was dressed appropriately for church, but her hair weave was ridiculous. It was long and straight and "hooker red." The lady wearing the nightclub outfit said, "Girl, I can't believe she didn't come back for the dinner." Keysha guessed that she was referring to Lynn.

The lady donning the "hooker red" weave said, "I don't know, but you see who's up in here trying to run things--the baby's momma."

"But you know who I want to see?"

"Who?"

"Malachi, don't they call him Mr. Nyree Shaw. You know he's Frank's cousin?"

"Girl, I didn't know that. I wonder if his wife is here."

"I don't think she's here. I've seen her before and I haven't seen anyone that looks like her."

"Well, maybe Malachi isn't here."

"I think he is. I want to see him. You heard about what happened to him?"

"Yeah, the streets say that Nyree's brother shanked him."

Keysha had heard enough and came out of the stall startling the two women.

"Malachi is the one pallbearer that was wearing the black suit with the black—and--white polka dot tie," Keysha said as she soaped her hands up and let the warm water rinse the suds away. She shook them dry and then towel--dried them.

"Is that your man?" one of the girls questioned.

Keysha grabbed the handle of the door and said, "No, he's my son," and let the door close behind her.

Both women looked at each other and smiled nervously. Finally, the woman with the "hooker red" hair weave said, "Girl, you never know who is who. You have to be careful about the conversations that you have in public restrooms."

The woman wearing the sleeveless, low-cut black dress said, "Who are you telling? His mother? She looks awfully young to be his mother. Come on, Girl; let's go see what we can see." She winked at herself in the mirror.

When Keysha finally returned to the kitchen, Malachi beckoned for her to come sit next to him at the family table.

"Dang, what happened to you? I thought you fell in," Malachi joked with his mother regarding the length of time that she had spent in the restroom.

"No," she said as she looked around and noticed that the two gossiping women that she had encountered in the restroom were looking at her and Malachi. She was annoyed and wanted to say something mean to them, but decided that this was neither the time nor the place to engage in a confrontation with anyone. Sipping from the cup of punch that Malachi had brought for her, she wondered if she were twenty years younger if she would have behaved as those two women had behaved.

"You're not going to eat anything?" Keysha questioned Malachi who seemed to be picking at the fruit on his plate.

"Naw, I'm good. You know I don't just eat anybody's cooking."

"Let's go," Malachi said to his mother. She placed a hand on his shoulder and asked him if he was feeling well. Since the stabbing incident, she had been overly concerned about him and doted on him. He had to admit that he was enjoying the attention and affection from his mother as he had not received it consistently as a child.

"I'm fine. I just want to go," Malachi told his mother.

She was glad because she had been ready to leave after she encountered those two women in the restroom. They gave family members hugs and told Francine to call them if she needed them. Then they exited the church.

Malachi felt as if he had been given a second chance at life. He wanted to hurry up and get back to his wife and be the husband and man that she deserved.

Twenty-Three

May 1996

Back in the Midwest, Nyree felt a rush of nostalgia as she perched on the steps of Marquette Park Pavilion, letting the warm spring breeze kiss her skin. She closed her eyes, taking it all in. "There's no place like home," she whispered with a smirk. This was her sanctuary—the one place she could sort through her mess and feel whole again. Her morning meeting with Nicole Rouse, one of the notorious Dilworths, had gone better than she'd hoped. Nicole was no stranger to handling ruthless divorces, and thanks to her, Malachi wouldn't be walking away with a dime of her assets. Nyree's life—and her name—would be her own again.

For three weeks, she'd been lying low, just savoring the quiet of home. But now, she was ready to re-emerge. When she pulled into Shaw Enterprises, a flash of cherry-red caught her eye.

A Lexus with Duval County plates. Colin. Her heart skipped, a mix of thrill and dread. *Right man, wrong time,* she thought, shaking her head. That was the story of her life. No use dwelling —she had business to handle. She straightened her shoulders and walked confidently toward the entrance.

Inside, it was like stepping back into the past. Same dark wood paneling, same hum of hushed conversations. And there, behind the switchboard, was Barbara, headset perched on her head, eyes widening at the sight of Nyree like she'd just seen a ghost.

"Hi," Nyree greeted her, a sly grin spreading across her face. Barbara blinked, mouth slightly open, clearly struggling for words.

"Nyree? I... I didn't know you were back," Barbara finally stammered.

"Don't be so surprised. You'll be seeing a lot more of me around here."

Barbara raised a brow. "So... are you moving back?"

"Oh, I'm back," Nyree replied, letting the weight of her words linger. "And I've got a few scores to settle."

Barbara raised an eyebrow. She had read all about Nyree's husband allegedly being stabbed in the parking lot by Kyle Shaw. Barbara could not wait to get home to tell her friend Cindy about Nyree. The gossip was endless today for Barbara. First there was a visit from Officer Simon Lillie trying to determine the where-abouts of Kyle and now a visit from Nyree. What could be better for the gossip mill? Even still, Barbara was not satisfied. She wanted to get more details and who better to get them from than the horse's mouth?

"So, how is married life?" Barbara questioned Nyree as she had heard that the night that Malachi was allegedly stabbed by Kyle, Malachi was in the club trying to talk to a female stripper from Chicago. Based on the few times that she had seen Malachi, he struck her as the kind of man who would be involved with a stripper. He looked like the type who would have sex with just about any woman that he wanted to, but he also looked like the type that would pay for it. She could never understand why men would pay for sex, especially when they had beautiful wives. Even though she could not stand Nyree, Barbara had to admit that Nyree was pretty. Maybe she was not putting out and that is why her man was trying to get with a stripper. Barbara did not think that was true. She thought that Nyree tried to play the innocent role, but believed that behind closed doors she was a different person.

"It is what it is," Nyree said, running her fingers through her hair. She spied the disappointing look on Barbara's face. Nyree knew that Barbara was not asking out of concern but in hopes of getting some juicy details about Nyree's personal life. Nyree was not a person who went around venting her personal problems to people. Even if she was that type, Barbara would be the last person on earth whom Nyree would trust. Telling anything to Barbara was like telling it to a tabloid.

"Oh, being that you have five kids and have never been married, you wouldn't understand what I'm talking about. Enough of the small talk. Is my father around?" asked Nyree impatiently.

Barbara felt as if she had egg all over her face. How dare this young prissy girl talk to her in this manner? That is what was wrong with the Shaw kids. They thought because they had money they could treat people any way. Nyree had always been haughty towards Barbara. She made Barbara feel inadequate.

"He's in a meeting and asked not to be disturbed," Barbara said humbly.

Nyree noticed that Barbara's tone had softened. *'Good. Every now and then you got to break these hoes down and give them a reality check. Hired help has to know its place. Oh my goodness, I sound like my mother. Well, the truth is the truth.'*

"Who is he with?"

"The new guy. I don't think you know him."

"You'd be surprised what and who I know. Buzz my father and let him know that I'm here and that I will meet him in the sports complex."

Barbara nodded her head as if to indicate that she would do it. Nyree stood at the desk tapping her finger impatiently on the maroon countertop.

"I would appreciate it if you buzzed him now, so I can get a reply. Thank you," Nyree spat with venom.

After Barbara contacted Edwin, Nyree strolled out of the front door and decided that when she came aboard, Barbara would have to go. That woman had too much of an attitude for Nyree. There was just something about Barbara that Nyree did not like. Nyree was not sure if it was because Barbara was on the heavy side and was always wearing low-cut shirts to reveal her cleavage, or because she wore seven gold chains around her neck that were always tangled? Maybe it was the ten gold bracelets that she wore on her right arm or the gaudy rings that she wore on each of her chubby fingers. The nails that were painted fluorescent colors with jewelry hanging off the tips did not help either. Nothing about Barbara said professionalism. She was the first person whom clients encountered when they walked through the door of Shaw Enterprises and she did not represent the company well. Nyree did not care if Barbara had been with the company for the past seven years, Barbara had to go. They might be able to find her a position in another part of the company. The sports complex might be a good place for her.

Twenty-Four

"Colin, I've been thinking... I want you and my daughter to work on the project together," stated Edwin Shaw.

"Mr. Shaw, in all due respect, this is my franchise and I think that I should be handling all the details."

"Colin, don't worry. My daughter is very efficient and thorough. I'm sure you will like her. I will arrange a meeting between you two. Say tomorrow, ten o'clock in the boardroom?"

Colin hesitated, holding back any further argument. It was clear Edwin Shaw wasn't budging on the idea of his daughter taking charge on the project. Colin had heard a lot about this so-called "daughter," and none of it made her sound like the type he'd want to work with. Being the new guy, Colin kept his head down and his ears open, soaking up the office chatter. If there was even a shred of truth to what he'd heard, he was in for a ride.

Barbara had painted a pretty damning picture: Shaw's daughter was rumored to be cutthroat—someone who didn't just break rules but rewrote them to suit her whims. Supposedly, she'd once married some thug from the streets, and when he wouldn't play by her rules, she went as far as putting a hit out on him. Then there was Shaw's son, who'd gotten tangled up in a murder plot that went sideways, leaving just enough speculation for everyone to stay on edge. Colin didn't know if all this was just smoke, but he'd learned one thing during his short time in Gary: the Shaw family wasn't one you messed with. And now he'd be working side-by-side with their wild-card daughter. He took a deep breath, wondering just what he was stepping into.

"I'm leaving for the day. I'll see you in the morning."

"We'll see you in the morning," Edwin responded as Colin walked out the door.

Colin continued down the carpeted hallway to Barbara's desk. He leaned over and smiled at her. "Barb, I'm gone for the day."

Barbara flirted. "This early? What do you have planned?"

"Nothing much. See you tomorrow." He

chuckled to himself as he walked to his car. Barbara tried too hard and she certainly was not his type.

A silver-colored BMW with Indiana license plate "BABYGRL" caught Colin's eye. Immediately he thought of Nyree. Her car had those same Indiana plates and she had said that she was from Gary. That would be too much of a coincidence, and he did not believe in coincidences. What if it was she? No, it could not be. Besides, her car was black, but she could have gotten it painted. He had secretly fallen for her, but she was a married woman. He was just fooling himself thinking that she would leave her husband and that there would be a happily-ever-after for the two of them. How many nights had he wondered how things would have been if only she were not married? He had learned long ago not to do that. Hadn't he done that with Adrianne and gotten burnt?

Adrianne was a beautiful girl on the outside, but a conniving witch deep down inside. The more Colin gave, the more she took, never giving anything back in return. When business began to prosper for Colin, he found himself taking more business trips and attending more meetings. Time became a critical issue for the two, but he thought she would understand that he was working hard now so they could have a better life. In the future they would be able to enjoy the fruits of his labor. Adrianne would complain that he must be with another woman and that was why she was always being placed on the back burner. Colin knew that he was a good catch and could have any woman he wanted. Yet he always tried to assure Adrianne that he was all about business and was very committed to her. Adrianne was insecure and did not believe him. Colin felt that was how she ended up in the arms of Jason, his fraternity brother. When he caught the two of them snuggled on the sofa in her condominium for which he was paying, it hurt him more than words could say. All Adrianne could do was blame Colin for neglecting her.

Colin was determined it was not going to happen to him. The next woman he got involved with would have her own money, be established, cultured and refined - like Nyree he thought. Why couldn't he get that girl off his mind? He could not believe the effect that she had on him. They had not been intimate, never kissed. The most that they had shared was a hug and she had hugged him like she was hugging her old grandmother or somebody. He had yet to feel the contours of her body. Still this girl was intoxicating. When he closed his eyes, he could still envision her face and smell that fragrance she wore, the one that made him feel tingly inside and sent jitters throughout his body. When he asked her about the fragrance, she said that it was a Nicole Bradley Candle Co original that had been designed especially for her. He had thought that she was making it up until he came to Gary and heard about Nicole Bradley Candle Co Fragrances. Many of his associates talked about Jahzara the perfumist.

From what he understood, the girl was dynamic. One of these days he was going to have to put her to the test and see what she could create for him.

He groaned as he walked through the door of his condominium and thought about having to meet with Edwin's daughter tomorrow. Maybe she was not as bad as everyone said. He would find out tomorrow. For now he would lie on his chaise lounge and flip through the channels to see if he could catch a baseball game.

Twenty-Five

Malachi regretted that the only person who was available on base to pick him up from Jacksonville International Airport was Kenya. However, beggars could not be choosy when they needed a ride. '*Where was Nyree?*' He wondered. He had called her cell phone and the house phone more times than he could remember and did not receive an answer. It had been so long since he had been home that he felt like a tourist. When Kenya pulled in front of the apartment building, she asked, "Is Nyree out of town? I haven't seen her car in weeks."

Malachi kept his face blank, giving Kenya nothing to work with. "She had to go away on some business," he replied smoothly. That seemed to do the trick; Kenya's curiosity was satisfied, and he thanked her for the ride before shutting the door of her SUV.

Taking the stairs two at a time, Malachi reached the twelfth floor, heart pounding with the thrill of finally being back in his own place. He'd been done with his mother's couch and her constant watchful eye weeks ago, but she'd insisted he stay until she was convinced he was "completely well." Now, here he was, ready to reclaim his space.

But as he turned the key and pushed open the door, a shockwave hit him: his place was empty—no furniture, no telephone, and definitely no food in the fridge. The only thing left was a massive black trash bag in the center of the room. He stepped closer, dreading what he'd find. Inside, his own soggy, mildewed clothes stared back at him, mocking his return.

Panicked, he ran to the closet, his mind spinning. Had he been robbed? Betrayed? Or was this some kind of message? The only item was his organizer. *'This can't be happening,'* Malachi found himself thinking. He had heard about people coming home to nothing, finding that their spouse had packed up everything and moved, but this was unreal. Malachi thought that he was having an out-of-body experience. Was this what people meant by divine retribution? He had returned to Jacksonville to make things right between him and Nyree and this is what he got. Why was it that every time he desired to do right, he was presented with an obstacle? Albeit he had not been a saint, he sure didn't deserve this. Did he deserve to be homeless and without clothing? All the clothing that he had was the clothes on his back.

He daydreamed about purchasing new clothing and replenishing his wardrobe. The daydreams were interrupted by the reality of his unemployment due to his having gone AWOL and being penniless because his wife had depleted their joint bank account. Where would he go? What would he do? Going back to Gary was not an option for him. Returning to Gary in his current state meant defeat for him. He had been down and out before, but not to this extent. Malachi prided himself on being resilient and resourceful, but this was going to be a challenge. This was war and Nyree had won the first battle, but he was determined that he would not be defeated. Hating to agree with his mother, he was beginning to see what his mother meant about Nyree and the Shaws. The more he thought about returning to Gary, the more it did not seem so bad. There was a score that needed to be settled. He had to show Nyree and Kyle that he was not the joke that they were taking him for. It bothered him when someone thought that they could walk all over him. All of his life he had to prove himself and now was no different.

Fumbling in his pocket he came across Bianca Bryant's card. She was the investigator who was now handling the case against Kyle Shaw. Officer Simon Lillie had been taken off the case and assigned to another one. *And to think I wasn't going to press charges because I thought I still had a chance with Nyree. That night we spent together was special. Obviously she doesn't share the same sentiments*, Malachi thought.

"Damn, she even took the phone with her," he said aloud to no one. To his dismay the battery on his cell phone had gone dead. Malachi walked out on the balcony and looked down on the cars in the parking lot. He thought about jumping from the second-floor apartment. Suicidal thoughts were becoming more and more pronounced in him, though he would deny them if asked. The suicidal situation with the knife had been an attention stunt that he had taken too far. Never in his wildest dreams had he imagined that Nyree would have called 911 about the situation. When she did not cave in and give him his way, he continued to play dead. It had been humiliating for Malachi to be put into the police car and taken to the psychiatric hospital. During the drive there, he kept thinking that the officers would just take him back to the base and everything would be fine. However, when they escorted him into the hospital and left him there he was sorry that he had cut his wrist. What had been meant to scare Nyree had backfired on him.

Four days in that place felt like an eternity. Going to groups to talk about his feelings had made him feel uncomfortable but having a bedtime was the worst. Nyree laughed at him when he told her that he had to get off the telephone because it was bedtime.

"What?" she questioned him about the comment.

"I said I have to go because it is bedtime."

"Ha. Ha. See what playing crazy got you - it got you a bedtime. Whoever heard of a grown man having a bedtime? Oh, well, obviously you have since you have one. Do they read you a bedtime story, too? Ha. Ha. I'm sorry, that is just too funny to me, a bedtime," she said and then hung up.

Her condescending comments had infuriated him so much that he went into the room and pounded his fists, causing a slight indentation in the wall. One of the nurses walking by observed the incident and told him that it was that kind of behavior that would prolong his stay at the hospital.

Malachi lit a Swisher Sweet cigar and smoked it while looking down on the cars. He visualized his body falling over the rail and hitting the cars below. Blood was everywhere and his neck was broken, but he was at peace.

He felt calm as he smoked the cigar. "Why do you smoke?" He heard the voice of his young cousin Jamal playing in his head.

"It calms me down," was Malachi's response.

Jamal had chuckled and said, "It's funny how the enemy has gotten our young black men fooled into thinking that indulging in alcohol and smoking makes us feel better. That's just a trick of the enemy. All you are doing is paying to speed up your death."

Jamal's words had reminded him of Nyree and her lectures. Malachi had not been in the mood for it, so he shooed his comments away in the same way that one would swat an annoying fly and said, "Go on, Man, with all that. You are making my high come down. Don't nobody want to hear all that philosophical bullshit."

Jamal simply laughed and as he walked away he uttered, "Hear me now or hear me later, but you will hear me. I just hope it's not too late."

The last phrase was replaying in Malachi's head now: "... hope it's not too late." What was that supposed to mean? Malachi wondered as he was hearing Jamal loud and clear now

Hey, Boo," Malachi said as he gripped the pay phone receiver in front of Burger King.

"Hey," Ciara said hesitantly as she watched Jeremiah eat the last of the chicken wings off the platter. Then she rushed into the bathroom so that she could speak more freely.

"So, you decide to return a phone call now? Where were you when your son was sick?" She scolded Malachi.

He sighed at her comment. Why did all of the women in his life feel the need to lecture him and give him the third degree?

"Look, why don't you come swoop me so I can come over there?" There was a long pause. "Are you still there?" Malachi asked.

Twenty-Six

Ciara sat on the toilet looking at the mint-green rug on the floor wondering what it matched in the bathroom. Everything else was either pink or lavender. "Yeah, I'm here."

"Well, are you going to come get me?" Malachi said.

Ciara did not know what to do. She had just started dating Jeremiah two weeks ago and things were going well. He had been reluctant to pursue anything with her when she told him that she had a child.

"I don't want any baby daddy drama," Jeremiah told her when she said that she had a child that was not even a year old.

"I can promise you that it won't be any drama. He's married," had been her response. Jeremiah looked shocked and did not try to conceal it, "Dang, girl. That sounds like drama. So, are you like a homewrecker?"

Ciara shrugged off his insensitive remark.

"Naw. He got married before I had the baby and he didn't tell me that he was getting married until two days before the wedding. But there is nothing between the two of us and he doesn't even come around to his son. I think he moved."

"What do you mean you think he moved? You don't know?"

"He's AWOL from the Navy and one of his boys said that he went home and hasn't been back."

Jeremiah had let his guard down and became involved with a woman with a child. It was something he said that he would never do. Ciara tapped her finger on the porcelain bowl and told Malachi that she would pick him up from the Burger King on Monument Road in about thirty minutes. Then she hung up. She flushed the toilet and washed her hands. When she walked back into the living room, she noticed Jeremiah watching a show on the Discovery Channel.

"Is everything alright?"

Ciara hastily said, "Yeah, I have to go pick up my brother. He has a situation and needs me."

Jeremiah raised one of his bushy eyebrows and said, "Oh, I can ride with you, if you want."

"That's nice of you, but it's kind of an

embarrassing situation, and I know that he would appreciate it if I came alone," she said while walking him to the door.

Feeling as if he were being pushed out of the door, he turned on his heel and said, "Well, I guess I'll talk to you when you get back."

Her mind was a million miles away and she was half listening to him. She smiled and said, "Oh, yeah," and pushed the door closed. Quickly she ran to the bathroom to touch up her makeup and brush her hair. She could not remember the last time she had seen Malachi and she wanted to be looking her best. Ciara wanted him to look at her once and see what he was missing. While she wanted to know where he had been and what he had been doing, she took delight in knowing that he had turned to her in his time of need- not his wife. It would be just the two of them because Camron was spending the night at her sister's house.

"So, whose ride is this?" Malachi asked as he reclined in the passenger's seat.

"It's mine." Ciara beamed at Malachi as she drove down Arlington Expressway.

"Yeah, right."

"On the boss it is." Ciara laughed.

Malachi lightly jabbed her in the shoulder. "Don't be lying on my nation. I'll have to 'f' you up."

Ciara rolled her shoulders back. "What's up with you? I was just kidding about the boss stuff. I only said it because you say it all the time when you want me to believe you. Anyways my dad bought it for me at the auction two weeks ago. He said that I needed a car to get me and Camron around."

"Where is my little man at?"

"He's with Kita."

"Oh, I know that's your sister but I can't stand her ass." he said with a scowl. "So, where are you driving me to?" asked Malachi.

"To my place," replied Ciara.

"Your place as in your very own crib?"

"Yeah."

"You go 'head on, Girl. You've been doing big things since I've been gone. It's good to know that my child support money is going to a good cause."

"Whatever." She said rolled her eyes.

"This is straight," he commented as he walked into her two-bedroom, one-story house. He went into the kitchen and stuck his head in the refrigerator as if he had put something in it. Disappointed that there was nothing inside that caught his fancy, he kicked the door closed. That was when he spied two wine glasses on the counter. One glass had red lipstick around the rim and the other did not.

"Make yourself at home," Ciara called from a back room to Malachi. "I'm going to jump in the shower. I'm hot as hell."

"All right," he called back and pounced onto the zebra-striped couch. He regretted having done so because he felt as if he were sitting on the ground. Ciara had no sense of style, Malachi thought. He had gotten spoiled living with Nyree. She would never have a couch or sofa, as she called it, that you would sit on and your booty would hit the floor. The apartment looked as if it had been furnished with items from the flea market.A ten-foot faux plant in the corner was hideous, but it did coincide with the zoo theme that she had in the living room. Flipping through the stations on the television frustrated him as he was unable to find anything that he wanted to see. The telephone rang once and he ignored it, twice and his curiosity was piqued. On the third ring he walked over to the breakfast bar where the phone and the caller ID monitor were placed. When he looked at the screen, he saw the name Jeremiah Floyd. Who was Jeremiah Floyd? It wasn't a name that he knew, so he decided that if it rang one more time he would have to answer it. It rang and he answered it.

"Hello," Malachi said in a deep voice with authority as if he was paying bills at Ciara's residence.

"Hello, is Ciara there?" Jeremiah asked not certain if he had dialed the right number.

"Yeah, she's here but she's in the shower right now. Who dis?"

"Ur...this is Jeremiah. Is this her brother?"

"Brother? Naw, this is Malachi, the father of her child. Carlos is in jail serving twenty on that murder charge."

"I see. Well, tell her I called."

"Will do, Man." Malachi hung up the telephone wondering if he had said too much. From the way the dude reacted to hearing about Carlos, Malachi suspected that he had provided the caller with too much information or at best with some information that the caller did not have prior to the conversation. When Malachi looked down the hall, still there was no sign of Ciara.

Listening to the running water, he was able to locate the bathroom. When he opened the door, the steam hit him in the face. He quickly got out of his clothes and jumped in the shower behind Ciara. He began caressing her breasts. She jumped so he had to hold her tightly to steady her balance because she almost slipped and fell. When he began circling her neck with his tongue, he felt her breasts perk up. The warm water splashed over their bodies as they washed each other. They were unable to contain their lust for one another, so they jumped out of the shower and ran to the bedroom to relieve their sexual tensions. After they climaxed, they just lay on their backs and stared at the ceiling until sleep fell upon them.

Ciara wondered if he had experienced such passion with his wife. *Wife? I wonder if I am going to burn in hell for this,* she thought to herself as she felt guilty for having indulged in such pleasure with another woman's husband. How would she have felt if she were married and her husband gave another woman the type of pleasure she had just experienced with Malachi?

Malachi looked up at the ceiling and then stared absently out the window at nothing. He had faked a climax which was something that he had never done before. The sex had been good, but Ciara was not his wife so it just did not feel right. Could it be that he was developing a conscience? Even still, he knew that he was going to have to do something that was going to be degrading.

He was in "dire straits" and had no one to turn to but Ciara. He needed money and a place to stay, so he would give her the best sex in the world in return for what he needed. Just thinking about it made him feel filthy and dirty. He was no better than a prostitute. This is what Nyree had reduced him to- a prostitute. Finally, sleep came to him. When he woke he was covered in sweat as there was no air conditioning in the house. Ciara was gone.

He tiptoed to the bathroom door and heard her whispering on the phone to somebody. Then she said, "I got to go, I think I heard him."

Quickly he scurried back into the room and slipped on his underwear.

When Ciara returned to the bedroom, he said, "So, who is Jeremiah, your little boyfriend?"

Her eyes bulged. *"Huh?* I don't know what you're talking about."

"Well, he called earlier and for some reason he thought I was your brother. I don't know why he thought that, but he did. So, I told him about Carlos being in jail."

"You did what? Who told you to answer my phone?" She was furious.

"I mean it just kept ringing and ringing and I felt stupid sitting there listening, so I answered it. Did I salt your game?" he said with a devious and satisfied look.

He was not quite sure why he took so much satisfaction in causing her grief. Maybe it was because his game had been salted so much that he felt the need to interfere with her relationships. Malachi was lashing out at Ciara, and he was not sure why as she had not done anything to hurt him. But that wasn't how life was- people picked on the one they viewed to be weaker but shied away from confronting the strong.

Suddenly, he realized that he was not thinking because this was the same person whom he had intended to ask for money. Well, so much for that plan. Now he was going to have to resort to what he did best- steal. Never before had he stolen from Ciara, but there was a first time for everything. Besides, what made her different from anyone else? If he stole from his mama, the woman who had given him life, and Nyree, the love of his life, what made Ciara exempt?

"Ooh, I hate you," Ciara said with a straight face. It was hard for Malachi to tell if she was serious or if she was just playing. If she was serious, he couldn't blame her for feeling that way considering what he had put her through and what he was going to put her through.

Ciara drove from work wondering where Malachi was as she had called home seven times today and not received an answer. She looked at the different gauges on the dashboard and realized that she was driving on fumes. As she pulled up in front of the pump, she contemplated using the twenty in her wallet for gas to get ten dollars' worth. However, if she did, then that would only leave her ten dollars until payday which was three days away. Finally, she decided to use her emergency credit card. She hated to charge gas, but since she was driving on vapors it constituted an emergency.

As she dug in her wallet she noticed that the card was not there. Now that was strange, because she always kept the card behind her license, and her license was there. *Calm down,* she coaxed herself. Haste makes waste and she figured that she was so anxious to find out what Malachi had been doing all day that she was overlooking the card. After looking through every single item in her purse she realized that not only was her credit card missing but her bankcard was missing as well. She wished that she could blame someone for stealing from her at the home improvement store where she worked but she could not. She always locked her purse in her glove compartment. Maybe she had left the cards in her other purse that she had taken to the nightclub on Saturday night when she and Malachi had gone out. After more thought, she realized that was impossible. All of the other items from the smaller purse were now in her purse.

"Well, I'll just have to break the twenty," she said as she began searching for the folded piece of currency in her checkbook. As luck would have it, that, too, was missing.

She had begun to cry out of frustration.

What was she going to do? She was ten minutes from home but seriously doubted that her car would make the journey. Her car sputtered. Not knowing what to do or whom to call, she dialed, hoping that Malachi would pick up the telephone.

The only answer she received was her voice mail. "I can't call Mom or Dad. I don't want them to know how irresponsible I have been," she said to herself. She also knew that she could not call her parents because when they found out that she had let Malachi stay with her for the past two weeks, they told her that she was dumb and stupid. Her response had been, "What's wrong with us wanting to be a family and having my son's father in the house?"

Her dad shouted, "Don't call me when he leaves you and gets tired of playing house. Where was he when your son was sick? Who bought you the car? Who helped you get that house?"

Pride would not allow her to call her parents. The only other person whom she knew that she could depend on in this world was her sister Kita. There would be a myriad of questions from Kita as to why she had not called Malachi. Kita had already asked Ciara why

Malachi could not watch Camron during the day since he was not working. When Ciara told Kita that he was out searching for work, Kita and the interrogation ceased. Ciara hated lying and making excuses for Malachi, but it was the only means of avoiding the third degree.

It took Kita ten minutes to arrive at the gas station. Ciara's self-esteem diminished when she saw Kita pull up with her two children and Camron. Ciara had never really liked pumping gas, but now she inhaled the fumes and was thankful to be able to do so. The simple things in life never give you such pleasure until you are unable to indulge in them. Ciara promised herself that as long as she lived, this would never happen again.

Although the speedometer on her green 1986 car was not functioning, Ciara was sure that she had to have driven at least seventy-five miles per hour all the way home. She was anxious to see Malachi, to hear where he had been and what he had been doing all day. In her opinion, a man without a job and without any money could not have been doing much during the day. In the past days, she became frustrated with his, "Let me get five dollars. Let me get ten dollars."

She wanted to tell him that she was tired of playing house and that he could go home to his wife. Finally, she had to tell him that he needed to seek employment or at least get a hustle. "Sell some T-shirts, cigarettes, something. But don't think you're going to nickel-and-dime me." If she was getting up going to work every day, certainly he could work. If she heard about what happened on the talk shows and the soap operas one more time, smacking him was going to be inevitable. Had she wanted to really know what happened on those shows, she could have set her VCR to record them.

"Malachi. Malachi," Ciara shouted as she closed her front door that had been unlocked when she opened it. How many times did she have to tell him to lock the bottom lock when he left? His standard response was always, "It ain't like somebody wants something up out of here." Ciara was well aware that she did not own much. However, the things she did were not exactly top-of-the-line items, but they were hers and she was proud of them. While he was criticizing her and making jokes, what was he bringing to the table?

Ciara cried like a baby when she realized that Malachi had gone and probably gone for good. He had taken her money, credit card, and self-respect with him and left her with a yeast infection. She blamed the yeast infection on him since she was not experiencing any of those symptoms prior to his stay with her. Now she knew what he was doing while she was at work-having unprotected sex with somebody and then having sex with her when she came home. This was the cruel wake-up call that she needed in order for her to cut her ties with Malachi. "A hard head makes a soft behind," her mother often said. Now, Ciara knew exactly what her mother meant by that phrase.

Twenty-Seven

Colin sat at the board table with his head in his hands. When he did business, ten o'clock meant ten o'clock not ten- twenty. He had been waiting twenty minutes for Mr. Shaw's daughter to make an appearance and he was becoming tired and agitated. Mr. Shaw's great idea was to have the two of them work together. One would have thought that his daughter would have at least had the decency to be punctual. From what Colin had heard about her, he gathered that she was a spoiled brat used to getting her way and having everybody waiting on her. He had worked hard to get where he was in life and resented people who hand things handed to them just because of connections. In a minute he was going to leave the conference room. The whole notion of working with this woman had him anxious and stressed out. Colin's head was pounding. He hated to wait for anything or anyone. Tina had told him to go into the meeting with a positive attitude, but it was becoming more and more difficult.

Colin looked at his watch. It was fastly approaching ten-thirty. "Um, Mr. Shaw, maybe we should reschedule this meeting, as I have some clients scheduled for later this morning," Colin said to Mr. Shaw.

"Good morning. Good morning. Please forgive my tardiness. I had a situation that I absolutely had to deal with," Nyree announced cheerfully as she entered the door and gave her dad a kiss on the cheek.

Colin looked at the woman in awe and Nyree's smile faded as she honed in on Colin's face. Edwin noticed the awkwardness between his daughter and Colin Jordan.

"Well, allow me to do the introductions. Colin Jordan, this is my daughter, Nyree Shaw Chandler. Nyree, this is Colin Jordan, owner of Beach Body Gyms. He is expanding his franchise in the Midwest and each one of our properties will have a Beach Body Gym."

"Uh-huh, I see. Can I speak with you outside for a moment?" asked Nyree.

"Colin, excuse us for a moment," Edwin said while eyeing Nyree curiously. Through clenched teeth Edwin asked Nyree why the sudden exit was necessary.

"Is this who you met while you were in Jacksonville?"

"Yes," Edwin said, expecting Nyree to have had something more important to say. "Is this what you called me out here to ask?"

"Yes. I mean, no. This is the person who you want me to work with?"

"Yes. Is there something wrong?"

"No. Let's go back in."

Colin tried to read Edwin's and Nyree's faces when they returned to the room, but they were wearing their poker faces, so he could not determine what might have been discussed when they left. Edwin handed Colin and Nyree a proposal of what he wanted to occur with the project and asked them to return in a week with the goals, ideas, and progress. Nyree cleared her throat. *"A week?* Do you really think that is sufficient time to…?"

Edwin waved his hand and shook his head. "Time is not on our side. We have competition out there. I am confident that the two of you will have something worked out by next week. Have a good day." Edwin smiled to himself as he shut the door and left Colin and Nyree at the table.

Nyree grabbed her purse and headed for the door when Colin said, "Don't you think we need to talk?"

"Maybe, but right now is not good for me. I have another appointment. You can schedule an appointment with Barbara if you want to talk to me."

"Schedule an appointment with you? What kind of stuff is that, Nyree?"

"Look, Mr. Jordan, you weren't so interested in talking to me when you left town without as much as a good-bye."

"I came by your job and you were hugged up with your husband, the one you claimed that you had no feelings for and from whom you were going to get a divorce."

"My marriage is none of your business and I know you're not talking when you told me that you worked at the gym. You never said that you *owned* the gyms."

"Your marriage is public knowledge. And I did work at the gym and train clients, so if you are trying to insinuate that I lied about that, I did not. I just didn't say that I owned the gyms. You weren't exactly forthcoming about your finances either…"

"Whatever, Mr. Jordan."

"Yeah, whatever."

Colin could not believe how infuriated he had become when she slammed the door as she left the room. How was he going to work with her if she behaved so childishly? He never expected Mr. Shaw's daughter to be Nyree. For that matter he never thought that he would ever see her again and that their encounter would be so unpleasant.

***

"Tina, you will never guess who Mr. Shaw's daughter is?"

"Who? Is she somebody famous?" replied Tina, Colin's sister.

"She's famous here in Gary. I told you about what some people were whispering about her in the office. Anyways, his daughter is Nyree."

Tina let out a chuckle. "Nyree? *Your* Nyree."

"She's not *my* Nyree, but it is the same Nyree I used to tell you about."

"What do you mean she's not *your* Nyree? You certainly could have had me fooled by the way you used to talk about her. It was Nyree this. Nyree that. What happened?"

"I don't know. Now that I'm here on her stomping grounds her attitude is totally different."

"You mean because her daddy is the boss, she is acting snooty."

"No, it's… I cannot really explain it. She treated me like a peon. She had the nerve to say that if I wanted to contact her about this project to schedule an appointment with her through Barbara. Can you believe that?"

"I find that hard to believe. Did you leave Jacksonville on bad terms with her?"

"You might say that. I told you about her husband making the scene at the apartment. After that I never really did see or talk to her again. I stopped by the bookstore to say good-bye to her, but when I drove through the parking lot she was standing next to her car embracing her husband. I just kept going."

"Well…"

"Well. Is that all you have to say?" Colin was hoping that his sister would provide more insight into the problem. She always had some advice and the best that she could do now was "well?" Tina decided not to say anything further about the situation. She knew that her brother had fallen for Nyree and the fact that Nyree was married did not help the situation.

Tina warned him that spending time with that married woman was not a good idea and although she wanted to remind him that she knew now was not the time to say, "I told you so." Tina thought about the business aspect of things and reminded Colin of his purpose for going to the Midwest.

"Colin, remember why you went to Gary. We are going to expand our franchises to the Midwest and eventually across the country. You two are going to have to put aside your personal life and get down to business. Now if you think it is going to be too much for you to work with this girl, then I'll come up there and handle the Midwest operations. You can come back down here and manage the Southern operations," she said with a smile.

Tina knew that Colin hated to fail or seem like he was running away from a situation, so his leaving would not be an option. In his sternest voice, he said, "No, you stay put. I can handle this."

Tina smiled. "That's what I thought. Well, I'll be looking forward to hearing from you this weekend. Love you. Later."

Twenty-Eight

June 1996

"Mr. Shaw, we have completed our investigation and have a complete report ready. Do you want to schedule an appointment for..." Amber of Dilworth Detective Agency asked. Edwin sat behind his massive cherry wood desk holding the telephone receiver in his hand while staring at the picture of him and Margo.

"No. Give it to me straight," Edwin said, half- annoyed that Amber would be so formal with him. He understood that she was new to the agency, but someone should have told her that he always received his reports verbally, and the written reports were hand-delivered to him via messenger.

Amber Sinclair drew in a deep breath and then exhaled slowly. She reminded herself to count to ten before speaking as he was really beginning to try her patience. Edwin Shaw was a valued client of the agency and if she made him angry she would never hear the end of it. Amber had only volunteered to take the case because she thought that it involved Malachi Chandler. She did not care what anyone said about him; he was a sexy brother and she believed that given the chance she could tame him. Even though she did not have the best track record with men, she thought it would be different with Malachi. To her dismay the case actually involved money transfers to a retirement community in Florida. When she found out, it was too late. Besides, this was her opportunity to redeem herself with the family as everyone had their eyes on her. Just because she had been placed on probation did not mean that they had to watch her like a hawk. Her mother, Hannah Sinclair, told her that she had brought shame upon the family by being involved in such a scandal and that she should be thankful to her great-grandmother for giving her the opportunity to work for the agency.

"I am thankful," Amber had whined, "but it's not a big deal. People get on probation all the time."

"Do you hear yourself, Amber?" asked

Hannah Sinclair.

"Yeah. What's the big deal?"

"The big deal is that you could have gone to jail."

"For what? I did not kill anybody. I just smacked Allen upside the head with the gun a couple of times and I bitch-slapped that woman he was with. Nobody disrespects me and gets away with it- **NOBODY.**"

Amber wanted to remind her mother like she had to remind Allen. Allen had been living with Amber and off of Amber's money. She had not minded when things were going well. However, when she received a phone call that he was at The Jukebox buying rounds of drinks for everybody in VIP and was hugged up with a girl with a bad weave, Amber got out of her bed and got ready. She slid into her size-four jeans, an old white sweatshirt, and combed her wavy locks into a ponytail. Then she braided the ponytail, twisted it around until it formed a circle. Then she secured the loose ends of hair under a rubber band. She placed all of her jewelry on her dresser in her jewelry box. This was her "going to battle" attire. It was not her modus operandi to go around pistol-whipping guys in clubs and smacking chicks with bad weaves. However, when a man thought that he was going to take her money and spend it on another woman, then her behavior became a little erratic.

"Amber, I can not talk to you when you are this irrational. If you had not been a part of the Dilworth family, you would have done some serious jail time for what you did," lectured Amber's mother.

"Ok, Ma, dang, would you give it a rest already? I did my community service and all that other stuff. Stop tripping. You would have done the same thing if you thought an imp was trying to play you," the twenty-two- year-old woman told her mother.

Amber sat behind the desk playing with long curly locks as she decided how to handle Edwin Shaw. She could just give him the information, but the problem was she did not like his tone or his arrogance. He spoke as if he were the king and she was the serf. She wanted to tell him that she was just as important as he was.

It bothered her that people in prominent positions thought they should be given special privileges. If the protocol at the agency was to make an appointment and to receive information, why should it be any different for Edwin Shaw? However, as she looked at the computer screen, she read that Mr. Shaw always received his information over the telephone. A messenger delivered the hard copy to his office or wherever he requested for it to be sent.

"Amber, are you still there?" Edwin asked. He had not heard her say anything in what felt like forever.

"Yes, Mr. Shaw, I am still here. I was reviewing the case note," she lied while trying to soften her voice. She felt like a fool now. If she had read the follow-up procedure prior to calling him, then all of this could have been avoided. "Mr. Shaw, we found out that the money that is being debited from your wife's account every month is going to Royal Springs Retirement Community in Jacksonville, Florida."

"Jacksonville?" Edwin said in a shocked tone. No wonder Margo had been reluctant to go with him to Jacksonville. She probably thought that when he invited her on the trip that he knew what she was up to.

"Yes," Amber said and then continued, "It seems that your wife has been paying for a Mr. Lucas Tate to stay there for the past five years."

"Who the hell is Lucas Tate?"

"Mr. Shaw, I have got to tell you before we continue that some of this information may be a bit shocking and disturbing. You may want me to send the report over."

"No, no, go ahead. I will behave, I promise. I don't mean to yell at you."

"Are you sure you don't want me to have one of our people deliver it?"

"I want to hear it first; otherwise, this old man will die from suspense. You don't want that, do you?" Edwin asked Amber.

She had to chuckle now because if he had asked five minutes ago, she would have prolonged providing the wait, just to see if he would die. Something told her that he was too mean and ornery to die. He had to be fifty-something, she figured. She arrived at the estimate because his son Kyle was knocking on thirty. Nyree had to be in her late twenties although she didn't look a day over twenty-one. Edwin was about six feet tall, with a medium build, brown complexion and jet-black hair that was slightly graying at the temples. His suits were tailored-made.

Amber was not sure how she knew that

detail about him, but she could tell that his suits were not store-bought. There was something about a man in a suit or a uniform that Amber found to be quite attractive.

Drawing herself away from her fantasies of Edwin she said, "No, don't go dying on me. So, Lucas Tate is your wife's father. Now I have to admit coming by this fact was difficult as the staff at Royal Springs did not want to divulge this information. Apparently, your wife, Margo, used to be Dr. Allyson Margo Tate who was dubbed the 'Love Doctor' in Tallahassee…"

"Slow down. You're telling me that my wife's father is alive in a retirement community which I am paying for and that my wife is going by a different name. She used to live in Tallahassee, although she led me to believe the first time she had ever been to Florida was with me when we took the kids to Disney World. This does not make sense. Why would she lie about this?"

"Okay, Mr. Shaw, now this is where it gets really interesting, so please sit down if you are not already sitting down. Your wife had been a stripper at one time to provide herself with college money. She became involved with a former client, Simon Wade. She had provided marriage counseling for him and his wife. They ended up getting a divorce and your wife and him became an item. According to reports he dumped your wife for another woman, and shortly after, he ended up dead. Your wife was the only suspect in the case but was found not guilty. She then dropped Allyson from her name, used just Margo, moved to Indiana, and I guess the rest is history. Now I am not sure as to how and why she reconnected with her father. I did meet her father when I did my undercover investigation at Royal Springs. Nice fellow. It seems that the only income he has is from the rich husband and his daughter, whom he hasn't seen in over thirty years. When I prompted him for more information, he became very agitated and defensive. That concludes my report. There are pictures and articles attached with the report."

"Thank you, Amber."

"You're welcome. Have a good day," she said and hung up the telephone.

Twenty-Nine

"Finally, you're here," Kyle greeted Nyree as she walked into the living room of their parents' home. Nyree was shocked to see Kyle there because her father had vowed that Kyle would never step foot into the home again. She was trying to brace herself for the news of someone's death. Whatever it was that her mother had to say had to be serious if Kyle had been allowed inside the house, although she suspected that her mother allowed Kyle access when her father was not around.

"Okay. Okay, I'm here. What was so urgent, Mother, that I had to get over here right away?" Nyree asked.

"Well, sit down. Stay awhile," Margo said.

Nyree just wanted to go home and relax. She desperately wanted this day to be over. Having to stop by her parents' home had not been on her agenda for today.

"Well, I had been keeping this secret and after over thirty years, I never thought..."

"Oh, my goodness, Mother, don't even tell me that you're pregnant," Nyree blurted out.

"No, it's nothing like that. Although, that would be much easier to say than what I'm going to say. Your father and I are going to get a divorce. I will be moving out within the next two weeks."

"What?" Nyree questioned. If her parents were going to get a divorce, it made her question if a thing called *true love* really existed. Her parents had their little spats, but overall she characterized them as having a storybook marriage.

"I knew it. I knew it. He's been cheating? Don't tell me he laid a hand on you. Did he? I will kill him. I swear it," Kyle said.

Nyree felt uncomfortable at Kyle's accusations about her father and the fact her father was not there to defend himself added to her uneasiness.

"No, this is my entire fault," Margo said.

Nyree's head was beginning to spin. Did she just hear her mother accept responsibility for something?

"I have kept a secret from him and you all

and I hope once I tell you all you will be able to forgive me. My father, Lucas Tate, is alive and well...," began Margo.

"What?" Both Kyle and Nyree chimed in unison.

"We have a grandfather that is alive. I thought you said he was dead. Where has he been all these years?" Nyree wanted to know. She felt cheated.

"He's been in Florida. I don't know what he has been doing all these years. I just regained contact with him five years ago. He saw me and Edwin on the cover of *Black Enterprise* and he located me and has been blackmailing me ever since..."

"Blackmailing you? Why would he do that?" Kyle asked.

"Look, let me tell you the story without any interruptions and when I'm finished, you can ask your questions. Agreed?"

Both Kyle and Nyree nodded their heads to indicate that they agreed to the request. Nyree walked over to the bar and made herself an apple martini. She had the feeling that she was not going to be able to handle whatever Margo was going to say in a completely sober state.

"My mother died like I told you all before. She left me a large sum of money for my college education. The problem was that when I graduated there was no money because my father had squandered it in bad business deals. He kicked me out the house when I asked about the money and at that point he became dead to me. I became involved with a guy named James who owned a strip club. I stripped for a while to make money and then James demanded that I stop stripping, and he paid my way through school. Those were some pretty dim years with James. I became a successful marriage counselor and was even nicknamed 'The Love Doctor.' I counseled a couple who eventually divorced. The man and I became involved with each other. His name was Simon. At his cousin's funeral, Simon brought another woman and announced his engagement to her. We were broken up at that time - about two, or maybe even three-weeks. I thought we were going to work it out. We didn't. Somebody killed Simon later that night. The police figured that I must have done it. There was a trial and I was found not guilty. You all cannot imagine my humiliation and when the newspapers got a hold of the story.

Well, I don't have to tell you all how cruel the media can be. Nyree, you know. I changed my name from Allyson Margo Tate to Margo Tate and moved from Tallahassee to Gary. After seeing that story on us, my father called here a couple of times asking to speak to Allyson. Each time he was told that he had the wrong number. He assumed that Edwin did not know about my colorful past so he's blackmailing me. For the past five years, I have been giving my father an allowance and paying for him to live in Royal Springs Retirement Community in Jacksonville, Florida. Edwin had the Dilworth Detective Agency investigate a debit that was occurring on our monthly bank statement and when he found this out, he told me he wanted a divorce. He said he did not know who he had married and just chalked up thirty years to irreconcilable differences. Can you believe it?"

"No," Nyree said as she clutched her purse. Her mother walked over to her and hugged her. "I knew you would understand, Nyree."

"No, I can't believe that you are acting like you're the victim here, Mother. We've all been the victims of your lies," Nyree said as she ran out of the house.

Sitting in her car she toyed with the platinum pacifier medallion that hung from her platinum chain. It had been a birthday gift from her mother. The inscription on the back read, *I love you, Baby Girl. Love, Mom.* Nyree did not know what to think. Had her mother been truthful in there with her and Kyle or had she told them half the truth in order to pacify them? Who was her mother? Allyson or Margo? Was her mother Dr. Jekyll and Mr. Hyde? She was always acting so prissy and looking down her nose at other people. She had a horrible past.

"Don't tell lies. There is no such thing as a small lie. A lie is a lie. What goes on in the dark will come out in the light," she could hear her mother's squeaky voice telling her while she was growing up.

Nyree laughed as she recalled how her mother had glossed over the part of her life when she used to be a stripper. She had mentioned it so casually. Margo had spoken about it the way one might speak about working at a restaurant or a library in order to obtain money to fund her schooling. And James, who was he? He had to have been pretty significant for her to remember his name.

Nyree wondered if he had been more than her boss. Perhaps Nyree would hire Dilworth Detective Agency to dig a little deeper. If the story had gone as Margo had wanted Nyree and Kyle to believe, then why had Margo's father blackmailed her? Nyree wanted answers. For Nyree, the story was not adding up.

Kyle watched Nyree back out of the driveway and speed down the street. He understood Nyree's anger, but he also knew what it felt like to have your back up against a wall. It was why he had not deserted his mother in her time of need. "Well, Ma, I don't know what to say. Far be it for me to judge. I love you and I'm here for you. Whatever you need me to do, consider it done."

Thirty

Margo hugged her son and whispered, "Thank you."

Margo hugged her son tightly, a quiet "Thank you" slipping from her lips. It felt strange to find comfort in him, the last person she'd expected would even try to understand her. She'd always carried guilt as a mother—guilt that she hadn't fought hard enough when the school system labeled him, placing him in special needs classes. She'd convinced herself that the stigma weighed on him, that it fueled his teenage rebellion, maybe even the lingering anger he still carried.

Deep down, she knew she could have done more, pushed harder, but fear held her back. She'd worried that opposing Edwin too much would drive a wedge into their marriage, and she wasn't about to let a man leave her again. Margo always said she'd be the one to walk away if it came down to it. But now, with her marriage crumbling, that fierce independence felt more like an empty echo.

Margo's emotions were a tangled mess of numbness, bitterness, and regret. It would be easy to point fingers—at Edwin, at her own father, who'd squandered her college fund and sent her spiraling down a different path. But she knew the hard truth: this was a mess of her own making, a bed she'd made decades ago.

***

"Why were you going through my bank statements? Why did you have the situation investigated? Why didn't you just come to me?" Margo had bombarded Edwin with those questions when he presented the evidence to her.

Edwin had stared her down as if she were a two- dollar whore and said, "Honestly, I don't know why I handled the situation in the manner that I did. It does not matter now. This is where it ends. This is where I stop playing the fool. All of these years, the joke has been on me, well, not anymore sweetie. It's over."

She cringed when he referred to her as "sweetie." He had called her "sweetie," knowing that was one of her pet peeves.

She prepared for a bitter divorce even

though he promised to be fair. His definition of fair differed from hers. They had worked together in business and, in her opinion, he had "screwed" a lot of people under the pretense of being fair.

That night he did not come to their bedroom. She had hoped that he would come to bed, they would talk and things would be like they had been in the old days. At this point it did not really matter. Neither one of them had been happy with each other in years, but neither one of them wanted to be the one to voice their concern.

The spice had gone out of their marriage right around the time Nyree graduated from high school. Edwin often stayed up late working on various projects and would fall asleep in his home office or in the guest room. Offers to accompany him on business trips had ceased. In many ways she had been happy that he had not invited her, because her excuses for not being able to go were beginning to sound just like that- excuses. Their sex life was practically non-existent. They had only had sex three times during 1995 and even then he had acted as if he were doing her a favor. Margo was tired of pretending to have orgasms, so it was just as well that they were not having sex.

Thirty-One

"Mom, I'm so sorry," Kyle said while trying to think of something more profound to say to comfort his mother.

Through tears and sniffles she said, "I am so sorry, too. My behavior is inexcusable and I hope that one day you and your sister will be able to forgive me. You don't know the agony that I have lived with all of these years. In a way, I'm glad that it is out. I feel as though a weight has been lifted from me. Enough about me; what's going on with you? Tell me this; tell me the honest to God truth. Did you stab Malachi? Whatever you say will remain between us."

"Will it remain between us?" Kyle asked not really sure if he could trust his mother. After all she had just admitted to having lived a lie for all of his life and most of her life. "Yeah, you can trust me."

Kyle wanted to tell her that saying the words, "you can trust me," generally did not add to a person's credibility. In fact, it had been his experience that those words caused one to raise an eyebrow and proceed with caution. Since she was in a vulnerable state, he decided not to tell her that. He tried to imagine her humiliation and how his father had ripped her apart. Kyle had thought that she was going to tell him and Nyree that Edwin was not his father. He would have been able to swallow that bitter pill better than the one she had just forced down.

"Yes. I did it. They do not have any witnesses who will say that I did it. But if I know Bianca, she will find somebody. Malachi was even saying that he was not sure that I did it."

"Bianca? The same Bianca that you used to date?"

"Yeah, she has it out for me. She's been snooping and hovering everywhere trying to turn up some dirt on me."

"What happened between the two of you?"

"Ma, I don't know. She started letting the 'm' word slip out of her mouth too much for me and talking about what type of ring she wanted. I couldn't handle it."

"I thought she got married."

"She did. I heard that she just recently

went through a bitter divorce with the guy. I don't know. I just wish she would leave me alone."

"If you were able to refocus her attention and divert it away from the case, at least until this thing blows over, then maybe…"

He smiled at what his mother had said. He liked the way she was thinking. "Then maybe the district attorney would not have a leg to stand on. That sounds so low-down and dirty. I like it. I like it a lot. You think she will go for it?" queried Margo's son.

"What's not to go for? You are handsome and you have money. She's vulnerable and probably feeling like she has something to prove, so she's going after you like a person deprived of food for five days would go after a steak."

"I don't know, Ma. She's tough and she's good at what she does."

"I'm not worried about her. My money's on you," replied Margo.

"Well, Ma. I'm going to get out of here. If you want to come stay with me, my door is always open. *Mi casa es su casa* and I mean that."

"I appreciate that. My place will be ready in two weeks, so I should be able to manage until that time. Besides, I would never dream of imposing on you."

"It's no imposition. The offer still stands. Where is this place?"

"Let's do lunch tomorrow and I'll take you there to see it. Your favorite restaurant tomorrow, at say noon?"

He smiled. She remembered his favorite restaurant. How could he say no to the *Beach Café's* cuisine? The thought of the fried catfish dinner had him already licking his lips. He wanted to know the secret to the recipe at the *Beach Café*, but he could attest to it being the best he had ever tasted. Some places had greasy catfish that tasted good. Although *Beach Café* fried the fish it was not greasy. "It's a date," he said as he hugged her and exited the house. He hopped into his 1996 Range Rover and coasted down the street while thinking about what his mother had told him. He was seriously considering calling Bianca.

Thirty-Two

Nyree and Colin sat at the table in the boardroom awaiting Edwin's entrance. While waiting, they discussed how much fun they'd had the previous evening at ESPN Zone in Chicago. "I really had a good time last night. My life has been so stressful lately, I really needed that," Nyree admitted to Colin as she grabbed her coffee mug and placed it to her lips.

Colin agreed with her assessment of the previous evening. "Yeah, I had a great time myself. I think you were the biggest kid there. You were jumping up and down and laughing and actually smiling. I didn't even know that you could still do that..."

Edwin brushed through the door. *"Do what?"*

Understandably, Colin felt a little embarrassed as he was unsure how much of the conversation Edwin had heard.

"Uh, smile." Colin choked.

Edwin smiled because he sensed some chemistry between his daughter and Colin. Now if he'd had to pick someone for his daughter, it would have been someone like Colin. He definitely would not have chosen Malachi. What sane father would have?

Edwin tried not to interfere in his daughter's life. His motto had been, raise your kids right and hopefully they will make good choices. Disappointment was an understatement when it came to how Edwin felt about Nyree choosing Malachi as a husband. Initially, he tried to dissuade her from marrying Malachi, but when there seemed to be no changing her mind he gave his blessing and prayers. Well, her saga with Malachi would be over next month and then she could move on with her life. He wished he could say the same thing about his marriage to Margo. Their lawyers had financial issues to deal with.

"Dare I ask what that means?" Edwin asked. He saw how uncomfortable his daughter and Colin looked. "Never mind; forget it. I called you all here to tell you that Harvey Miller accepted your bid and proposal. Congratulations! He just signed the contract.

Let's have dinner tomorrow night, my treat at *Wing Wah*."

"It's a deal," Nyree said. He would not get an argument from her. She absolutely loved *Wing Wah's* cuisine. In her opinion, no one in the world had better Chinese Food.

"My schedule is free," Colin answered, trying not to appear overly anxious.

Nyree and Colin had been waiting for Edwin to appear at the restaurant for thirty minutes. However it didn't seem that long as they had been laughing and talking. It felt good to be on good terms with Colin. This was how she remembered their relationship. They had been working so closely together the past couple of weeks that it had been hard for either to be cruel to the other. Colin had admitted that he had been jealous when he saw Nyree in an embrace with Malachi in the bookstore parking lot. She had admitted to being jealous when she saw him at church with Tina. Colin had doubled over in laughter when she confessed.

"How was I supposed to know that was your sister? You never said much about her," Nyree had said.

Nyree looked at her watch. "I wonder

where Daddy is? I hope he is okay." Colin saw the panic in her face and assured her that there was need to worry. "Excuse me, I need to take this," she said as she pressed the talk button on her cellular phone to answer the incoming call.

"Daddy. Where are you?"

Edwin was taken aback by the question, even though he knew that was a logical one. He sat on the edge of the bed with his robe wrapped tightly around him thinking what he would say. He stifled a cough. "I'm at home. I'm not feeling well."

"What was that?" Nyree questioned as she thought that she heard laughter in the background.

"What was what? Probably just a bad connection," he said, turning to Amber while placing a finger to his lips to indicate that she needed to be quiet. "You all enjoy dinner and have them charge it to the company credit card. I wish I could be there with you, but enjoy it for me. Love to you." Edwin hung up.

Nyree looked at Colin and then back down at her phone as she placed it in its carrying case and dropped it back into her handbag. The conversation with her dad seemed a bit peculiar.

"That was my dad. He says that he is not going to make it and that we should have dinner anyway. He said that he was not feeling well, but something just did not seem right. If he were calling from home, why did the phone number come up as 'unavailable' on the screen?"

"What are you now, like 'I Spy' or something?" Colin said in a joking manner as he observed the suspicious look on his dinner companion's face.

"No, you don't know my dad like I do. I know when something is not right."

"You don't think he is in the hospital and just not telling you."

"No, I think he's up to something else. Never mind, let's not let it spoil our evening."

"So, what are you going to order? What do you recommend?" asked Colin as he opened his menu.

Thirty-Three

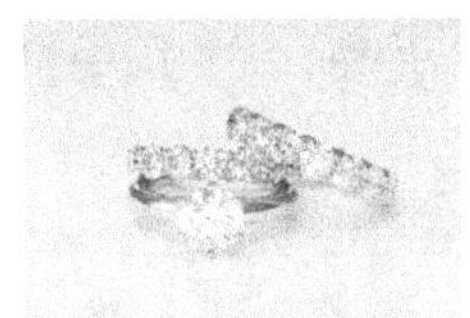

"So did she buy it?" Amber asked regarding Edwin's lame excuse he had given to Nyree. In her opinion he had not sounded too convincing. If it had been her dad on the phone she would have given him the third degree. She disliked being lied to and despised that she had been the cause of Edwin lying to his daughter.

Amber felt a tinge of guilt because of it. He did not have to lie. *'If she had been in his shoes, how would she have handled the situation?'* she wondered.

Edwin rolled his neck around in a circle, inhaled deeply, and let his breath out slowly. His body was longing to go back into the misting room of their suite. "I don't know. I think she was going for it until she heard you giggle. That's one thing about Nyree, not too much gets past her," Edwin said about his daughter. Amber massaged his shoulders as he lay on his stomach. She thought about his last statement. *'I wouldn't exactly say that there is not too much that gets past her, considering she has a cheating husband',* Amber thought. Then she remembered that her assessment of Nyree may not be fair, because she, too, had been the victim of a man who tried to be a player.

"Oooh, that feels good," Edwin told Amber.

"I know. I got that magic touch."

"Have you ever thought about being a masseuse?"

"No, actually I haven't ever thought about working."

"Why is that?"

"I guess I never really had a need to work. I have everything handed to me and I never had the desire to work a conventional eight-to-five job. I do my modeling thing, and that's about as much of a job as I would want. I don't even do that every day."

"What about the investigations you do? You have a way of getting information."

"I like doing investigations on my own terms. I could not do it every day and I would not want to do every case."

"I see. I want you to have dinner with me and my children this weekend."

"I don't know. Do you think that is such a good idea?"

"If I didn't think it was a good idea, I would not have suggested it. So what's the problem?"

"I mean they may resent having me around."

"Are you uncomfortable with our age difference?" He had thought about it. He was old enough to be her father. Some of his friends had grandchildren her age, but he knew what he wanted - and it was her.

"No. I was thinking that they might have a problem with me as your divorce is still pending. I am the one who delivered you the information about your wife that is causing you to get the "divorce." She paused. "Are *you* uncomfortable with our age difference?"

"How does that one singer say it? Age ain't nothing but a number and going down..."

"Hold tight on that. I don't get down with all of that."

"Maybe that's because those youngsters you're used to dealing with had no clue," he said to her as he jumped into their private twenty-two-foot swimming pool in their suite at the Sybaris.

Edwin hoped that Colin and Nyree were enjoying their evening, because he surely was enjoying his. Although he had only been seeing Amber for two weeks, it was difficult for him to imagine what life was like prior to her. Who would have thought he and this sassy girl, who had conducted an investigation on his wife, would have become an item?

Thirty-Four

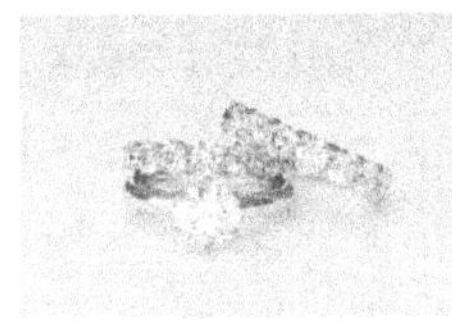

Amber turned up the jets on the Jacuzzi as she recounted her first encounter with Edwin Shaw.

"Mr. Shaw, Amber Sinclair is here for you," Barbara had told Edwin.

"Tell her that I will be with her momentarily," Edwin had responded. He smiled as he sat behind his desk, propped his feet up, and stretched out in his oversized mahogany, leather chair. All of the work that he intended to do had been completed, so he could have brought Amber into the office, but he figured that he would make her wait.

Amber sat in the waiting area and had to admit that she was impressed by the peanut-butter soft leather chairs, glass tables, and leather throw rugs on the hardwood floors. The soft jazz playing in the background added to the ambience, but Barbara, the receptionist, detracted from the atmosphere. Amber looked down at her watch and thought, *'He can come any time now.'* The thought of leaving the documents with Barbara was tempting. However, Barbara struck her as the type that would unseal the envelope without so much as a tear, remove the documents ever so carefully, read them, place them back in the envelope, and reseal it. Then she would be on the phone calling "Pookie," "Ray-Ray," and all her nieces and nephews with the confidential information. Amber would leave with the envelope before she left it with Barbara. That would be all she needed to hear. "What were you thinking about leaving the envelope with the receptionist? You cost us our reputation as a reputable and confidential agency and we lost Edwin Shaw as a client," is probably what her family would say if she left the precious contents with Barbara and the information was leaked to the public. There would be no one to blame, but herself, and she could not live with herself if that were to happen.

Edwin was walking toward her and saying, "Come on back, Ms. Sinclair."

It's about time, she thought. She followed him down the hallway and noticed the other offices, all of which were nicer than hers. She was making a mental note to have someone come and decorate her plain, boring offices. They were approaching the end of the hall and wouldn't she know that his office was the ostentatious one at the end. Why did she have to go to his office anyway? She had briefed him on the phone. It would have been perfectly fine for him to take the envelope in the lobby and for him to have given her the check there as well. Maybe he did not want the transaction to occur in front of Barbara.

He motioned for her to sit in one of the leather chairs facing his desk.

"Why?" she screamed in her head. *I just want to get my check and get out of here. I cannot continue with this nice tone for too much longer. He does not care for me and I don't care for him, but business is business,* she thought.

"All right," she said as she sat down in the chair which was more comfortable than it appeared. There was silence and she did not want to be blunt and say, "Give me my money." But if it came down to it, she would. She was not above asking for what she wanted.

"You have a nice office here. This is my first

time here at Shaw Enterprises and I am really impressed," she found herself saying. Although true, she was unsure why she was making small conversation.

Shocked by her statement, he responded, "I could give you a tour if you'd like."

When she took him up on the offer he was even more shocked. Initially, he thought that she was being nice by commenting about the facility. But, as they walked around and she asked questions, he could tell that she was genuinely impressed and interested. When was the last time a woman had been genuinely interested in what he had to say?

Margo only feigned interest in his projects until she heard about how much revenue would be generated. Then she would become fully alert. Amber, however, was different. It was as if she were soaking it all in.

"Edwin, you know what I like the most about your facility..."

"No, tell me," he said, genuinely wanting to hear what she had to say.

"Well, the fact that you have a daycare, cafeteria, and gym on the site...this shows that you really value your employees. Well, I'm just going on and on. People say I talk too much."

"Not at all; I like listening to you talk," Edwin said. He then wished he could have taken the words back because Amber was looking at him as if he were some kind of pervert.

"Well, I know that you probably have a lot of things to do, so here is your check and thank you."

Amber looked at the check as he handed it to her. She gasped at the amount. Edwin saw the look on her face and asked if something was wrong. Amber swallowed hard, trying not to stutter, but she could not help it. "It's written for seven thousand dollars. The fee was five thousand."

"I know. That's my tip."

"*Tip?* I'm not complaining, so please don't think I am. I mean, that is very generous of you. Do you always tip like this?" Amber was curious as she had never received a two thousand-dollar tip.

"No, I don't usually but you went above and beyond the job. I wanted to show my appreciation for your hard work." He tried to conceal a smile when he saw her blush at the statement.

'I wish more people showed their gratitude in that manner', she found herself thinking. "Thank you so much, but I can not accept such a generous tip," Amber politely said.

Edwin smiled at her courtesy. It was good to see that she was not money-hungry like most of the people that he did business with, but he genuinely wanted her to have the tip. "You will offend me if you do not accept it," Edwin told her, "and you don't want to offend an old man, do you? I mean it could cause me to have a heart attack and die."

If he insisted that she have the money, she was not going to argue. After all, she prided herself on being "nobody's fool." What was a girl to do in a situation like this?

"Mr. Shaw..." she began but was interrupted.

"Now, now, what is all this 'Mr. Shaw' business? Call me Edwin."

"Well, okay, Edwin. You don't look old to me. I doubt that you are going to die any time soon, but in an effort not to offend you, I will accept your generous tip."

"Well, good," he said, wanting to say more but not sure exactly what. There was something about this young girl that caught his fancy. She had awakened feelings in him that lay dormant.

Uncomfortable by the silence, Amber announced, "I better get going. I'm famished."

"Really, so am I. Would you like to grab something to eat with me?" he asked before he knew it.

Amber stammered, "That's nice of you, but I really don't want to impose."

How would you be imposing? You're hungry. I'm hungry. I am going to eat. You're going to eat, so why not eat together? Unless you had plans... Oh, I feel so embarrassed," Edwin said.

"No, I don't have plans. I'll take you up on that offer, I hate eating alone," she said.

Now he was blushing. "Oh, you don't have to say that to be nice."

Amber looked at him and placed her hand on her imaginary hip. "Edwin, I'm not being nice. I am hungry and I would enjoy your company over dinner. Now come on, let's go. I've been sucking in my stomach, pushing it in with my fist hoping that you wouldn't hear it growl; but if I don't get something to eat soon, I am afraid it is going to roar louder than a lion."

"Well, then we had better get going. How does Chop's American SteakHouse sound to you?"

"Great, I'll follow you." He agreed, but secretly hoped that they would have ridden in the same car as he was enjoying being in her presence.

They had been seated in a private section of the restaurant.

"They have the best shrimp and lobster in the Midwest. Try some," he told Amber as he munched on salad.

"No, thank you," Amber declined his offer.

"Don't be shy. Try it, you will love it. You said that this was your first time here."

"Edwin, I don't eat shrimp and lobster."

"Oh," he said, sounding disappointed, "are you allergic to seafood? If so, we can dine somewhere else."

"No, I'm not allergic to it. I just don't eat scavengers of the water," she said a little more forcefully than she had intended.

"Interesting... Is there other food that you don't eat?" he asked with interest and she mistook for sarcasm.

Placing her fork down in her salad, she

rolled her eyes and asked, "Are you trying to be funny?"

"No, not at all. I really would like to know for future references."

"I don't eat pork. I limit my beef, chicken, and poultry," Amber told him.

"Is this due to religion?" Edwin wanted to know.

"I would say spiritual reasons. If you look in the Bible in the book of Leviticus there is information. There are other books too. However, you will find Biblical principles to support why one should not eat these things. If you read the book, *How To Eat To Live* by Elijah Muhammad, it will explain these foods."

"Are you a member of the Nation of Islam?"

"No, I am not, but some of the things that they discuss, I agree with. I don't define myself by my affiliation with a particular religious group. I read a lot. They know me quite well at Your Black Bookstore on 46th and Broadway. They always show me love and treat me like family," Amber told him. They had spent the evening talking about religion, politics, clothing, and various topics. They each felt as if they had known each other forever instead of hours. They were the last customers to leave the restaurant. It had been a good first impromptu date for both of them.

***

Bringing herself back to their moment now at the Sybaris, Amber smiled. She had never dated a man as old as Edwin and was beginning to wonder why. Why had she spent so much time accepting whatever came her way? Many men were intimidated by her family's wealth and her on-and-off-again modeling career. When she did find someone who was not intimidated by either, he tended not to measure up to her standards. Allen had once told her, "All the things that you want a man to do and have are just not going to happen. You better take what you can get or you're going to find yourself alone."

She was ashamed to admit that she had believed that crap and settled for Allen. As she and Edwin playfully tossed water on each other she knew that she deserved better and did not have to settle for less. Edwin was everything that she had wanted in a man. She could not allow herself to get too close to him as he was still married.

Even now she couldn't believe she was here with him. She remembered his invite and what she had said to him, "I'll go with you to the Sybaris but no...," she stammered.

Edwin had laughed and told her, "I'm not one of those young bucks that you're used to dealing with. I can be in the presence of a beautiful woman without having to have sex. I won't lie. I do find you attractive, but more importantly I respect you and your feelings. You have made it clear to me how you feel about being sexually involved. When my divorce is final..." She had interrupted him and put a finger to his lips. The word "divorce" always led to his speaking about Margo, and today she did not want to hear about his dreaded, estranged wife.

Thirty-Five

Margo entered Shaw Enterprises and walked past Barbara without speaking. Barbara wondered what was eating at Margo, as they always exchanged pleasantries. Now Margo was acting like Nyree and that was atypical behavior for Margo. Barbara had heard people remark that Margo could be very difficult to deal with at times, however, that had not been in the years that Barbara had worked at Shaw Enterprises.

Where was the newspaper? Barbara wondered. She had a good mind to call the *Midwest Vein* and complain about not receiving the paper today. It was only eight. If they had not received a copy by nine o'clock, then she would call and make a complaint. This was unlike their carrier. Maybe he was sick today, but still that should not have had an impact on their service, Barbara thought.

"Edwin, what is the meaning of this?" Margo questioned when she threw a copy of the

Midwest Vein on his desk as he rushed the person on the other end of the telephone off the line.

Edwin tried to pretend that he didn't know what his wife was ranting and raving about. It was difficult as the headlines read in huge bold print, **THE SCANDALOUS SHAWS.** The paper also showed several pictures of him and Amber having conversation and dinner. The bottom half of the paper displayed Nyree and Malachi's wedding pictures and then Nyree and Colin having what appeared to be intimate conversations. Malachi had also given an interview to the *Midwest Vein*, which Nyree jokingly referred to as a rag. She had stated that she hated the paper so much that if it was the only thing available to wipe her behind with, she would not use it.

Edwin recalled having said to her jokingly, "Well, let's just hope it never comes down to it."

Nyree had responded, "I know, right. I would hate to get diaper rash."

Boy, had they chuckled about the paper that day. Of course it had been when reporter Rayna Summers had done the piece on Nyree and Malachi. She had really spoken poorly of Malachi in the article. Now she attacked Edwin and

Nyree and made reference to the incident that had occurred between Malachi and Kyle. She had even given Malachi an opportunity to vent about the Shaw family.

'That ungrateful bastard', Edwin had thought after reading Malachi's cruel comments. Why hadn't he been informed that Malachi was in town?

"Margo, you are not to come in here unannounced. This is a place of business, not a place for you to exercise your tantrums." Pushing the newspaper back in her direction and ignoring the newspaper issue.

Margo fumed at the statement. *'How dare he talk to me in that manner?'* She would not be treated in this manner; after all, she had helped to build the empire.

"Edwin, I will not be treated any kind of way. This is embarrassing, my husband parading around with a girl young enough to be his daughter. In fact, she is younger than your children. What are you thinking?"

"Margo, I don't answer to you. In the future you are to be buzzed in like any other client."

"You will answer me. I am still your wife and I refuse to be buzzed in…"

"Margo, let's, as the kids say, 'keep it real'. You and I have not been happy in a long time. We were just going through the motions. *Wife?* You're my wife in name only. Please understand if you cannot come here and behave in a respectable manner, I will have a restraining order put in place."

Margo placed both of her palms on the desk that she had purchased for him five years ago, and leaned forward so that their noses were only centimeters apart. Staring him in the eyes she asked, "So are you screwing her?"

Edwin returned the stare into her red eyes. She had been crying and for that he was sorry. He hadn't wanted her to be hurt by the newspaper article and would have given anything not to have had those pictures and the malicious story printed.

"Margo, leave while you still have some dignity."

Pushing him in his collarbone, she said, "No. I will not leave. Are you screwing that girl? How long has it been going on?"

"Sit down and lower your voice. I have not, and am not, currently involved sexually with her or any other woman." It was the truth. During the years he was married to her he had never been unfaithful in any way. There were many opportunities and women who had flaunted it in his face, but he never indulged himself in such activities. His marriage vows meant something to him, and he knew the pain that his mother, Lula, had experienced. He vowed he would never treat a woman badly. It bothered him that Margo felt that she was being treated badly now. He was not cheating sexually with Amber, but emotionally; however, he would not admit this to Margo. What about his feelings? Had she ever considered how he would feel if and when he learned the secrets of her past? He could divulge that information in the divorce hearing, but he told his attorney, Nicole Rouse, that he would like to have as amicable a divorce as possible. He wondered if it were possible to have such a thing. Nevertheless, he did not bring up his wife's past if he could avoid it. Now if she wanted to play dirty, then he would be forced to play dirty, but he had hoped that the lawyers could work things out and keep it out of the media. It was his fault that he was on the front page of the *Midwest Vein*. By not going to local establishments and by going to Chesterton this one time, he thought that he was being careful.

"Not that I owe you an explanation, but here goes. We're just friends," Edwin told her as she blew her nose into a blue tissue that she had taken out of the box on the edge of his desk. She wanted to believe him, but she did not. At least, he had tried to spare her feelings by not rubbing it in her face.

"Well, I have work to attend to. Like I said, next time talk to Barbara before coming back," Edwin instructed Margo as he tried to get her to leave without being rude.

Standing up and picking up his favorite golf ceramic off his desk and throwing it at the wall, she announced, "That's what I think of talking to Barbara before I come back. I helped build this company and I will not be treated like some type of stalker," she yelled.

"Margo, I own this company. This company existed before I even knew you. Yes, you helped to advance it, but it is mine, totally mine, and the legal documents are so tight that you can't touch the company. Now, leave before I have you escorted from the premises."

She was furious at his statement, but decided to leave as there had been enough scandal in her family for one day.

"Have a good day," Barbara said to Margo as Margo breezed past her desk and out of the door.

Once in her car, Margo screamed at the top of her lungs and punched the steering wheel of her pineapple-yellow Corvette. She dialed Brooklyn Bradley for information about her divorce settlement. Brooklyn was as fierce an attorney as Nicole Rouse. Margo had wanted to retain Nicole's services, but Edwin had retained her services before Margo had an opportunity to do so. In fact, the divorce papers had been served the day after Edwin presented his findings to Margo,

"Brooklyn Bradley," the attorney announced in a pleasant tone.

"Brooklyn, this is Margo Shaw."

"Yes, good morning, Mrs. Shaw. I was going to call you to come in today to look at the agreement that Nicole and I have reached so far…"

"Brooklyn, Edwin tells me that I am not entitled to any of Shaw Enterprises," stated Margo.

"Mrs. Shaw, why are you talking to him about assets? That is why you pay me and may

I remind you, that you pay me a pretty penny. If you are not going to let me handle matters, why have you secured my services?"

"Skip the legal lecture and tell me if I am entitled to any of Shaw Enterprises."

"Well, Margo, technically you are not. Whoever drew up the contract and papers regarding Shaw Enterprises made very clear who is entitled to ownership. That is Edwin and his mother, Lula, and at the time of either one's death the ownership is to be transferred to Nyree and Kyle initially. However, it seems that when there was the issue of misappropriation of funds on Kyle's part, he was taken out of ownership."

"So what are you saying? I'm going to be broke?"

"By no means are you going to be broke. Edwin is willing to split some of the subsidiaries and projects that you two worked on, and I am sure that you will find your monthly allotment to be more than generous. You have to remember that you do have a practice, so no judge is going to give you everything."

"How much is the monthly allotment?"

"Fifteen thousand dollars."

"*Fifteen?*"

"Yes, the house that you moved into is paid for."

"Is that the best you can do?" Margo asked even though she was more than satisfied with what she heard. However, if she could get more then that's what she wanted.

"That's the best, Mrs. Shaw. Now if you have some particular things that you want other than what you have already stated, let me know and I will go back to the drawing board. I just figured that you all would want this to be quick and speedy and not long and drawn out.""It sounds pretty good. I will come by and review the papers. Now that court date is set for August first right?"

"Yes. Well, Deana will be here to review the documents. Make sure you sign off and then all we have to do is wait for court."

Thirty-Six

Shutting and locking the door. Edwin settled into his chair behind his desk. He quickly dialed Amber. "Amber, how are you doing?" Edwin asked.

"I'm fine.Why?" Amber asked. Edwin realized that she must not have heard about the newspaper article and when he told her, he imagined that she bolted up in the bed.

"I'm heading home. I can't believe this," she whined.

Edwin told her that she should stay at the suite as they had it for another night. They should not allow the media to ruin their plans. She agreed. This would give her another day away from her family and the million questions with which they would bombard her and answers that she probably would not have. As soon as she turned on her cell phone, it rang and she answered it. After hearing her mother's high-pitched voice, she regretted having turned her phone on and having answered the call.

"What is the meaning of this? What are you thinking, young lady?" Hannah Sinclair asked.

"Ma, it's nothing, dang. You know that newspaper will get a sliver of something and turn it into a big to-do," Amber told her mother.

It was difficult to comment as she had not read the article, she told her mother. Why did she go and say that because her mother began reading to her word for word what the article said? "Oh, Ma, please. I will sue them for slander. All we have ever done was have dinner," she said while purposely omitting their time at the Sybaris.

Even though it was innocent, she knew that her mother would not believe it. *Heck,* she thought to herself, *I would be inclined not to believe it either. But, it has just been a relaxing experience.* She couldn't help but smile as she reflected on the spa treatments that Edwin treated her to. He insisted that she first have the spa manicure, followed by the Sea Spa Deluxe pedicure and for the finale the European Rose Body Mud Mask. She had been in heaven and was floating on cloud nine and was determined not to let anyone stress her out. Not even her mother.

"So where are you? I have been calling you all morning," her mother inquired. Not wanting to divulge that information and not wanting to lie, she told her mother that she had just awakened. She really needed to go to the restroom and would call her back later. She hung up without saying good-bye.

Thirty-Seven

"Hello," Nyree groggily answered. *'Who could be calling at…What time is it? Eight forty-five? It seems earlier than that,' Nyree* thought.

It had better be an emergency. Some people did not have the common decency to call at a good time. She did not care if the sun was up and had been up for hours, she was tired. Her evening with Colin had gone into the wee hours of the morning.

"How can you sleep at a time like this?" her best friend, Aris, asked.

Normally, Nyree would try to figure out what Aris was talking about, but she was too exhausted to play along with her.

Pulling the cover up tightly over her head, she said, "Okay, I give. What's going on?"

Aris could not believe that Nyree was playing it so cool. "Girl, don't tell me you're still sleeping."

Nyree was annoyed and figured that if Aris

could tell that she was asleep then Aris should have been courteous enough to, number one, apologize for interrupting her sleep, and number two, get off the telephone.

Nyree let out a sigh to indicate that she was annoyed. "Yeah, I'm still asleep. What is going on? I'm too tired to guess."

"What's going on is that I am supposed to be your best friend but I had to find out about Mr. Colin Jordan from the *Midwest Vein.*"

"What are you talking about?"

"You better open your door, pick up the paper, and read it. I'm sure your phone is going to be ringing off the hook," Aris told her and then hung up.

Whatever it was, it had better be good, Nyree thought as she climbed out of bed and placed her feet in her fluffy, pink house shoes. She rubbed her eyes as she tried to bring things into focus. Everything appeared blurry. It seemed like her eyes did not want to fully open. Where had she left her robe? She found it draped over the chair at her vanity in the master bathroom. The bathroom was massive with his-and-her sinks, whirlpool tub, separate showers, and her vanity station. There was still space to place something else in there.

Barefoot, she ran down the spiral staircase with only her T-shirt and panties. She hoped that none of her neighbors were up and about. She was going to open the door a tad to reach for the paper and ease herself back in the doorway. Nyree was pretty sure that her plan to grab the newspaper had worked; however, after she had it in her hands and began to scoot back in the doorway, she felt several flashes of light dance across her face. Did the reporters ever take a break?

Slamming the door and resisting the urge to kick herself for having gone to the door half-dressed, she darted into the kitchen area. A cup of coffee would soothe her nerves, but she decided against it as coffee tended to irritate her acid reflux disorder. She settled for a glass of orange juice, the lesser of the two evils. After drinking a glass of freshly squeezed orange juice, she removed the newspaper from the plastic bag.

"What in the world...!" she screamed loudly. How dare they invade her privacy with these pictures? There really was not a story; it was more speculation about what could have been going on between her and Colin.

They even interviewed Malachi and he had spoken as if he had first-hand information. He portrayed himself as an innocent victim. "Poor, poor Malachi," Nyree said.

When I finish with him, he will be sorry he ever crossed me, she thought. How could he give the *Midwest Vein* an exclusive interview, knowing how badly she despised its journalism ethics and knowing that he was lying?

Why had she expected anything different from him? Hadn't he proven himself to be a consistent liar without ethics and morals? And the *Midwest Vein* wasn't that the same paper that had described him as being a "money-hungry man who could not be trusted due to his criminal past? Yet they quoted him as if he were a credible source. They had sunken to an all-time low in order to sell newspapers.

This was yellow journalism at its finest. "Smut sells," she said to herself as she picked up the telephone to call Colin. She knew that he probably wished he had never met her. If she were him she would wish that she had never met her. *Now why did I move back home? For peace,* she reminded herself. When was that going to occur? Her life had been just as chaotic here in Gary as it had been in Jacksonville. The only difference was she did not have to deal with "baby momma drama."

Thirty-Eight

"Malachi, you must be feeling real proud of yourself," Monte said with sarcasm.

Malachi gripped the telephone tightly, trying to comprehend what his brother was saying to him. His intuition had told him not to answer the telephone without looking at the caller ID, but he had done so anyway. This would be a lesson. Check the identification screen before answering the telephone. In his opinion caller ID was the best invention in the world. Too bad he didn't take advantage of it consistently.

He stretched his long body out on the air mattress trying to get comfortable. It was difficult to relax as he was used to sleeping in a bed. Even the bed on the ship had been more comfortable than this mattress. It was too low to the ground and did not provide any support for his back. It always aches when he gets up from sleeping.

He tugged at his thin sheet, hoping that it

would provide him with some warmth because there was a cool morning breeze blowing through the partially cracked window. The faded, yellow full-size sheet had been his favorite while growing up. His mother had encouraged him to discard it many times, but he could not part with it. For him the sheet was just as important as it is to the *Peanuts'* character, Linus, and his blanket. The sheet really did need to be washed so that it would have that fresh fragrance. However, Malachi was afraid that if he were to wash the linen, it would disintegrate in the washing machine.

Malachi rolled his eyes at the thought of having to listen to Monte. Monte's holier-than-thou attitude was really starting to rub him the wrong way. Lately, Monte was the expert on everything. He had hoped that Keysha had not told Monte that he'd borrowed money from her. As far as he was concerned, that was an issue that did not involve Monte unless Monte was going to repay the debt. He was sure that wasn't going to happen. If Monte was going to give him the "if you don't work, you don't eat lecture," he knew it by heart and could recite it.

At nine o'clock in the morning Monte

would just be wasting his breath. What was wrong with Monte calling this early anyway? Didn't he know that Malachi's day didn't start until three o'clock in the afternoon? Malachi slept until about noon or one o'clock on most days, then grabbed a bowl of cereal. On a good day he would fry bacon and eggs-depending on what Keysha had in the refrigerator. After eating he would iron his clothes, shower and shave, and make a few phone calls. About three o'clock in the afternoon, upon completing his rituals for the day, was generally when he would leave the apartment and go visit friends.

"Proud of what..." Malachi began to ask when he was interrupted by the beep from the other line. He clicked over to answer.

"Boy, you big time. You made the front page and you're not dead nor did you kill anyone. That's real good being that you from the 'hood and all," his friend Derrick told him.

Malachi responded casually as if he always were on the front page of the newspaper. "Oh, yeah, man? I haven't even seen it yet. Look, I got my brother on the other line, I'm gonna hit ya back," he said, rushing Derrick off the phone.

He knew that there would be no end to

Keysha's complaining if she were calling right now and the phone line was busy. She did not like to hear excuses as to why the line was busy when she called home. If you were to tell her that you had been on one of the lines with Bill Clinton, she would respond, "So. Don't be tying my lines up."

Sometimes she would call home just to see if the lines were tied up. If Malachi passed the test that would be good. If he did not pass the test, then he had better get ready to hear about how he needs to get his own number if he wants to use three-way services or talk at length with one person while another person is holding the line. "All right, I'm back," Malachi announced after he returned to Monte.

"Do you have any dignity? How much did the *Midwest Vein* pay you to sound like a whining chick? You conveniently left out all the dirt that you did," Monte told Malachi.

Wiping the corners of his mouth, he said, "Man, go 'head on with all that. It's too early in the morning for all that yakking," Malachi said.

"Man, it's nine o'clock. It's not early."

"It's early to me. I didn't get in until five this morning."

"You're going to keep running the streets

with those low-lifes and you're going to get killed for real," Monte said, making reference to the stabbing incident that had occurred in the parking lot of the Jukebox.

Here we go, Malachi thought. The last thing he wanted to hear about were his poor choices of friends and his brush with death. He could probably stomach the conversation regarding his peers, no pun intended, but discussing the stabbing literally made his stomach hurt.

"Yeah, yeah, right, man. I'm sleep. I'll holler at you later," Malachi told his brother and hung up the telephone before Monte could respond.

The telephone rang again, but Malachi didn't answer. He even turned the ringer off so he would not be disturbed. That's how celebrities handle annoying callers, right?

Thirty-Nine

Nyree pulled her car close to the bumper of the white compact car in front of her. She wondered what type of car it was; she would never know because the name had fallen off years ago. It was making a loud, sputtering noise. She wondered if the car would die when its driver informed the guard at the gate what apartment he was visiting and provided the resident's telephone.

Nyree figured that the guard must be new because he was actually dialing the telephone number. Generally, the guards would wave callers through the gate, but not this one. No, he took his job seriously since he asked the driver more questions and redialed the number. Nyree thought that she was going to be sick from the dark smoke that was coming from the vehicle's tail pipe in front of her. There was no doubt in her mind that the vehicle would not pass the emissions test that was required for renewing license plates. Finally, the yellow bar went up allowing "Old Smoky" through.

As the bar lowered, she rolled up to the booth, smiled at the guard, and pointed to the vehicle that had just gone through to indicate they were together. He motioned for her to roll her window down. "I'm with him," she told the guard.

He grinned. "Oh, okay. Next time tell him to let me know," he informed.

Nyree smiled. "I will. He is so goofy. I don't know what he's thinking about." She was happy that he pressed the button to allow the bar to go up.

She sped past not allowing him enough time to write down the information from her tag. There was to be no record of her visit with Malachi. She had no intention of giving the *Midwest Vein* its feature story for tomorrow.

Once she reached Keysha's door, she began pounding like a maniac.

"What the hell wrong with you?" Malachi asked when he opened the door. "Don't be banging on the door like you, the feds," he said, looking past her into the dimly lit hallway to make sure she did not have the feds with her. He had dibbled and dabbled in selling drugs from time to time to put a little money in his pocket. Lately, dealing was taking money from him as opposed to adding. He had only been selling marijuana to his friends, but he was giving it to them on credit or at a discount.

He chuckled when Juan had said, "Man, let me get a nick."

"A nick? It ain't even worth my time to bag a nickel," Malachi had told him.

"Suit yourself, I'll just holler at my boy. Benny down the street. He'll give me a nick. I mean I was just going to deal with you since you are my boy and all," Juan told Malachi knowing full well that Benny would have slapped him for saying something so absurd.

Malachi went against his better judgment and succumbed to Juan's request. His rationale was that five dollars was better than nothing. Just yesterday he had given Juan a nickel for three dollars. Times were really hard.

"Well, come on in," Malachi told Nyree. *What does she want?*

"Are you that desperate for money that you would sell lies to the *Midwest Vein*?" Nyree asked.

After reading the article he felt like a low-life and a crybaby. Everybody had assumed that he had been paid for his story. He was too embarrassed to say that he had suffered this shame at his own expense.

"I didn't lie. He is your boyfriend, isn't he?" Malachi asked, hoping that she would say, "No."

Her red eyes stared at him absently. He had never seen so much hate in a person's eyes as he saw in hers now.

Where had the love gone? What could he say? He wondered if she was here to make amends. He could hope, couldn't he?

"Nyree, I didn't catch you two in a compromising position on our anniversary?"

She was sure that he had not come up with that statement. Rayna must have crafted that. Tightening her lips, she said through clenched teeth, "No, you didn't catch us in a *compromising* position. I mean, what was your purpose in talking to her?" Nyree genuinely wanted to hear his answer. *What had he hoped to gain from talking to Rayna?*

Shrugging his shoulders, he said, "I just wanted people to see another side of Polly

Purebred."

"So, you would lie on me. How could you tell her that my father was a cheater? After all he did for you, you just go and lie on him?"

"I didn't lie. I mean, I'm pretty sure he has not always been forthcoming with the truth. Probably doctored some documents, you know?" Malachi said with a smile as if he accomplished a great feat by making misleading statements about her and her father.

It was useless talking to him. His version of reality and the truth was distorted. He honestly did not see anything wrong with what he had done.

It may have been a little vindictive, but in his eyesight, not wrong. She had been standing by the door the entire time, so she grabbed the doorknob and opened the door. He wanted her to hurt and ache like he did. Did she know what it was like for a twenty –six- year old man who had traveled around the world and lived in luxury with his wife to have to return home to his mother? Did she know what it felt like to go from sleeping in a bed to sleeping on the floor until he was able to get an air mattress on which to sleep? She did not know how it felt to come home to an empty apartment. Had all of the clothing that she owned ever been destroyed in a single instant? He did not think so. Why couldn't things be the way they were before he joined the Navy?

In retrospect, joining the Navy had been the biggest mistake of his life. "Look, I've hurt you and you've hurt me. We could call it even now and stop before someone gets hurt again. We could make up and get a place of our own..." Malachi told her as she moved closer to walking out of his life for good.

Nyree shook her head. Some people simply did not get it and he was one of them. It was like the lights were on, but nobody was home. "Malachi, do you even hear yourself? I know you can't believe half the shit that you say. Why would I consider getting back with you? What do you have to offer?" she said in a sincere tone, not trying to be malicious.

Boy, she knows how to tear a brother down. That's what's wrong with Black women nowadays, they don't support their Black men, he thought.

"Can I use your restroom?" she asked, holding her knees together as if that would keep urine from seeping out of her bladder. *Where did this urgent need to urinate come from?*

He pointed her in the direction of the restroom where she was headed. After arriving, it was beginning to feel as if she were going to have an accident as she struggled with the button on her jeans. Once she had the button undone, she had to fidget with getting the jeans down past her hips. All the while she had her legs crossed and was slightly bouncing as she tightened her uterine muscles to prevent leakage. "Please, God, don't let me use it on myself," she whispered as she finally got the jeans down and squatted over the toilet.

Never had she been so grateful. At twenty-seven, she knew she was too old to be urinating on herself. She felt relief and then became alarmed when she realized that her menstrual cycle had begun. What was she going to do since she did not have any sanitary napkins in her purse? She opened the medicine cabinet to see if she could find something. Then she looked under the sink. There was nothing that would aid her situation. *Oh my goodness, she probably doesn't even get a monthly anymore. I just need something to tide me over until I can get to the pharmacy to purchase some sanitary items.* Then she decided to look in the area of the restroom where the soap, tissue, and other toiletries were stored when she found what she needed.

A knock at the door startled her. She wondered if Malachi had heard her rummaging through the contents of the bathroom. "Nyree, is everything all right? I thought I heard something fall," Malachi said.

"Yeah, everything is fine. I just accidentally knocked over a can of air freshener."

He looked at the door and shrugged his shoulders. "We don't have any air freshener, do we?" *'Will he go on and get away from the door, so I can tend to my business?'*

"I'll be out in a second," was all she could say.

"It's about time," Malachi said when Nyree finally surfaced from the bathroom.

"I gotta go," she announced without warning.

Malachi found her behavior to be a little disturbing. "Well, what about what we were talking about? What about us getting back together? We can even go to counseling to work this out."

He said everything he thought would win

her over. Much to his avail, nothing was working.

"It's a little too late for that now. When I wanted to work on this marriage you were too busy doing your own thing. You were unreceptive to what I wanted…"

"So what is this? Payback, huh?" he yelled out of frustration and anger at himself. "You think that I am going to just let you walk out of here? Sit down," he said while pinning her back against the door and placing both of his hands over her head.

Her forehead was under his pectorals and she breathed in his cologne which for once did not have an intoxicating effect on her. She pushed him in his stomach, but he didn't move. "Malachi, move. I really got to go," she said, trying to pry herself away from him.

"Where do you have to go? Are you going to see your *boyfriend?*"

"No, we've been through this before. Look, I don't feel well. I really need to go home."

Malachi disregarded her statement and continued talking until she darted for the bathroom. He heard her vomiting. This time when she returned to the living room, he did not interfere with her attempts to leave. Her eyes were red and watery and it was evident that she did not feel well. "Call me when you get home so that I know that you made it home safely," he called to her as she bounded down the stairs and out the building.

Forty

"Where were you last night?" Bianca asked as she walked around Kyle's house like she owned it. She was looking for a clue that another woman might have been over there last night. There was no evidence. His house was spotless as usual. He sat in front of his big-screen television watching a tennis match.

"Bianca, I told you that I was at my mother's house. I didn't even think that you cared," he said nonchalantly. Ever since they had started dating again, Bianca had wanted to keep tabs on him.

"I'm not going to be anybody's fool again," she would say when he asked her why he was being bombarded by questions. According to her she could have avoided the heartache that she had suffered when they broke up if only she had asked the right questions.

He wanted so badly to tell her that was not

true. "A man is going to do what a man is going to do. If a man is going to be a dog, he is going to be a dog and no amount of questioning and interrogating is going to stop him from being a dog," he wanted to yell.

She just did not get it. She thought that she was controlling the situation when in reality she was creating a problem that did not exist. Maybe this was why things did not work out between them. He didn't need to be with her every waking moment of the day. For her, if they were not together, then she needed to be talking to him or knowing what he was doing.

"I bet you were at your mother's," Bianca said in a tone that sounded to Kyle as if she were trying to start an argument.

'I will have peace and quiet in my home. I will have peace and quiet in my home. I will have peace and quiet in my home', he said to himself before he responded. There used to be a time when he would have been yelling and cursing and at the point of destroying anything of value in his home. Now he repeated the peace and quiet mantra before acting impulsively. "Bianca, I was at my mom's. I have no reason to lie. Now if you are going to be disagreeable, I am going to have to

ask you to leave."

She was taken aback by his behavior. *Has he just flipped the script on me?* she thought.

"It's not like I don't have a reason for not trusting you," she said as she snuggled next to him.

"What's that supposed to mean?"

"I mean it's not like your family isn't plastered across the front page of the *Midwest Vein.*"

"You know that is really low that you bring that up at a time like now. Bianca, I thought that you cared about me and this relationship, but now I see it's all about you, **you, YOU!** I'm going to have to ask you to leave."

"Fine, I should have known this was not going to work."

"I should have known this was not going to work," he said more to himself than her as he walked her to the front door and watched her exit.

***

It had been his mother's idea to woo Bianca and the charges would disappear. The problem was that he had been wooing the wrong person. He needed to woo the district attorney and that was not going to happen because the district attorney was a man. Even after learning that Bianca could not get the charges dropped, he continued to see her to make sure she did not find any information about that night in the parking lot.

Kyle learned from her that Malachi said he was not sure who had stabbed him. Later, Malachi would tell Bianca that he would say that Kyle had stabbed him just to get revenge on the Shaw family.

Kyle had been clever enough to get that conversation on tape. His attorney, Nicole Rouse, said that she would use the tape as evidence in court if need be, but she was almost sure that the case would not go to trial because there was no evidence to support the claim. She had smiled and patted Kyle on the shoulder and said, "Funny, how no one wants to testify that they saw anything."

"I don't know what you mean," he had said sheepishly.

In her office, overlooking Lake Michigan, she sashayed past him and he felt his heart skip a beat as she said in a sultry tone, "I think you know full well what I mean. Have a good day, Mr.

Shaw."

"Call me Kyle."

"Have a good day, Kyle," she said, causing ripples to run down his spine.

***

It had given him great pleasure to slam his double wood doors behind Bianca as she walked out of his home. Why had he ever given her the time of day? Why had he wasted her time as well as his? What had his mother been thinking? Isn't this why the family retained Nicole Rouse so that she could handle their legal battles? The telephone interrupted his thoughts.

"Hello."

"Kyle, this is Nicole. I have great news for you."

"Funny, I was just thinking about you. But, yeah, what's the good news? You're going to be my future wife?"

"Such a kidder, you are. No, seriously, the charges have been dropped."

"How did you manage that?"

"I get results. That is what you pay me for."

"What are you doing tonight?"

"What?"

"Look, I have an extra ticket to that play

Unforgotten Memories at West Side. Please don't make me go alone."

"A handsome fellow like you … I'm sure you will be able to find someone to accompany you." She chuckled.

Nicole did not believe in mixing business with pleasure. Look at what happened to her cousin, Amber. Amber was on the front page of every newspaper with Edwin Shaw. How had that happened? The last she had heard, Amber and Edwin had been butting heads over the investigation, but from the pictures in the paper, they looked to be getting along just fine.

"Don't make me beg. I will. *Puh-leeze.*"

"Will I get Nachos with peppers at intermission?"

"Is that all you require? I can do that. So it's a date."

"I would say "date" but …yeah, I'll meet you in the surge area at six forty-five," Nicole told him, hung up the telephone, and began wondering why she had agreed to attend the play with Kyle Shaw.

She could pick up the telephone, call him back, tell him that she had just checked her schedule and realized that she had a prior engagement, but she decided against it. *What the heck, it just might be good to get out and have fun,* she found herself thinking. Besides, she could not recall the last time she had been out and had fun. With her it was always work and more work.

Forty-One

June 1996

Nyree woke up at six-thirty in the morning with the aid of a very loud alarm clock. She felt void of energy. Yesterday she had thrown up three different times after her visit with Malachi, so she figured that was the cause of her lack of energy. She had a slight sniffle, but nothing that concerned her enough to make an appointment with her family physician. Still, she put on a pair of cotton pajamas and drank straight from the bottle of a generic nighttime cough syrup. The generic brands worked just as well as the pricey name brands. In some cases the generic brands worked even better.

Summer colds could be the worst, so she was going to get an early start and ward it off with medication before it hit her hard. If one considered her unbearable by nature, she would be doubly unbearable if she were to catch a summer cold. It was difficult for her to believe that she felt as if she had not slept in days, considering she had gotten to bed at nine o'clock last night. That was the earliest that her head had made contact with a pillow since her return to Gary. Dragging herself into the bathroom, she sat on the toilet to collect her thoughts.

When she woke up it was seven-fifteen. She could not believe that she had fallen asleep while using the toilet. This was bizarre, unexplainable behavior. Even more bizarre was the fact that her cycle did not come last month and then it arrived late yesterday, but she had been happy that it arrived. Now it was gone, nowhere to be found. She had experienced irregular menstrual cycles in the past, but never had her cycles been this irregular.

Brushing her teeth had never been so laborious. The taste of the toothpaste was sickening and caused her to vomit yellow bile. As much as she had vomited yesterday, she was sure that whatever had been in her system that was causing her to feel ill, should have been long gone. "Oh, now, come on, tell me this is not going to be a repeat of yesterday," she said while balancing herself on her knees and gripping the sides of the toilet.

After she was able to stand and make it to her bed, she reached for the telephone.

"Hello, Barbara, this is Nyree. Please clear my schedule for today. I will not be in."

"No?" Barbara questioned, hoping that Nyree would offer more details.

"No," Nyree tried to say firmly but instead it came out weakly.

"Are you sick? This is not like you to miss two days of work back to back," Barbara said.

Suddenly, Nyree felt like a child trying to account for too many missed days of school. Then she realized that she was Barbara's boss and did not owe her an explanation.

If she had been feeling better, she would have put Barbara in her place and reminded her of the employee slash supervisor roles, but Nyree did not have the energy to do so.

Instead she said, "Barbara, hopefully, I'll see you tomorrow. Have a good day." Barbara sat and stared at the phone for a moment.

Forty-Two

Hell must be getting ready to freeze over. The "ice princess" actually acted like a human being. I better circle today's date on my calendar because this is not likely to occur again in this millennium, Barbara thought.

Colin strolled past his office and was headed to Nyree's office when he heard Barbara yell to him, "She's not here today."

But I'm here if you need anything. I mean anything, she wanted to say. How could she get his attention and let him know that she was interested in him with out sending the message that she was desperate? *Forget it. Some people have all the luck,* Barbara thought. She could envision herself walking on the white sands of the Caribbean with him, her kids calling him "Dad," him placing a diamond so huge on her finger that it weighed her hand down.

"Barbara. Barbara..." Colin was standing

across from her practically yelling.

"Huh," she said to him trying to drag herself out of her daydream.

"I said, can you add toner to the copy machine? Are you alright? You look a little zoned out."

"I am really tired. I don't have much energy."

"Yeah, you do look tired." Colin then regretted having commented when she gave him what he called "the evil eye." If looks could kill, he would be dead and buried.

"Gee, thanks, that is what every girl wants to hear- that she looks tired."

Come on with the quick save, Colin said to himself. He smiled. "No, I didn't mean it like that. I meant you just don't seem like your normal vibrant self, that's all. Why don't you come over to the gym later on and let me create a regimen for you? That will boost your energy." Reluctantly she agreed only because this would allow her an excuse to spend some time with him away from the office. She had to wonder if he was indirectly calling her fat.

Forty-Three

Nyree focused intently on the clock. She waited one minute before looking at the urine stick of the home pregnancy test. Her fingers were crisscrossed behind her back when she tiptoed to the sink and approached the stick that would determine her fate. It was funny how this little stick would answer so many questions and rule out some possible answers to those questions.

There were two lines that were pink. Barely pink; but as far as could be determined that color was pink. In her midst of anxiety, she had forgotten what the lines and color meant. According to the instructions, one blue line meant that one was not pregnant. Two pink lines meant that one was pregnant; no matter how faint the pink was, it was an indication of pregnancy.

"**NO!**" She screamed and cried at the same

time.

'*Wait a minute. Wait a minute. Let me back up, the lighting in here is horrible. Tomorrow morning I am going to have someone come out and do something about the lighting in this bathroom. This is ridiculous, that the lighting can be this bad,*' she said to herself.

She tried to walk under every angle of light hoping that one ray of light would cause that faint pink on the stick to appear blue. No matter which bulb she approached and at what angle she twisted her body, the color did not change.

What was she going to do with a child? Yeah, she had complained a time or two that her biological clock was ticking, but she could have sworn that it had come to a screechy halt when she saw those pink lines.

I don't want to be pregnant. What can I do to erase this? How can I reverse this? She remembered in junior high school hearing girls say that if you douched immediately after having sex, you couldn't get pregnant, or if you did a handstand, you wouldn't get pregnant. It was funny how a touch, a smell, or an incident could bring something that had occurred over a decade ago back into remembrance.

What she would not do, to rewind to that night in April and do a handstand and an immediate douche after that hot and steamy evening with Malachi, just to prevent this agony she was experiencing right now.

She convinced herself that since she had taken a generic pregnancy test that it could not be accurate. "Yeah, yeah. See, it's generic and it's off. The reading is not accurate. Some generic things are fine, but not a pregnancy test," she said as she stared at herself in the mirror and wiped her tears.

"Nope, I'm not pregnant. It's a false positive," she said to herself.

She put the stick in the box and threw all the contents into the plastic bag that was lying on the floor. Then she washed her hands, tied a knot in the bag, and walked into the den where Colin was sitting on the mink throw rug in front of the fireplace. The melodic sounds of Maxwell were playing and the scent of vanilla and lavender candles filled the room. She wished that she could take advantage of the ambience he had created.

"Is everything okay? I thought I heard you yell," he said to her.

"Yeah, I thought I had lost my... oh never mind," she told him. He looked at her with a raised eyebrow as he spotted the plastic bag in her hand.

"Where are you going with that bag?" he asked as he noticed how tightly she was gripping it.

"This bag..." she stuttered, "Uh, I'm going to take it out to the trash."

"I'll take it out," he volunteered.

"That's okay. I'll take it out. I need to get a little fresh air," she said as she rushed out of the patio door and to the outside trash can that was provided to residents by the city.

When she returned she quickly washed her hands, poured herself a shot of Jack Daniels, and offered Colin a drink which he declined.

"Nyree, what's up? You're drinking? Now I know something is up. You never drink hard liquor. The most that I have ever seen you drink was one of those sweet frozen drinks. I really wouldn't consider that drinking because you can't even taste the alcohol in those. So are you going to tell me what's up?"

"Nothing. I just felt like a shot, that's all." She wasn't sure if she sounded convincing as the warm, brown liquid warmed her insides as it seeped down her esophagus and into her stomach. The way it burned going down she knew it could not be good for an acid reflux condition. Drinking the liquid was her means of trying to convince herself that she was not pregnant. A pregnant woman in her right mind would not have a drink because they would be concerned about the unborn baby. However, her logic was that she could have a drink because she was not pregnant and did not have an unborn child. She only had to worry about her liver, kidneys, and health, and such a small swallow, in her opinion, would not kill her.

"All right, if you say so. I still think that you should schedule an appointment with the doctor to find out why you've been throwing up so much. Do you think with your condition that you should be drinking?"

"What condition?" she questioned very defensively. Did he think that she was pregnant? Was it possible that he knew the contents of the plastic bag that she so readily discarded?

"Your throwing-up condition. I mean since we don't know what is causing you to vomit, I thought that adding liquor to your system may not be in your best interest."

"Oh, yeah, you could be right," she said while trying not to appear worried. It bothered her that she was lying about her condition.

'Well, *it is not a total lie because I'm not one hundred percent sure about the results,*' she told herself. Was she obligated to tell him what was going on in her mind and her body? If she were to tell him that she and Malachi had shared a steamy moment back in April, it would alter their relationship. How do you tell the man whom you love that you are carrying another man's child in your womb? Their relationship had just returned to normal- like it had been prior to the anniversary fiasco that had occurred in Jacksonville with Malachi. She was not sure that she wanted to alter things since they were going so well.

Forty-Four

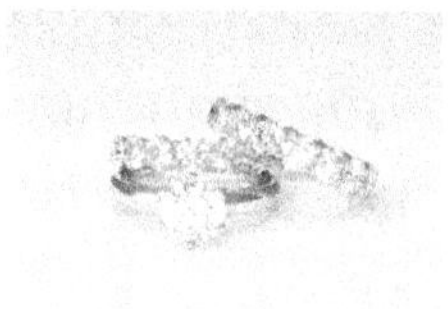

July 1996

Nyree's face practically hit the ground when she opened her front door to see Malachi standing there. Normally she would have tried to conceal her frustrations, but lately she had been saying the first thing that came to mind. It was as if someone had stuck her with a needle containing a truth serum.

"What the hell..." she had begun saying when she found herself face to face with Malachi at the door.

Brushing past her, not waiting for an invitation, he said, "Happy to see me?" he asked while handing her two dozen long-stemmed roses from her favorite flower shop.

Holding the roses from *Petals* close to her heart, she inhaled the scent. She was flattered that he remembered her favorite flower shop.

Then she took a moment to think if he

had asked her if she was happy to see him, or if he was merely making a declarative statement. *It had to have been a question*, she told herself. In her opinion, he just was not that cocky to come to her home with that much boldness. But then again maybe he was because he surely did not wait for an invitation.

"Not really," she said, trying to keep him in eyesight because she did not want any of her precious items to come up missing, due to his sticky fingers.

He looked like a kid in a museum. "Damn, you living large," he commented.

Placing her right hand on her hips and allowing her abdomen to relax, she rolled her eyes at him. Malachi disregarded the look and said, "Looks like somebody hasn't been working out. What does Mr. Exercise Man have to say about that?" Malachi commented hoping that he would strike a cord when he made the remark about Colin Jordan.

What kind of name is Colin Jordan? He had asked many times. "Sounds like a weatherman," he had told Monte. Monte, being Monte, responded by saying, "Man, stop being a hater. At least he has his own money."

"Well, at least I got these muscles by working out and not taking steroids," Malachi had boasted to his brother while modeling his muscles.

"I'm pretty sure he works out. I doubt that he takes anything."

"Man, get off his nuts. He takes steroids, dog. That's a fact. Why do you think he sells all those shakes at his health clubs," he had told Monte.

Nyree interrupted Malachi's daydreaming by tossing the bouquet to him which he barely caught.

"You're here because…"

He hated when she talked to him as if he had difficulty comprehending. Sometimes she made it worse by doing sign language gestures and enunciating every letter in a word. She sounded like a record whose speed had been slowed down.

"I'm here about this," he said while showing her the letter from the courthouse indicating when he was to report for the divorce hearing.

"And…?" Nyree hoped to hurry Malachi on his way before Colin showed up. She did not want Colin to see Malachi there. It would be an uncomfortable situation and would only add to Colin's insecurities. How many times had he told her that she was a married woman, and that she could drop the divorce at any time and go back to her husband?

"And I don't want a divorce," he said sincerely while imagining himself walking around the house wearing a robe and a cigar hanging out the side of his mouth. He thought about his current living situation with his mother, and the possibility of living with Nyree. There was no comparison. Like the old people say, going from life with Nyree back to his mother was like 'going from sugar to shit,' and boy oh boy was it bitter!

"Well, Malachi, it's not about what you want. It's about what I want. One week from today, July 15, I will be a single woman. I will be rid of you. Now I have to get ready to go, so please don't let the doorknob hit you where the good Lord split you."

"What?" He was puzzled.

"Well, let me break it down to you. In the words of Martin Lawrence, 'Get to steppin','" she told him while pushing him out the door.

"You're willing to throw away all these years we had together for what?"

"Don't go there with 'all these years we had together.' If our time was so sacred, then why did you cheat and not just get one- but two- babies? Don't talk to me about what we had. It's over and I cannot begin to heal until I have some closure."

Malachi watched her as she spoke those hurtful words that had not been spoken with venom. She had spoken as if she were having an out of body experience. Detached - that's what she was and Malachi knew that it was truly over and that whatever she had felt for him in the past was gone.

Once more he tried to convince her to give them one more chance. "But I love you. Tell me you are not doing this so that you can be with dude."

"Malachi, for once in my life, I am doing something for me. I need to move on with my life to be happy, and this is the only way I know how. This is not about anyone but me. Now please leave or I will have you removed, but it would be nice if we could behave like adults and not have to involve anyone else in our business."

"Fine," he said as he heard the door slam

shut behind him angrily. He walked down the circular driveway to the 1964 Mustang that Frank had willed to him.

Forty-Five

"I should be going," Nicole told Kyle as they both put the finishing touches on the sand castle that they had been building together.

"It's still early. Come on, you can stay a little longer," Kyle told Nicole as the breeze from Lake Michigan whipped past them.

"No, I wish I could. I have court tomorrow morning with your sister and I want to go home and review my notes. It's the last case I have before I take my much needed vacation."

"Live a little. Just a little longer," he begged.

"I'm sorry," she said as she brushed the sand off her legs and feet with her beach towel. She began gathering her beach bag as she prepared to make steps to her car. He snuck up behind her, grabbed her by the waist, turned her around and said, "What if I kidnapped you and refused to let you go?"

She smiled at him. "What if you kidnapped me tomorrow evening?"

"Sounds like a plan. So if you were to be kidnapped, where would you like to be kept beyond your will?"

"Cancun. Cozumel. Pina coladas, margaritas…oooh, I got to go."

"Be ready to go to Mexico tomorrow evening."

"I will," she said as she trekked through the sand and raced him to the parking lot. He let her win and smiled when she boasted about not being a rotten egg because she had made it to the parking lot first. They were good for one another, for they brought out the less serious side of each other.

Forty-Six

Although it was cold enough to make a snowman in the courtroom, Nyree felt herself sweating profusely when the judge asked her if she was pregnant. She tried not to panic as Nicole had briefed her it was one of the standard questions. "No," she had said in a hoarse voice that caused Nicole and Malachi to look at her in an alarmed manner. Nicole thought that the temperature in the courtroom may have affected Nyree's voice and Malachi figured that Nyree was tired of people making comments about the weight she had put on.

He had to admit that he liked her better with a little more meat on her bones.

Nyree was ecstatic when she heard that the divorce had been granted and her name had been restored. She could hardly wait to get home to take off the pinstriped suit she had worn to court. The waistband had dug into her stomach. She was sure that there was a ring stomach due to the tightness of it. Malachi walked out of the courtroom like a dog with his tail tucked between his knees. Nyree had laughed at the thought of him thinking that he was entitled to her money. "Your Honor, my client does not have anything to give the defendant. The court should note that everything she has is in the name of Edwin Shaw. In terms of alimony the request should be denied. Records indicate that the defendant is unemployed due to dishonorable discharge for being AWOL."

Nyree walked slowly down the hall of the courtroom feeling ambivalent about the outcome. She was happy that the divorce had been granted, but sad in many ways because she had given her heart to Malachi and doubted that she would ever be able to give one hundred percent of herself to anyone again. Her heart could not endure heartbreak. As she walked to her car, she saw Malachi at the bus stop. "What happened to your car?"

"It needs some work. It's down," he said.

"Good luck with it." She could have given him a ride, but that is how their relationship had begun in the first place, him making an effort to see her despite the fact that his vehicle was inoperable. Life was funny like that, she thought to herself; sometimes you just come full circle.

Forty-Seven

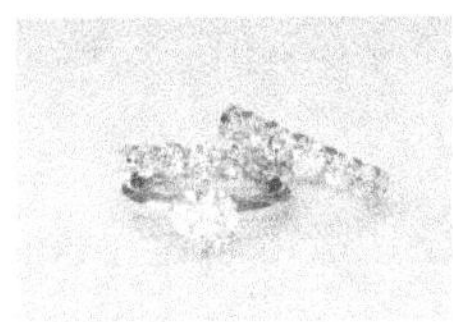

The only people in the gynecologist's office were Nyree and the receptionist. Nyree tugged at her oversized Guess overalls as she absently watched *Family Feud.*

"Ms. Shaw, I'm sorry about the wait. The doctor had to go to the hospital to check on a patient. He should be here shortly," the receptionist told Nyree.

Nyree politely nodded her head. She had cleared her schedule for the day so it wasn't as if she had anything to do. She was just tired and would have rather been at home with her head buried in her pillow.

"Due date is January 20," the doctor told her as he spun that circular wheel in his hand. "Here is a prescription for prenatal vitamins. You are to take them every day. I'll see you in three weeks."

Nyree sat on the table in the room and

stared at his back as he left the room and shut the door. *This is unreal. I have got to be starring in somebody else's life. He didn't just tell me that I am pregnant?*

Two over-the-counter pregnancy tests and blood work could not be lying, but Nyree was having difficulties facing reality. What would she do with a baby? She liked to do what she liked to do. If she wanted to take a trip in the spur of the moment, that is what she did. She did not know the first thing about being a mother, and, furthermore, she did not have the desire to be a mother. Nevertheless, she was having a baby. She would have to tell her family and Malachi. Seems that Malachi was not out of her life.

Forty-Eight

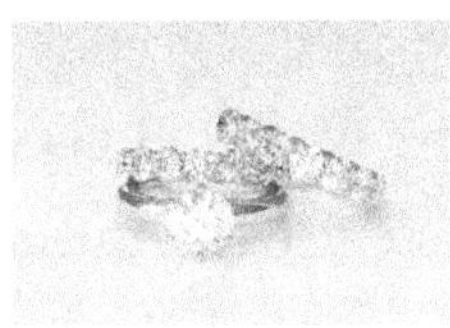

"Malachi, I'm pregnant," Nyree told him over the telephone.

Malachi laughed. He had the audacity to laugh after it had taken her a week to muster up the courage to pick up the telephone to call him and tell him the news. Initially, she had thought about not saying anything but remembered how he felt about his own father. She thought who was she to deprive him of being in his child's life.

"Yeah, right? Stop playing," he yelled over the loud music and laughter in the background.

"It's real. I was just calling to tell you. You do what you want with the information."

"You are for real?" he said, realizing that she was not joking.

"Yeah, I got to go," she told him and hung up before he could say something to make her angry. Her grandmother had told her to remain in good spirits and to view her baby as a blessing, not a burden.

"God doesn't give us more than we can handle," Lula had told Nyree who was not sure what she thought or felt. Everybody had good advice, but it was Nyree's drama that Nyree had to endure.

Colin had tried to conceal his hurt when Nyree told him that she was carrying Malachi's child. She watched his Adam's apple go up and down as he swallowed. "Congratulations. That's great."

Colin felt a sense of hurt. He felt like she had cheated on him even though she was married and had been intimate with her husband. *When did it happen?* He thought. Had they been intimate during the time when he and Nyree were not speaking? What difference did it make? He asked. She had slept with someone else. It made sense that she would, but he found it difficult imagining her being intimate with another man. In his eyes she was perfect and without flaw; but the fact that she had been with another man, and a dog for that matter, knocked her off that pedestal he had placed her on. *Try not to look disappointed*, he thought.

"I guess. I don't know," Nyree said as she

shrugged her shoulders and wondered what he was thinking. It was difficult to read the blank expression on his face. She desperately wanted him to say something. Nyree wanted to hear something positive and reassuring from him.

"So, what did Malachi say?"

"Nothing really. He thought I was making it up at first."

"And when he realized that it was real?"

"Nothing. I hung up. I just wanted him to know. I know that ultimately this is my baby and all the responsibility falls on me as I am the mother, so I have to deal with it."

Colin had reached over and put his arm around Nyree. "Look, you're not alone. I'm here for you and our baby. I let you get away from me once, but not again. I got to tell you I wish it was my seed growing inside of you, but how can I say I love you and not accept your child."

Nyree wiped her tears away as she lay on his rock-hard chest. It was the first time he told her that he loved her and she would remember this moment forever. For once in her life, she felt like everything was going to work out for her. She let out a long deep breath and closed her eyes.

Excerpt From My Love Won't Last Forever: Chaotic Bliss

There had been a time when Tyler Woods did it for her, when he had been the answer to all of her questions. There had been a time when all he had to do was walk into a room and her underwear would instantly become moist. Now when he walked into the room, it was all she could do to keep herself from screaming. She hated to admit it, but there was a borderline hate thing going on with her. He was still sexy to her. His skin was as smooth as a baby's behind. His arms were chiseled beyond perfection, and his abs and obliques were right out of a fitness magazine. Every now and then, when she thought about him, her heart would skip a beat. Despite all of his wonderful qualities, she resented anyone who thought that they were going to make a fool out of her and that's what he was doing right now, trying to make a fool out of her. He was rattling on about his friends and her jealousy of them and the time he spent with them.

"No, Boo, it's not that. You're just not

going to tell me that you were out until six o'clock in the morning having beers with the fellas." Aris was interrupted by the sound of a person clearing his throat. She immediately spun around in her chair and found herself facing the most gorgeous man in the world. He had to be six foot three, two hundred pounds with about seventeen percent body fat. He had a milk chocolate complexion and pearly white teeth. *I wonder if his teeth are naturally that white or if he has had some whitening treatments? I would love to touch his bald head right now. Umph- umph. It should be a sin for a man to be this fine.* When she caught her breath, she spoke lowly into the phone so her unannounced visitor would not hear and said,

"I'm going to have to let you go."

Solomon James liked that comment. He tended to have that effect on women. Somehow he could change their course. When she placed the phone onto the receiver he smiled and said,

"Yeah, you need to let that go. Anything that has a beautiful woman like yourself screaming like that can't be good for your health," Solomon James stated coyly while using two fingers to massage his goatee and smiling a devilish grin. *I wonder if you would be good for my health, sir.* Aris did not have an answer for that question, but she was going to attempt to find out. Standing up behind the hand made oak desk that had been given to her as a gift from one of her clients, she looked the man in his soft brown eyes and said in her harshest voice,

"I don't take advice from strangers. Who are you?"

He opened his mouth to speak, but she dismissed him with a flick of her wrist. She pressed a button on her phone and called, "Erin. Erin?" After moments with no response from Erin she said, "What do I pay her for?"

Solomon smiled again and said, "I had a one-fifteen appointment with you. I'm Solomon James."

"I see. Unless my watch is wrong and I doubt that it is, you're fifteen minutes late." She frowned on gross tardiness as such. Most times she was running five minutes late; but fifteen minutes late said to her that this person did not care about her, her time, or what she had to do. One of Aris's pet peeves was waiting. She hated to wait for anyone or anything. All her life she had been waiting.

* 9 7 9 8 9 8 7 3 0 7 8 3 0 *